THE 40TH DAY

DEIRDRE GOULD

The 40th Day

For Rickey and Melissa E.: Thank you for letting me
shamelessly use you to rebuild the world

And for all of the readers who loved all of these characters
as much as I did. These books wouldn't exist without
your support.

ONE

Christine slowly realized she'd long ago lost all sense of where they were. They walked through another grimy, damp intersection that looked the same as all the previous ones. Marnie held the map in front of her, glancing up only long enough to note the next section of tunnel. Christine's legs were tired and she could feel the muscles wobbling on the edge of a series of cramps. Stress and the pregnancy sucked away her energy. Marnie paused to mark where they'd been again, streaking a red pen across the filthy map. Christine bent down to rub her calf muscle, trying to coax it into relaxing. She'd have to see if she could find some source of potassium when they got to the surface. Maybe that was why she'd suddenly had such strong cravings for meat. It was something she hadn't really missed in years. Except for eggs from the handful of chickens she and Sevita had kept, meat wasn't available. But she'd been dreaming about hamburger all week. Rare hamburger. The kind that mushed and bled in the middle. Christine stood up. *No good thinking about what doesn't exist anymore,* she told herself. *Get yourself and Marnie out of these filthy tunnels and into fresh air and there's a protein bar in the pack for you.*

Marnie turned back toward her. "It's not so much farther. We're getting near the power plant tunnels, there should be an exit in a few blocks, we can peek out and see if it's safe on the street."

Christine nodded and followed after her down the long tunnel. It stretched on and on. The thicker dark and the quick chilly breath of openings at her side never failed to make Christine nervous, expecting some dark creature, something oozing infection and skeletal to come shambling out of an intersecting tunnel to grab her or Marnie. The girl seemed unconcerned though, jumping only at the infrequent pop of gunfire or thud of something moving on the street above them. The dark, the seeping rotten leaf smell of stagnant water, the rustle of rodents didn't make her hesitate at all. Christine wondered about her life Before. It wasn't the first time since meeting Marnie that she'd thought about it. But she didn't ask. *Nobody* asked in the City. A person was how they acted after arriving. It was too dangerous to be nosy about what had happened, what they'd done before walking through the massive entry gate. It was never a happy story. Christine tripped and went down onto the muddy floor, her arms stretched in front of her to protect her from slamming her belly into the cement.

"Whoa," said Marnie, reaching to help her up, "Are you okay?"

Christine wiped her arms on the front of her pants, trying to clean the slimy grit from her skinned elbows and scraped forearms. "I'm fine," she said, "Just clumsy."

Marnie swung the flashlight around. "What'd you trip on?"

"I don't know. It didn't really felt like I bumped into anything, more like I got tangled up in my feet. Must just be tired. I'll pay more attention to what I'm doing."

Marnie helped her get up and retrieved Christine's flashlight. "Do we need to do anything for the baby? Did that hurt it?"

"The baby is okay. It wasn't a bad fall and it's still very early."

Christine finished brushing herself off and hitched her pack a little higher as she started down the long tunnel again.

"Why did you— wouldn't it have been easier to adopt?" Marnie asked, and then quickly added, "I know that's too personal, you don't have to answer that."

"We wanted to make sure that if the plague came back someday, maybe centuries later, there'd be humans with immunity. So Sevita and I agreed to the pregnancy, so our baby would have two Immune parents. We didn't know a different strain was out there until after. It wasn't so hard, the City arranged it all, I just had to go to the hospital one day for an hour and it was done."

"I didn't mean *how* you did it. I meant— I don't know what I meant. Maybe that babies shouldn't be born anymore. Maybe that having a baby is dangerous. For you *and* the baby. There's not enough medicine, not enough food. Never enough of anything. Except people hurting each other. Maybe we aren't supposed to make more of us."

Christine frowned. "That's pretty cynical for someone so young. Yeah, I guess things weren't great. Especially outside. I'm sorry for what you've been through. For what we've all been through. But the City has been secure for a few years now. We didn't have excess, sure, but everyone had enough. Some things are scarce, like medicine and some foods, but that isn't going to change for a while. Should we just let ourselves run down to extinction because of some lean times? Why go on at all?"

"But you don't even know if your baby is immune. Maybe it's infected right now. Maybe it's going to kill—"

Christine turned to face the teenager behind her. Marnie stopped talking. "Sorry," she mumbled.

"It's not infected," said Christine. "Not yet anyway. It won't be in danger of infection until delivery. That's how the bacteria works. By then we'll be far enough away that we'll never have to worry about infection."

Marnie nodded.

"Look," Christine continued, "I know this is scary, especially at your age. But women have been doing this for millions of years. Through plagues and wars and starvation. Is it right? I don't know. Would it have been better if the baby were an accident instead of planned?

Maybe it's selfish. Maybe it's not fair. But the world needs babies. It needs hope or what's left will fade away. *I* need this baby. It can't bring Sevita back, I know that. It can't undo what's been done. But the baby's world won't be what happened eight years ago or a hundred years ago. Its world will be what happens once it opens its eyes. And those days are still ahead. I have to believe those days are beautiful and loving and worthwhile. Without this baby, those days are just an empty span of waiting to die, immune or not." She stopped for a moment. "I'm sorry for whatever you've been through Marnie," she said, "and I wouldn't blame you if there were days where you wished your parents hadn't made the decision to have you, that it's all more grief than it's worth. But it wasn't always this way, and someday it *will* get better, for you too. There are good reasons that we keep holding on, even when it seems pointless. One day, you're going to wake up and the sun's going to seem warmer and the food's going to seem better and you'll find your purpose again. We all will. Maybe it's in someone you haven't met yet. Maybe it's in doing some real good in the world. You'll find it. So will this baby. As difficult as it is to believe, someday, this will all be worth it —" She stumbled again as something launched into her from a side passage. She hit the side wall of the main tunnel with a thud. Marnie yelled and jumped after her.

Christine slid down the wall as she struggled to keep the man on top of her from biting. She pushed his jaw up and away and flinched as his hands flailed and scrabbled across her. He was growling but it turned into a deep gurgle as saliva pooled and dribbled from his jaw. She could tell he was smelling her and it only made him hungrier. Marnie yanked on his shoulders trying to pull him off, but the man just shrugged her off.

"Marnie, no! Stay back!" Christine yelled. She tried to wriggle out from beneath him, the grit from the floor grinding and smearing into her back. She tried to kick, but he straddled her legs and sat down. His hands seemed to remember their purpose and began closing around her neck. Marnie swung her large pack, aiming for the man's head. It hit his shoulder and he rocked back for a second. He reached up and yanked the pack from Marnie's arms and threw it behind him while Christine twisted and broke partially free. He shrieked, upset at the near escape of his prey. He clamped down on Christine's arm with one hand and turned his face, slavering, back to her. Christine panted, pushing his face as far upward as she could.

"Help! Somebody help," Marnie yelled, not knowing who she meant to call out to. "What do I do?" she asked, hovering over the man's back. Christine didn't answer, her face flushing red in the bright halo of her dropped flashlight. She just grunted and strained as the man above her snarled and twisted, trying to get closer. Marnie glanced around. There'd been no weapons in the bunker, not even a kitchen knife. A pair of scissors had been all, Marnie had looked, missing the hunting knives that had been confiscated at the City gate. She'd left the scissors behind. She'd thought the other people would need them more. And now she had nothing. She glanced down at Christine. There was more bend in the other woman's arm, and her chest heaved with exhausted, whooping breaths. The man was going to kill her in only a minute or two

I should run, Marnie thought, the idea growing from her very bone. Christine groaned. She glanced up at Marnie, and the girl could see that Christine knew she was about to give up.

"Run," she wheezed, echoing Marnie's own instinct.

Marnie shook her head, unsure whether she was denying Christine's command or her own. She groped for her pack in the side tunnel and pulled it out by a strap. She could hear Christine gagging as the man's grip tightened around her neck. Marnie leaped onto his back. Christine let go of his face, tearing at his hands as she choked. The man lunged forward, mouth stretched wide in a roar. Marnie dropped the pack's canvas strap over his head and pulled back. The strap pulled against the man's throat and Marnie yanked backward, using her body weight to force him up and away from Christine's skin. He released Christine's neck, trying to pull the strap away. Marnie spun the pack until the strap closed behind his head in a completed loop. She twisted it farther as the man stumbled off of Christine and flailed, trying to reach the pack behind his head. Christine scuttled away, still wheezing, while Marnie clung on. The pack swung and rocked as he struggled to stand and Marnie was lifted off her feet, but she didn't let go. For a few seconds, he tottered and then bashed into the tunnel wall. Marnie yelped as her shoulder hit and bruised. The man slowly collapsed to his knees, clutching at the strap that cut into the skin of his neck.

"Stop," panted Christine. "Stop Marnie, that's enough."

"What?" asked Marnie, staring at her.

"You'll kill him. Stop."

Marnie didn't let go. The man slumped forward more, his shoulders touching the floor as he gasped for a tiny breath. "He's going to kill *us*. I can't stop."

"He's just sick, Marnie. You have to let go. He's a human being."

"What do you propose we do with him? If I let go, he'll be up in a matter of seconds chasing us again. Even if we lose him somehow, he'll just wander around until he finds someone else to hurt," she grunted. The man's gasping stopped. It would only be seconds now until brain death.

Christine was crawling toward her. "Let go, Marnie, we'll tie him up. I'm sure he's got a family in the City. They'll care for him until the Cure—"

Marnie shook her head and tightened her grip. "There's no Cure, Christine. You said so yourself. If we tie him up, we just leave him to a worse death by slowly starving."

Christine bent forward to look at the unconscious man's face. "I know him," she said, "He's an electric plant worker. He came in for chemical burns last year. I treated him. He's just sick, he's not evil, Marnie. I know him."

"Not anymore. He's not who you think. He doesn't know *you*. He tried to kill you. He'd keep trying. They all try. Don't you remember what they are like?"

The man was dead now. Marnie was sure. She slowly untwisted the pack and slid the strap out from underneath him. His head dropped the rest of the way to the cement with a thunk. Christine slid a dirty hand over her eyes. "You didn't have to do that. He was a human being. You can't just kill people, there's always another way."

Marnie adjusted the pack on her back so that it sat flatter. "Yeah, he was a human being. He wouldn't have wanted to live that way. I wouldn't have wanted to live that way. Another way wouldn't have been kind. You think your wife enjoys eating innocent people alive?"

Christine stared up at her. "Sevita isn't eating people."

"Wake up!" shouted Marnie, her voice ringing like cold metal from the tunnel walls, "If she's still living, then she's eating people. If she's not, then someone else showed her the same kindness I showed this guy. You can't go on thinking we can just knock em out and leave them or— or lead them home on a leash to their family. They aren't the people that they were!" she kicked the man in the side.

"He's not Henry anymore, so get up and dust yourself off. There's going to be more and we have to save ourselves."

"Henry?" asked Christine, confused.

Marnie ignored her, picking up the flashlight and shoving it into Christine's hand before wiping off the dampened map and heading off down the tunnel.

TWO

He wasn't a brave man, he could admit that to himself, though the others insisted he was. Reckless, desperate not to recover from a second madness as he had the first, yes. That's why he had volunteered. It meant he'd never have to come back. The others would make sure of that. He wouldn't be left to recover in some strange house with no explanation except his nightmarish memories ever again. But it wasn't free, that assurance. What he'd have to do in the coming weeks… Vincent paced the long, grassy lane between the wire cages of the quarantine camp. Moonlight outlined each small square in the wire mesh and made the small tent where Father Preston slept glow in the dark field. The two men in the wire cages lay still under their tiny squares of tarp. Vincent softened his footsteps as he neared them. How could they sleep? He couldn't. He hadn't been able to quiet his mind enough even to say a proper prayer in weeks. Not since the barn meeting. Not since he'd realized what must be done. He hadn't been able to sleep either, not really. Instead, he'd drop from exhaustion every other day for a scant few hours and wake unrefreshed and more strained than ever.

The mumbled panic-stricken pleas that took the place of his normally thoughtful, peaceful devotions made him ashamed, but it didn't make his fear subside. He'd hidden it well from the others. He still hid it from the slowly sickening pair of refugees that he was caring for. But alone, when all of his work was done, the terror choked him and he resorted to begging, to bargaining, to everything he knew wasn't really prayer.

You know I'm not afraid to face You, he'd begin, his feet wearing away the long, smooth grass as he traveled the length of the camp over and over again. *I know there is no hiding from You. What I've been, what I've done. And I know Henry was right. There isn't anything we can do to*

lessen the harm we've caused, no matter how long we live.
Vincent wrung his hands and paused halfway up the lane.
*I'm not afraid to die. I'm afraid of what has to be done
next. Is this murder or is it self-defense? I'm afraid of what
I'm going to become. I need help. Help me.* He went back
to pacing, trying to erase the feeling of cowardice and
shame his thoughts produced.

The bell hanging in the silo clanged and echoed
over the farm and down into the quarantine camp. Vincent
turned to look down the road. A cluster of flashlights
bobbed and wavered. *Help me,* he pleaded again, and
headed down the dirt path as the light in Father Preston's
tent brightened and shadows began to move inside. He
could see it was a large group from the number of lights.
For a moment, he thought about switching on the small
radio he carried to call for help. He couldn't expose anyone
else. If they were looters or worse— well, he guessed that
he wouldn't have to worry about what would happen in a
few weeks.

The lights drew closer and Vincent could hear the
dragging shuffle of several tired feet. "Hello," he called,
still several yards from them. He didn't want to startle
them. The shuffling stopped abruptly and Vincent found
himself soaked in the bright glow of overlapping flashlight
beams. He tried to force a smile. He was glad he couldn't
see them, these people he was meant to kill. "Where are
you coming from?" he kept his voice casual, as if crowds
normally walked the road in the middle of the night.

"Are we at the Cured Colony?" asked a voice.

"You're close to it," offered Vincent, squinting
against the light. "Where are you coming from?" he asked
again.

"Look, you can't turn us away. We've nowhere to
go. There are women and children—" shouted a man.

Vincent raised one hand to calm him. "We aren't

going to turn you away. Are you from the City?"

"Yes," said the man hesitantly, "but you can't send us back there. There were riots— half the soldiers are dead. People went crazy— just like before. Just like the Plague. The soldiers keep trying to round them up, to put them somewhere so the rest of us can be safe, but there aren't enough of them anymore. We had to leave. You have to help us."

"Of course. Of course we'll help you. We've been expecting you—"

There was a murmur of relief and a few sighs as the small crowd surged toward him.

"But we have to protect the people who are already here," Vincent continued.

"Please," said a woman stumbling forward, "we've been walking for days. Most of us haven't had anything to eat in almost a week—" She was carrying a sleeping boy whose arm hung crooked in a sling. Vincent gently reached out and lifted the child from her.

"I'm taking you somewhere safe, where you can rest. There will be food and medicine, but you've all been exposed to the new disease. The people at the Colony haven't been. We have to quarantine you. We'll take care of you, but you *must* cooperate."

"But we aren't sick!" cried someone.

"It's a precaution. What if you brought it with you on your clothes or on your skin? Do you want to risk turning the Colony into the same nightmare you just left?"

"What about you? Now you are exposed. Maybe infected."

Vincent nodded, wanting to close his eyes, wanting to flee. "I'm staying in the quarantine camp with you. When we're all clear in a few weeks, we'll go rejoin the Colony. Together. In the meantime, I'll do what I can to help. Are you ready?"

The woman nodded, and Vincent hoped she was speaking for all of them. He didn't wait for people to protest or threaten violence, instead he turned and carried the boy up the trail and back to the quarantine camp. The others followed closely behind. Father Preston was waiting at the entrance. Vincent brushed past him with the sleeping boy, hoping the other priest would let them at least get through the door before launching into his faith healing bit. He placed the boy gently down in one of the small tents and turned its lantern on. The others crowded into the cell around him.

"You can't expect us to live here," protested a man. "I admit things may not have been great in the City for you Cureds, but we didn't make you live in tents. You had as good as we did."

Vincent looked up at him. "I promise you, this is the very best we could do with the time we had. The people up in the Colony are living in tents and plywood sheds too. You'll see in the morning. Most of the people up there are hoping their families are coming here, that their friends and loved ones will rejoin them in a few weeks. They *want* you to be comfortable. They want you to come home to them. Whatever we have, we are sharing."

The man looked stricken. "This— this is how you've been living? You left the City for this?"

The boy's mother knelt beside Vincent and stroked the child's cheek, gently lifting sweaty strands of hair away from his skin. She looked up at Vincent and smiled. "I'm sure it won't always be this way. We can make better lives here, when we're out of quarantine. It's better than what we left."

Vincent stood up. "Let's get everyone to where they ought to be, and then Lisa and I will get you a meal and do what we can if you have injuries." He paused for a moment, "Is anyone here a doctor or nurse?" Nobody answered. "That's okay," he said with a tight smile, "I just had to check."

"We don't need a doctor," said Father Preston from the back of the crowd. Vincent could hear the satisfied smile in his voice.

"I meant for other ailments, Father Preston," Vincent sighed. "These people are tired and hungry, we'll talk about things in the morning." He hoped it would forestall any more miracle talk. He led them out of the cell, sorting them into tents and taking their names. A few tried to protest the separations until he tried gently to explain that it was for their own protection. Most were too tired to bother arguing at all. The mother, alone, pleaded to stay with her sleeping son.

"He's sick," she whispered, when Vincent and she were alone again. "The others don't know." She wiped away tears. "I know he's going to turn. I know there's no cure. But the soldiers would have taken him. They are taking anyone who might be sick. At first they said it was a vitamin deficiency, that they were taking people to get injections of vitamins. But the sick people never came back. And in a few days, the Infected started popping up on the streets, the ones who had hidden from the soldiers or who didn't seem sick at first. They couldn't hide what was happening anymore. I know they *tried* not to hurt the Infected. They *tried* to avoid shooting them, some of the soldiers got hurt rather than killing their own people. But it all ends the same, doesn't it?"

Vincent started to shake his head but the woman just smiled. "You don't have to pretend. I know what's going to happen. I didn't come here to hurt anybody, I meant to leave the group days ago, but I didn't know how to do it without terrifying my son. I just wanted a quiet place for the last few days of it. I just wanted to hold him until— until I can't anymore."

Vincent squeezed her hand.

"You're going to— you're going to get rid of the ones who get infected, right? So they don't make anyone else sick?"

Vincent nodded. "We don't have much choice."

"When he goes, I go."

"But you might be Immune."

She patted his hand. "Mothers are never immune to what their children suffer from. I'm going to stay with him. I go when he goes."

"Okay," said Vincent. He handed her two mismatched bowls with food in them. "Does he need anything for his arm? We don't have any doctors, but I do know a good deal of first aid."

The woman shook her head. "It happened when we left. I made a sort of cast, but— well, it doesn't much matter anymore, as long as he isn't in pain."

Vincent nodded and turned to leave. He could see Father Preston talking to someone in a cell far down the lane. He turned back to the woman, almost hating himself as he said, "Don't give up yet. Where there is life, there's hope. Miracles *do* happen."

The woman teared up again. "I can't expect a miracle. I don't deserve one."

Vincent quietly backed out as she bent to kiss the sleeping child's cheek. He locked the cell and glanced back at Father Preston. *I don't deserve a miracle either, and here I am, pleading for one,* he thought. He watched the other priest for a moment, trying to conquer the deep dislike and unbelief he had for Father Preston. *Keep my miracle. Make his real. For all their sakes. Make his real.*

THREE

The abandoned gas station's windows flashed in the afternoon light. Seeing it again made Nella uneasy and depressed. As if she were stuck in one long loop that had closed around her when she wasn't looking. She hadn't wanted to come this way. She knew Frank would have avoided it too, if they could. The world wasn't the regular, organized net of roads it had been. If they hadn't retraced their steps, Nella wasn't certain they'd ever find the farmhouse. She still doubted there was anyone there to find.

It had taken a few extra days to skirt the City's barrier and Frank had insisted on keeping it barely in sight, as if the concrete wall, itself, oozed the Infection through its pores. But the perimeter had changed and they'd accidentally missed the Smuggler's entrance. They found themselves forced closer to the Barrier as they neared the main gate where the forest clustered thickly around the road. It was a shock as the trees gave way to a wide band of flat tar that ended abruptly on one side in a tumbled hill of debris. The smashed metal of a vehicle poked through a huge mound of rubble. The massive chunks of cement left holes scattered throughout the pile. Some were large enough that people had tried to crawl through. Nella could see some of them stuck there, halfway between the City and the open world. Half a dozen maybe. Most of them didn't move. Shot or crushed, they'd been dead for some time. One of them saw her, though, and reached out to her with one arm. The other arm was pinned behind its body. Frank pulled Nella farther from the rubble.

"What if they're Immune?" she whispered.

Frank shook his head. The person reached out to her again. Nella tried to take a step toward the rubble, but Frank held onto her hand to stop her. "Don't Nella—" she looked angrily back at him. He let go, but he shook his head again. "Please don't. Even if it's an Immune, we'll never be able to unbury them. Don't get sick for nothing."

She hesitated. The person strained forward, trying to push its way free. "We can't just leave them— it must hurt."

Frank rubbed a hand over his head. "There must be someone inside taking care of them. They did for the others."

Nella tried to peer through the small gaps in the concrete. She couldn't see anything but the empty street. "Maybe whoever was helping is gone."

A faint moan came from the person above them. Nella looked up. It was still reaching for her. "Can you hear me?" she called. Frank felt his stomach clench with panic. He wanted to tell her to be quiet, for goodness sake, not to draw attention. He looked around, expecting a flow of people to burst over the top of the mound, like a dam suddenly breaking.

"Please, just tell us your name?"

The person groaned again, this time using its outstretched arm to grab onto a nearby rock. It tried to pull itself forward.

"No— don't, you'll hurt yourself, we'll come and help you." Nella shrugged off her pack and started climbing the jagged pile of concrete, picking her way quickly around the twisted spikes of rebar that poked through.

Frank dropped to his knees beside her pack, too afraid to waste time arguing with her. He fumbled in the pockets for a few seconds before his hands closed over the small gun she kept. He stood up, checking it as the person in the rubble let out a howl of pain. Nella stopped to look up. She was almost within reach, if she just reached an arm up— the person's face turned down toward her. Most of its features were covered with soot and dried blood.

"I'm coming to help," Nella tried to soothe it.

"Don't touch it, Nella. Get back," Frank shouted.

Nella turned to look down at him. He was holding her gun. The howl of pain turned into a shriek and Nella whipped around. The person was reaching for her, it's pinned shoulder twisting too far, the angle all wrong, and the person started to slide forward, screaming in pain.

"It's an Infected, please, come back," Frank was yelling behind her. She ducked away from the outstretched arm. There was a clunk and then a rattle as a few chunks of debris loosened and fell away. She glanced up and saw a screaming mouth above her. Unnerved, she slid away and down the loose stones. Frank didn't wait. He shot and missed, once, and then again. Nella was beside him as he shot the third time. The person's arm flopped onto the rubble and the screaming stopped.

Frank pushed the gun into Nella's hands. "It was an Infected," he said.

Nella was silent, looking at the weapon.

"It was an Infected," Frank insisted, "and we couldn't do anything for it. You were right, we couldn't leave it that way. It would have taken another day to die. We couldn't—"

She caught one of his hands in hers and squeezed it. "It's done," she said, when he had stopped. He took a deep breath and nodded. She knelt and tucked the gun back into her pack, taking the moment to think.

She looked back at the rubble that had once been a bustling front gate. Then she looked back at Frank. "You have to trust me," she said, placing a cool hand on his flushed cheek, "I made it a long time without anyone looking after me."

"I know, I know. I'm sorry. I thought you'd get sick —"

"We might. Maybe we already are. But I'd rather

spend the last few weeks of my life helping people and trying to be a decent human being than hiding from everyone and everything for the rest of it, hoping not to get infected—"

Frank shook his head. "That's because you don't know what it's like. It's *not* the last few weeks of your life. You go on and on, month after month, hurting people. More than the few you would have helped before you turned. Killing them. Destroying families. I can't let it happen. I can't let us get sick."

"But if we go into the City— if we do what you are planning to do, destroy it so the Infection can't spread, we *will* get sick, Frank. You understand what we're talking about?"

"I'll find a way. You can't get sick. Anything but that." He pulled her into a hug.

"And if I do?" she muttered into his shoulder.

"Then I won't let you suffer as I did."

She was quiet for a moment, the logical part of her realizing she ought to be horrified that he was willing to kill her, the rest of her oddly comforted by it.

"Let's go," she said at last, "we can't help anyone by standing around here. I think we can reach the top if we go slowly." She let him go and began picking her way up the mound again.

"What? Where are you going?"

She looked back down at him. "To find Christine, of course."

"No— the plan was to get help first. We have no biosuits and we have nothing to defend ourselves with."

"We can't just leave her in there, she's waiting for us. We're right here—"

"She's *safe*. Safer than us. She's tucked away in that bunker, she's got food and water and electricity. She's fine. All she has to do is stay put. We'll go get help and a way to stop this thing first. Otherwise, we'll just be dragging her and us into possible infection or attack." Frank shook his head. "I know you want to see her. I know you are missing Sevita too. But if we go get Christine now, we might not make it to her. Or we might get her sick. We just have to go a little further, and I know we'll be able to help."

Nella turned to come back down, peering back through a small hole in the rubble for a few minutes.

"She's *safe*," said Frank again. Nella nodded and took his hand as he helped her down onto the street. They turned away from the slumping Barrier and the silent City and walked up the empty road.

They had reached the abandoned gas station almost at dusk. Frank stood for a long moment looking down into the station's tire pit. Three small piles of rubber glowed in the ruddy sunset. Nella remembered making them a few months prior, burying the abandoned remains of three unknown people who had died while Infected. The store was as empty as it had been the first time they'd seen it, but multiple footprints and campfire rings around it told Nella that it had been used several times by travelers in the past few months. Had they been fleeing the City or trying to enter it? The question unnerved her. How far had this thing spread?

"We should go somewhere else," she said. "It looks like there's been lots of traffic here in the past few days."

Frank frowned. "I don't remember there being any other real shelter between here and the farmhouse, do you? A couple of places that were falling down, but that's it."

"If we go a few miles farther out before we head to the farmhouse there should be some empty neighborhoods —"

"Then we risk getting lost. Or running into strangers. The people that came by here had to go somewhere. They didn't get into the City if that's where they were headed. And if they were escaping, they won't have gone far."

Nella looked nervously into the large empty store. The sun was setting but the City's soft glow was absent. It would be dark, so dark in an hour or two. Any light, even from the tiny back room where she and Frank had slept before, would be like a neon sign to anyone in the area. Even the woods would be preferable. In the open, they wouldn't be trapped if something, *someone* found them. "It's warm. We'll find somewhere, not on the road, not where people can find us."

Frank shook his head. "We *know* there are Infected in those woods. One bit you last time."

"That was miles farther. And those Infected were almost dead when we found them. And those had to have been kept somewhere. Nobody is left, no Infected could have survived this long on their own."

"We don't know how many new Infected escaped the City, Nella. Here, we'd have a door or two between us and them. We don't know how many people are just desperate because the City has collapsed. There's no more trade, there's no more security, and there's nobody enforcing peace in the area. Seeing two people on their own, we'd be vulnerable to anyone that wanted to rob us. If we stay quiet, nobody will know we're here. It's obvious to anyone looking at this place that it's been stripped clean a long time. Nobody will come in looking for food or supplies if they don't know we're inside."

Nella hesitated, but she knew he was right. She followed him into the station and flipped the lock on the glass door.

"Better not," said Frank, seeing her hand on the door. "If someone tries it and finds it locked, they'll think there is something valuable in here and they'll get curious.

If it's unlocked they'll pass by."

She unlocked the glass door. "All right, but we're locking the store room. If anyone gets that far, I want some warning."

Frank nodded. They closed themselves into the small stock room, the late summer air stifling in the windowless closet.

FOUR

Christine thundered through the thick underbrush, scraping herself on the thorns of a wild raspberry patch as she tried to follow Marnie toward the road. She stank from her struggle with the man in the tunnel, her arms and back still covered in drying muck, and she was so exhausted that she stumbled frequently. But she knew something was wrong. Off. Maybe it was the pregnancy. Maybe it was the stress. All Christine knew for sure, was that a few days earlier she would have had no trouble keeping up with or leading the teen. Emergency work had kept her in great shape for years and she'd worked hard during her pregnancy to stay healthy and active. There was no real reason she should be so exhausted. Or clumsy. Marnie was standing still ahead of her, waiting for her to catch up. Christine reached her, gasping for air. The girl handed her a bottle of water she'd packed from the bunker.

"How close are we?" asked Christine between gulps. The water tasted tinny and warm and Christine fought to keep herself from vomiting. She thought she'd left the morning sickness behind a few weeks before, but the heat and the faint odor of sewage that still clung to them from the tunnels made her nauseous.

Marnie stared at the map trying to place them. "It's hard to tell. The map doesn't have the wall on it. It must have been made before everything."

Christine squinted up at the dark Barrier. She didn't know either. All the panels looked the same and she was used to seeing the other side anyway. "Look, I need a rest, and I'm sure you are as hungry as I am—"

A woman's voice floated in the distance and Christine fell suddenly silent. She grabbed Marnie's arm and pulled her down into a crouch. They waited for a second, and the woman's voice came again, but it was too far to hear what she was saying.

"I'm going to go look," whispered Marnie.

"No, not alone."

Marnie peeled Christine's hand off of her arm. "You're too tired, you are making too much noise. I lived out here a long time. I know what I'm doing. I have to see if they are dangerous before we get too close. Stay here, I'll be back before you know it."

"No—" hissed Christine, but Marnie had plunked her pack on the ground beside them and was already moving quickly through the thick trees, the golden sun threading through the shadows as she slipped silently away.

Christine sighed and sat on the leafy ground, too tired to protest or follow.

Marnie heard a man's voice yelling and sped up, running lightly over the knotted, lumpy ground, falling back into the rhythm and instinct of her years at the Lodge. She wished again that she had a weapon. There was a scream of something in terrible pain and Marnie flinched and tripped over a raised root. She went sprawling and heard the man yell again. She was on her feet just as a gunshot was fired. A second and a third, like stronger and stronger echoes came from just ahead as she scrambled forward, sliding into a crouch just behind the tree line. A mound of rubble interrupted the smooth wall of the City. Marnie could see the huge gate she had entered through. It twisted and rippled outward like the steel petals of a giant metal morning glory. A man and woman stood in front of her. They were looking at a corpse in the rubble and the man tried to hand a gun to the woman.

"It was an Infected and we couldn't do anything for it," the man said quickly. "You were right, we couldn't leave it that way. It would have taken another day to die. We couldn't—"

The woman took the gun and then held his empty hand in hers. "It's done," she said. She knelt and tucked the gun back into her pack.

Marnie watched her face. She didn't look shocked that the man beside her had shot someone, but she didn't look triumphant about it either. She just seemed tired. Sad. Like Marnie's mother had looked, the day she left the Lodge.

As if she had suddenly realized she had come to the end of things. As if she had no choice but to follow the path in front of her, thought Marnie, and her eyes filled with sudden tears, the first she had for her mother in years. The couple was talking about going into the City. Something about destroying the Infection. Marnie listened closely. Did they have a cure? They talked for a few more moments, but turned away and walked down the road. Marnie knew she should run back to Christine, but she was torn. What if she lost them? *Why do I care?* She asked herself. She was going back to Henry. She and Christine would be safe. She didn't need to worry about cures or the City or anyone else. Besides, she didn't know anything about the couple. They could be dangerous. They could be Looters or they could be scared of being infected and shoot her just for coming from the direction of the City. It's what she'd do, if she were in their place, Marnie admitted to herself. The couple disappeared over the top of the long hill. Marnie made her way back to Christine, trying to convince herself she'd made the right choice. But her mother had made a different one. Her mother had died to bring the Cure to the Lodge. To save Henry. To save Marnie and her father.

Christine was sitting on the ground where Marnie had left her, the contents of both their packs strewn about her. She held a large foil pack in her hands and was frantically trying to chew it open, but it was too thick.

"What are you doing?" asked Marnie.

Christine looked up and dropped the packet into her

lap. She wiped some saliva from her chin and her face reddened with embarrassment. "It's— I was very hungry. It's the baby, it needs things we don't have anymore. I know it's weird, but I've been having these cravings for meat for a few days. I found the jerky packet and I was so relieved—"

Marnie reached down for the packet. She twisted the foil and the packet easily tore open. She handed it back to Christine.

"Thought you were the adult here," she muttered, too low for Christine to hear. She started stuffing equipment back in their packs. There was no way they'd catch up with the couple now. Marnie was almost relieved that the choice to follow them had been taken from her. Anything that meant she didn't have to think about her mother, about her past life at the Lodge was a relief. Christine choked on a piece of jerky. Marnie turned to look at her. The other woman acted as if she'd been starving. *Never getting pregnant,* Marnie told herself. *Not even if I was the last woman alive.*

"Are you okay?" Marnie asked.

Christine chewed the last bit of jerky, swiping her fingers along the bottom of the packet to get any crumbs. "I wish it was fresher. This was tough and dry. Is that all of it?" she asked.

Marnie nodded and Christine burst into tears. "I don't know what's wrong with me," she said, "I'm sorry, Marnie. I should be taking care of you, we should already be at your friend's camp by now, but I'm so slow and clumsy. I've never been like this before. And hungry. So hungry."

Marnie felt a pang of guilt and knelt near her, patting her on the shoulder. "It's just the baby. It's okay, we'll get to the camp and I'm sure they'll have something there. Henry said there was plenty of food. A few more days, that's all."

She helped Christine to her feet, and they packed up the rest of their supplies without speaking again. Marnie led them to the road just as the sun was slipping behind the large hill. Christine stood for a long moment in front of the rubble. No light leaked through the pile, and the only sound were sharp chirp of crickets in the field beside the road. She touched one of the broken shards of concrete. Somewhere, beyond it, her wife was suffering. And Christine was about to leave her behind. She glanced at Marnie who was pacing the width of the road. Maybe she should go back. She got Marnie this far, and the teen knew way more about life beyond the wall than Christine did. She could go back, back to their little apartment and see if she could find Sevita. Christine could keep her safe until they developed a cure. But her friend Nella's words echoed in her head. "Chris," she'd said, pressing a small, glittering key to a gun chest into Christine's palm, "if it starts again, don't hesitate. It's not going to get Cured next time. They're not going to come back anymore." There had been such finality in her face. "They're not coming back anymore." Christine sighed and turned back toward the road, her mind saying a final, silent goodbye to Sevita and hoping she'd find Nella, somewhere soon.

"The last time I left the City was before the Plague. Before Sevita. Everyone I know, everyone who was left, is behind that wall," said Christine.

"You know *me*," said Marnie.

Christine smiled, turning toward her. "That's true," she said, "and I'm glad you're on this side of the wall with me."

They walked up the long hill. Even Marnie was exhausted by the time they reached the top, but the road stretched out in the twilight, either side unbroken emerald of trees and brush. "I passed some buildings when I came.

Should only be a few more miles. Can you make it?" Marnie asked.

"Now that we're on the road, I want to get as far from the City as we can," said Christine. "Never know who is also fleeing, and I'm hoping you haven't been exposed yet. Touching that man in the tunnel wasn't good, but he didn't breathe on you or drool on you. I hope you are still safe. Let's keep it that way."

Marnie nodded and they walked on.

FIVE

Sweltering darkness. And a loud noise. Nella remembered a loud noise, but not where she was. The dark was suffocating. She couldn't even tell if her eyes were open. She gasped a great, panicked breath. She was drowning in the dark. Her hands flailed in front of her, as if she could find the shore and something closed around her left arm. She wasn't alone. Another stuttering breath, but before she could let it out in a scream of terror, a hand pressed over her mouth. And then a stream of heat and damp in her ear.

"It's okay, it's okay Nella," whispered Frank into her ear, taking his hand from her mouth and pulling her closer to him. He brushed the hair away from her face, his voice vibrating in her ear. "It's just me, it's okay. We have to be quiet now. There's somebody outside."

There was a thump from outside the door. Nella felt a jolt of adrenaline stab into her. Frank tightened around her.

"There's a door here," came a girl's voice. Nella could hear clicking metal and was grateful she'd insisted on locking the door.

"Never mind," said another voice, "it's way too late to be wandering around. Besides this is right on the Cure route, there won't be anything left here, even in the back."

"But it's safer back there, no windows. Besides, if it's empty why is it locked?" The metal clicked again.

Nella felt Frank's leg pass over her own. "What are you doing?" she hissed.

"Trying to find the packs," he whispered.

"Above us," she whispered back. "But there's no other door. We can't leave."

His arms left her as he searched for the pack. She felt untethered, lost. There was a bang and a shudder. Nella sat up, desperately trying to see anything in the dark.

Another bang and shudder. Nella covered her ears with her hands. The next bang leaked through anyway. Frank pulled her back toward the far wall. He held an arm around her.

"You're only going to wear yourself out," came a voice. The banging stopped. "Even if you get it open, you'll break the lock and it'll be no safer than out here."

"But why's it locked?"

"Who knows? Maybe it's a contraband drop off point. Or maybe someone locked an Infected back there a long time ago. Or maybe it's nothing. Just habit, left over from Before. A self-locking door unless you have the key. I'm too tired to care. You should be too. We still have a long way to go tomorrow."

"Yeah," yawned the girl, "guess you're right. I just feel so exposed out here."

"We haven't seen anyone for hours, and everyone knows this area has been picked clean. Nobody's going to bother us."

A few scuffling noises and then silence. Nella still felt panicked, the damp sauna air still pressing on her chest. If only she could open the door to find the sunlight streaming through the glass, the cool morning breeze filtering through the drafty window corners. Frank's hand dropped into her lap. She let her fingers graze over it.

"Careful," he whispered, "gun."

"You're getting way too comfortable with that," she said.

"I know. I can't help thinking everyone is a threat."

"Everyone was a threat before, but when I met you, you said you'd never be able to shoot anyone."

"When you met me, I wasn't sure if I cared to stay alive. We risked so much, worked so hard— how did this happen?"

"The only people that know are probably dead or Infected, Frank. This isn't our fault."

"We have to stop it. Do you think the people out there are from the City?"

"We saw the gate— I don't think anyone's successfully come out that way. The only holes large enough already had bodies in them. And we saw the harbor. All the boats are gone."

"There are other exits. Small ones."

"Yes."

Frank lifted his hand, the gun still in it, and leaned forward. "They could be carrying the Infection. They'll spread it—"

Nella reached out, trying to find his arm in the dark. "They could be Immune. They could be coming *to* the City. They've done us no harm." Her hand found his shoulder.

"Yet," said Frank, "but if we let them go, they'll infect other people. It will just keep spreading and spreading. Nowhere will ever be safe again."

"Frank, people have been infected for two months now. In all that time, you think nobody came to the City to trade? Or that no scav teams left? No one decided they wanted to see what this Cured Colony was up to? The ground around the station was littered with camp trash. The people in the next room might be from the City. But they aren't the first. And probably not the last. For all we know, we could be infected too. We were covered in blood from the woman in the cooler. *We* could be spreading it. You can't just eliminate anyone who *might* be infected."

"So we're just supposed to sit here and let it happen?"

"I don't know what we're supposed to do. I don't have any answers either. I'm just trying to remind you that those are human beings out there. Just like you and me. Maybe they are *good people.* Maybe, if they are sick, they'll recover and beat it. Or maybe they are Immune. Or maybe, Frank, they are just sick. Not evil, just sick. I know you've said if it were you, you'd consider it mercy, that you wouldn't want to be sick again. But if there is a cure someday— isn't there enough life left to make survival worthwhile? Isn't what we have enough?"

She felt his arm relax and droop. He slid away from her and she heard the slow zip of a pocket opening. Then he was back, pulling her back to the floor with him. She felt a deep sigh shudder through his chest, though he was careful to stay quiet. "What are we supposed to do?" he asked.

"For now, we trust Sevita. We go find this colony, and see what they think. We have to believe the disease is contained. We need help, Frank. Not just warm bodies, but real, human community. We can't do this alone anymore. It's too big. Maybe, if we hadn't done it alone before—"

"I thought you said this wasn't our fault."

"It's Robert Pazzo's fault," she spat, feeling the name like a bitter, rusted nail between her lips. "But that doesn't make the mess any easier to clean up."

"First we're going to have to figure out a way out of here. They may try the door again in the morning."

"Hopefully, they'll just leave. Let's not borrow trouble," Nella yawned. "We've got enough already."

SIX

Henry squinted at the crowded field.

"These people are going to get sick, Henry. We're all on the same water. If we don't move the facilities, the waste is going to draw pests or we're going to have an outbreak. It was okay when we had just the latrines across the road and the house toilet, but there are too many people here now. We have to do something, and it's got to be fast. I've seen it before. A few days, a week maybe, with this many people and those latrines will be full. That's not to mention what poor Vincent has to do with the quarantine waste. Those plastic barrels aren't going to last him forever." Amos crossed his arms and sighed. "And that's not even addressing the issue of water."

"We're working as hard as we can. We have to get these people into houses and the rest of the wall up, even if it's only on the field side. We can't just let people wander in, that defeats the whole point of quarantine."

"So does cholera and dysentery. We have to get this done."

"We just don't have enough hands."

"Ask Father Preston's people. I respect a person's right to pray, Henry, but they've got to do more than that. I don't think there's anyone telling them what needs to be done. Vincent could have, but— what about Gray?"

Henry shook his head. "Something's wrong with him. I don't know what he wants from Father Preston, but I don't buy him as a true believer for a second."

"If he wants to eat, he can work. And get the others working. Have them dig new latrines. No—" Amos stopped for a second. "No, if your gut says he's bad news then I trust it. If he does the latrines, he could make us sick if he wanted to. Have him finish the wall with his people. That's simple enough."

"I can do the latrines, if you tell me where they

ought to go. I've no idea how all this works. Didn't bargain on all this when I dragged you out here."

Amos grinned. "Yeah, well, nothing like a practical education. We'll do it together. The others can handle the farm. You get people organized. I'm going to take Rickey and the truck for supplies."

Henry hesitated. "There might be Infected out there."

Amos nodded. "I know. But some things we aren't going to be able to do ourselves. I have to find some pipe for irrigation or we're going to be out of clean water in a week. And the latrines have to be lined with something, or we might as well not dig em." He clapped a hand on Henry's shoulder. "This isn't exactly how I planned it either, but I'm still glad to be here. It's going to be hard work to get us through the winter, but believe me when I say that I've been through worse without the help we've got now. I've dealt with the Infected before, I won't let us bring the disease back. We won't go far. You worry about getting those people working on the wall."

Father Preston's people had clustered around a large canvas tent, mingling only with the others during meal times. Vincent had told Henry that he thought they could be steered away from idolizing Father Preston, if only after he had gone to the quarantine camp, but Henry hadn't seen much difference in the past few days. He wasn't sure how much good a handful of people were going to be anyway. There'd only been twenty, including Father Preston when they arrived and they hadn't even taken care of themselves very well. He wondered if they knew how. Most of these people had been sick since the outbreak. Maybe the past few weeks with Father Preston had been their entire experience in this new world. Henry understood what that was like. But he and the others hadn't waited to be rescued either. These people seemed to be waiting for permission to live. He hadn't even seen anyone enter the large tent that had been the priest's, though some of his people were reduced to sleeping in the open field without even canvas over them. A few people glanced furtively at him as breached the circle of their camp, but nobody stopped him. Henry looked around for Gray, but didn't see him. Henry doubted *he* was sleeping under the stars. He lifted the flap of Father Preston's large tent. It was mostly empty, though it was clear from the unmade bed and the small pile of clothes that someone was still living inside of the tent. Henry was about to leave and ask one of the others for help finding Gray, when a flickering glimmer on the table caught his eye. It was a slim tube standing up from the wood. Henry walked over to it, curious. What he thought was a tube turned out to be a needle, a dart stuck deep in the table, silky fronds on the top fluttering in the slight breeze that flowed through the tent. He pulled at it, twisting it carefully out of the wood until it lay across his palm. It was definitely a tranquilizer dart. Henry rolled it over his hand. Had Father Preston found it in front of the farmhouse? Was it the one that had cured Vincent? They'd found them in a small pail in the bathroom when they'd awoken. The people that had cured them had carefully brought them into the house and covered them with blankets. They'd left food and a letter, but they'd taken out the darts. Vincent didn't seem like the type to hold on to that type of memento. Who had brought it here? And why?

"So you've found us out," said a low voice behind him. Henry turned to find Gray smiling at him. "I wonder what you intend to do."

"Do?" asked Henry, his mind scrambling to figure out exactly what he had "found".

"I don't know you well yet, Henry, but what you did at your little Colony meeting told me you were a smart one. I knew you didn't believe Father Preston's miracle malarkey any more than I did. But you were sly enough to play along. I just haven't figured out why. Was it your priest? Did you want him out of the way? Killed two birds with one stone, eh?"

Henry's hand closed around the dart. "Vincent is my *friend*," he said.

Gray smiled and held up both hands. "Sorry, didn't mean to offend. Just figured his fairy tales might be as dangerous as Father Preston's. But I'll admit, Vincent seemed more practical than that. If he was such a good friend, why'd you let him go stay in Psycho City? Why didn't you tell him Father Preston was full of it?"

Henry began to realize that the dart didn't belong to him or his friends. "Vincent didn't need me to tell him. He didn't go because he believed that Father Preston works miracles. He went because somebody had to. Because he wanted to save anyone he could. The Immunes. Because if he didn't go, I'd have shot everything that got near the wall. Father Preston was going to go regardless of what we said. Vincent tried to stop him. Tried to reason with him. We didn't have this to show him, though." He twisted the dart between his fingers. Gray's grin grew wider. Henry's teeth ached and he realized he was grinding them. "We played along in the meeting because we thought you *believed*. We thought we could help your group, but only if we respected what you knew as truth. Why did *you* play along? Why didn't you tell us about the darts? Why didn't you tell us you've had contact with the City? Now we've risked the entire Colony—"

The grin dropped from Gray's face. "Whoa. Hang on, we didn't have contact with the City. Never even been near it. I wasn't ready to take them there without finding out the situation first. We stopped here first because our numbers were close and you weren't well organized.

Frankly, I knew we could match you, if you threatened us."

Henry was uneasy. He hadn't realized their vulnerability had been so obvious. "Who cured you then?"

"Not me. I wasn't one of you, not ever." Gray sneered. "There was a fight. Father Preston was trying to take over this hospital, full of Infected. We were going to train 'em up, make them useful and take care of them. They were starving and locked up in tiny cells. The people who had them couldn't see that. They didn't want to accept that they were wrong. They turned the Infected loose against us when we came to take them. There was a fire and lots of smoke, and the last thing I remember is this skeleton-thing running out of the smoke at me. It was an Infected. I tried to take him down without hurting him, but then this woman stabbed me in the arm with that thing—" Gray pointed a finger toward the dart in Henry's hand, "and then a big guy punched me hard enough to knock me out. When I woke up, I was inside the hospital with Father Preston and the others. That's it. No City, no Plague, no need to panic."

"Why should I believe you? You lied about the dart, why should I believe anything else?"

Gray shrugged and the grin crept back. "Would you rather believe the alternative?"

Henry set the dart down on the little table, his limbs suddenly heavy and useless. Gray was right. He was either lying, and they were all already dead, or he was telling the truth and only the quarantine camp was exposed. Either way, there was nothing Henry could do except continue as if they were going to survive.

"Besides," said Gray, "You can ask any of the others. They can tell you we've never gone near the City and they weren't lying about their Cure. Or at least, they don't know that they are lying. Father Preston and I were the only ones who knew about the dart. And Father Preston was delusional about it anyway. Still," he said, picking up the dart and twisting it between his thumb and forefinger, "Father Preston's version *does* keep them loyal." He looked up at Henry. "Don't know what they'd do or who they'd listen to if they ever found out that Father Preston wasn't the miracle worker they thought he was. Some of them probably wouldn't believe it, they'd join the priests down in Psycho City just to prove it. Some of them might run off for the City. Some of them might just decide to lay down and die."

"You're asking me not to tell them? Why? So they can keep being duped by you? So you can keep using them as your personal servants?"

"You *need* them, Henry. You need *me*. It's only been a few days since Psycho City opened up. There're only a few people in there right now. What's going to happen to your Colony when more start showing up? Who's going to make the food to feed them all? Someone's got to eliminate the ones that turn when Father Preston's 'miracle' doesn't work. And bury them. And take care of the healthy ones up here. And defend the place from being overrun or looted. And finish building houses for the survivors before winter comes. That's a lot of 'ands', Henry. You think your little Colony can do it all by itself? I can help you. These people believe I'm Father Preston's right hand. They'll do anything I ask. Anything, Henry. When it comes time to risk somebody to remove the Infected from the quarantine zone, who would you rather do it? Melissa? Rickey? Or some gullible hick from hundreds of miles away that you don't know? Someone who will think he's shooting a sinner so irredeemable that even Father Preston couldn't save him. Who'll have no guilt afterward. Unlike your friends, who'd be haunted if they survived. And when it comes time to touch them, to move the bodies and bury them, are you going to dig the pit and toss em in? Or you going to let good ol' Gray pick one of the more useless ex-zombies to do it? Someone who doesn't fit or can't farm or isn't a natural survivor?"

"I might need them, but I don't need *you.* And they don't need you either. They deserve the truth. And they deserve to hear it from someone who is like them—" Henry took a step toward the tent flap.

"But you aren't like them. *Think* for a moment, Henry. Think of the people who trusted you and followed you out here. *Those* people are the ones who are like you. Not Father Preston's flock. Your people *survived.* You know what it's like to do what you have to. To eliminate threats. To make use of the resources available to you. Even after the Cure, you live with what you've done, what you have to do. You make tough choices. I can respect that." The nasty smile on Gray's face said otherwise. "But Father Preston's people— they haven't done what you did. They never killed. They never felt the slick, slippery chew of raw skin between their teeth. They never woke up and found themselves ripe with filth, rotting in all the broken places. They're soft. Shielded. Not ready. They spent the past decade being fed and cleaned and doctored in a hospital where they couldn't hurt anyone. Not even themselves. You are more like the *Immunes* than you are like these people. They are practically pets, Henry. They aren't going to make it. They'll only drag the rest of us down. But they don't have to. They can be useful. But only if you let them be. Let them have their delusion. None of them would thank you for telling them the truth. They're *happier* this way." Gray held out the dart in his palm, offering Henry the choice.

Henry had a fleeting wish to snatch the dart and stab it viciously into Gray's grinning face. He picked it up carefully between two fingers instead. "I need your people on the wall. It needs to be finished this week. When you are finished, you'll report to me or to Amos for your next task. I'm keeping this." He held up the dart. "I might need that wall up, but it's not going to come at the price of slavery. If I see you misusing anyone—"

Gray shrugged. "I'm just a simple, devout man, remember? If 'foreman' is too ugly, think of me as a caretaker instead. This needn't be unpleasant, Henry. I think we understand one another now. You'll see I'm not so different from you in time."

"Just get to work. I've my own tasks to attend," Henry growled and stepped out of the tent.

SEVEN

Henry swiped a crusty rag over his forehead, but it only pushed the dirt and sweat around rather than lift it away. Amos was on the other end of the trench angrily stabbing at the dirt with his shovel. "It's not right," he said.

"Nothing is anymore. I don't like it either, but what are we supposed to do? He's right. If we tell them, they'll fall apart. Some of them will come around, sure, eventually. But we don't know what kind of things were demanded of them in the name of 'faith' before they got here. We don't know anything about them at all. Gray compared them to house pets, said they'd just be a liability if we didn't use them the way he saw fit."

"That's a bullshit excuse Henry, and you know it. If a child came to us, you wouldn't throw it out just because it couldn't kill to defend itself, would you? If Marnie came— the Marnie you remember from Before, what would you do? We can't operate that way. I didn't come along for that."

"I'm just trying to be practical. Children grow up, they learn. And maybe these people will too, but what if they don't? Are we just supposed to keep feeding them while they cower behind a wall and pray? They've already been kept that way. That hospital held them for almost a decade. The way they remember living, the way they know from Before, it doesn't *work* anymore. Even if we all want it to. I don't make the rules. We're back to survival of the fittest now, and these people are weak."

"No. You're wrong. The world needs peaceful people. The world needs innocence. If we go back to might makes right, we may as well put down our shovels and lie down in this pit, because we're already done. Survival of the fittest, Henry? The Plague *won*. We should be extinct. And we will be if we don't protect people like them. We should be *happy* that these people didn't have to do what we've done. I'd say that's a miracle in itself. One I'd give my life protecting. These people aren't useless. They might be the most important ones here. These are the people that are going to rebuild civilization, not old worn out soldiers like me, or shell-shocked survivors like you. We've forgotten how it's *supposed* to be. If everyone is a fighter, then who is raising the crops? Who is treating the injured and helping babies be born? Who's digging the latrines?" Amos held up his shovel. "We can't do everything ourselves forever, Henry. Something's going to give. We *need* them. And we need them now, not six months from now after they've come to grips with having to fight. And not duped into sacrificing themselves either, the way Gray wants."

"So you think I should tell them, then?"

"Shit, no," said Ricky around a cigarette. He knelt between them, laying long lines of brick along the wall of the pit. "What good would that do? That'd destroy whatever innocence they had. Gray was right about that part anyway."

"So what do we do?"

"In a few days they're going to realize that Father Preston's miracle power has dried up," said Amos, "wouldn't it be best if we told them before they find out the hard way?"

"Amos, you're a smart guy," said Rickey, rocking back onto his heels to rest his back, "but there's a big difference between being sad that a miracle didn't work for someone else and finding out you aren't really, truly special enough to have had a miracle work for yourself. These people feel chosen. Like they have a purpose besides just surviving. Like they were picked out by hand. And you just agreed with them, not a moment ago. You said we needed to protect them. That it was going to be them, and people like them that rebuild the world, while we spend our time scrabbling by. You take that miracle away, you tell them they've been tricked, and they're going to lose that feeling of being special. They're going to question their purpose. And then they scrabble in the dust like us. We don't tell them and Father Preston can't perform, they'll just think either those other people weren't special enough or that Father Preston has lost his stuff. Doesn't change how they feel about themselves."

"If we don't tell them, then they remain under Gray's thumb. He can use them as he wants, whenever he wants." Henry scowled and threw another shovel load into the bucket.

Rickey shook his head. "He's got more to lose than we do and he knows it. We expose him and they'll lynch him. He's going to test the limits, don't get me wrong, his kind always do. But if we make it clear that we value these people, that we're making it a priority to protect them, he'll have to back off. He's in a bad position and he knows it. He *let* you find that dart. He was counting on one of us to find it. Because he's talked you into second-guessing yourself. He's talked you into feeling guilty for something *he* did. Well, him and Father Preston, anyway. Can't fall for it, or you'll stop pressuring him to treat them better."

Amos leaned on his shovel, heavy with worry. Henry thought he'd never seen the other man looking so worn. He tried to blame it on the lack of light in the narrow pit, but he knew it was more than that. "Gray's got to go," Amos said, his voice a low whisper, "Not today, not for a little, but he can't stay. One way or another, he's got to go. He'll twist this place otherwise. He'll turn us against each other, just so he can climb up the heap a little. I can agree to keeping the dart secret, but Gray's got to be dealt with. And I don't mean exile. You thought Phil was bad, but this man's far, far worse. He'll just keep coming back. We can't let that happen."

Rickey dropped a brick with a thud into the soil and swore. He stubbed out his cigarette. Henry just nodded. He began pulling the basket rope to raise the dirt he'd just dug. Rickey wiped the dirt from the brick and stared at the drying mud where it was meant to go. "How come it's always us who have to do the shit work?" he said softly. Henry knew he wasn't talking about digging latrines.

Amos scraped his shovel over the floor. "So that there are other people in the world who can stay clean. So we aren't *all* dragged down into the muck."

EIGHT

It was so fast. He'd expected it to take longer. To be more of a struggle. Something in him rebelled. It *should* be harder. It should have *hurt*. But there they lay, the mother and the son, arms and legs still gently bound as they lay on the plastic sheet. The mother's head had rolled toward him. Her expression was peaceful, blank. It was *wrong*. The boy's face was turned toward Father Preston who was still shaking in the folding seat next to him. Vincent wasn't even breathing heavily. His hands didn't shake. He had expected a sudden snap of agony in his chest, as if the act of severing the boy's head also severed his soul. But the misery and guilt had come in the days before. All he felt now was a quiet relief that it was finally done, that the final, irrevocable step had been taken. Part of him was a little frightened that he didn't feel more. He knelt beside the bodies and wiped the blade on the plastic sheet before sliding it into his belt. He gently arranged the bodies and began wrapping them tightly in the plastic.

"What have you done?" gasped Father Preston at last.

Vincent didn't look up. "What nobody else was going to do for them."

"They didn't have to die."

"What would you have done?"

Father Preston stood, raking his fingers through his hair. "I was *curing* them."

Vincent sank back on his heels. "You were trying, but we both know that nothing was helping the boy."

"I just needed more time. Your doubt has undone everything—"

"The world is filled with doubters. Bigger doubters than me, Brother Michael. It's never stopped a miracle before."

"Don't call me that. You are no brother of mine.

You've broken the most sacred law. You are no priest. Faithless, wicked, you are my mortal enemy. You are no longer part of the church."

"I know," said Vincent quietly, "it comes from a higher authority than you, Michael. It had to happen. It will continue to happen. You will see. Your miracle won't work here. We have to think of the days ahead. Of the Colony. Of your people and my friends on the hill. There are no more miracles coming, Michael. We have to save ourselves."

"Do not speak to me. Never speak to me again. I *will* cure these people. I was not given this gift to have it fail now—"

"Perhaps you were mistaken about your gift. Perhaps there was some confusion—"

"Stay away from me. You're in league with Gray. I should never have trusted him. But I won't fall into despair because of him. Or you. Stay away. You are unwelcome, unwanted. Keep your bloody hands to yourself," Father Preston was hissing with rage. He fled the small tent. Vincent was still for a moment and then slowly returned to wrapping the bodies for burial.

He knew Father Preston wouldn't expose him. It would mean admitting that the miracle had failed. Still, Vincent waited several hours in the small tent for the camp to fall silent around him. He didn't care what the others thought of himself, but he didn't want the deaths to cause a panic in the quarantine camp. Near midnight, he slipped out, wheeling the barrow back through the dark pathway to the tent. He placed the bodies inside, the mother's legs hung out of the end, though Vincent tried to gently bend them into place. He wheeled the barrow quietly past the other cages, their occupants all sleeping. The only light was from the watch fires that capped the ends of the Colony's now finished wall. There was little fuel to spare for lights in the quarantine camp. That suited Vincent. He didn't want to be seen. He didn't want to be distracted. The quarantine fence ended in a large circle. The waste buckets were dumped into a hole here, because it was at the bottom of the hill and couldn't contaminate the Colony's water. Vincent didn't want to bury them here. Not among the filth. But he didn't trust himself outside the fence either. Despite his memory of how it happened the first time, the Plague was like an ax above him, waiting to fall at any second. He had to stay inside the camp. His own sanity demanded it. He set the barrow as far from the waste buckets as he could. A large crabapple tree grew just outside the fence, its old crooked limbs hanging over it and over Vincent. It would be a quiet spot, that much he could give them. It would smell sweet in the spring with plenty of blossoms and again in the fall as ripe fruit spilled onto the ground.

Nonsense, Vincent thought. *Just bodies. The mother and boy are gone. They don't care what happens now. Just lumps waiting to turn back into dirt. Get it done.* He chopped into the grass with a shovel and it released a gentle scent of growing and green. The ground was hard and stiff with years of unchecked grass growth, but soon Vincent broke through to softer earth and soon had a pit large enough. He carried them gently, mother first, then son, into the grave and then sat down on the edge to rest. Vincent looked up at the dark silo that towered over the Colony's wall. He knew someone was watching the road from there, even if he couldn't see them. He wondered who it was. He pulled the walkie-talkie from his pocket and turned it on. The click and sharp static startled him, even though he'd kept the volume low.

"Anyone home?" he said quietly.

"Vincent, is that you?" Henry's voice crackled through the small speaker and Vincent smiled with relief.

"Yeah, it's me. I just needed someone to talk to."

"Are you okay? Have— have you noticed anything?"

"I'm not sick. Not yet." Vincent could almost feel the sigh of relief traveling through the small radio, though Henry didn't transmit. "But the first one finally turned."

There was a long silence. "I know you wanted to believe he could do what he said, but— this isn't a shock is it Vincent?"

"No. I've been dreading it. It finally came."

"Does he realize what he's done now? Is he ready to cooperate?"

"No. He couldn't face it. Days and days, he tried to cure them. He wouldn't give up, I'll give him that. He was exhausted at the end. He just collapsed. I— I took care of it."

"I'm so sorry." Vincent swiped the back of his hand over his good eye. The radio crackled again. "I'm not supposed to tell you this. I don't know who else can hear us, but I want you to know for sure that you did the right thing. We found a Cure dart. Someone cured the others, someone from the City. Some part of him knows it wasn't a miracle. He and Gray both knew. He couldn't do what you did, Vincent, because he's a coward."

"It doesn't make what I've done any better. The cardinal law, Henry. The one unforgivable thing. I'm damned."

"No, what you did was mercy."

"It was murder. It's for God to decide life and death, not me."

"Maybe God *did* decide. Maybe he just used you to do it. Maybe He's decided for all of us, but we can't know. If you are damned, then we all are. There was no choice. There's no return this time. Just madness and suffering and infecting others. Think of it as self-preservation. That's allowed, right?"

"I'm an evil person. It doesn't matter how I justify it. I've done a terrible thing. And I can't even repent, because I mean to go on doing it, when necessary."

"I'm coming down there. I can't ask you to do this. We didn't really think far enough ahead about what we were asking."

"No, Henry, I've accepted my role. There is no reason for you to become ill too or to share this burden. I just needed someone to talk to. I was just lonely."

"We're missing you here too. I feel like I've lost my conscience. Like you were the voice of our better selves. I hate that you are there without a friend. Isn't there anything I can do to help you? Sitting up here is driving me crazy."

Vincent took a deep shuddering breath and stood up on the edge of the pit. "I know you aren't religious Henry, but knowing someone was praying for me, that my name still reached His ear, even after I turned away, that would bring me a great peace."

"If it will bring you some comfort, then there won't be a day that I don't pray for all of us and you in particular. Goodnight, Vincent."

"Goodnight Henry." Vincent clicked the radio off and began filling in the pit with the cold soil just as the horizon began to lighten in the approaching dawn.

NINE

Christine watched the sparkle of dust floating in the morning sun. Marnie was awake, looking at the map again, but Christine wasn't ready to go yet. She'd pretended to still be asleep when Marnie had shaken her shoulder. She was slow. And it was getting worse. She'd stumbled more and more after they left the tunnel. She slid one hand gently over the top of her belly. She'd heard that women grew clumsy, lost their balance during pregnancy. Even that their thought processes were impaired. But was it the baby? Or something else? After Marnie had fallen asleep, Christine had lain awake wondering what was behind the locked door in the back of the abandoned station. Maybe food that the looters had missed. Maybe more jerky. She could still feel the stringy pull of the pieces she'd had earlier, the salt and spices still tingled as she licked her lips. She told herself there was nothing back there, just an empty stock room. Even if the looters had been in too large a hurry to clean it out, the scav teams that hit it later from the City would not have left anything behind. But in the dark, the thought of the jerky grew until the clench and rumble of her empty stomach had woken her in the early morning. It had taken a few seconds to realize that she'd bitten through her bottom lip and was sucking the salty blood from the cut. Christine had shut her eyes again, wondering if she'd missed signs of the Plague, dismissed them as strong pregnancy cravings and symptoms. She pushed the thought away. She should have turned by now, shouldn't she? Sevita had said a week and it had been two. *Sevita said a week until things got bad in the City, not a week to infection,* she thought, as a panicked cramp squeezed her core. *Could I have been that far behind Sevita? Are there still people turning now?*

And the baby? Was there any way to save it? *What for?* She asked herself, *Marnie was right. No reason to bring a baby into this misery.* But Sevita had been so happy. Christine could still see her sweet smile when the test had come back. She could still hear the melody of the lullaby Sevita sang with her cheek against Christine's stomach. But Sevita was gone. And the baby would end up an orphan. Like Marnie. Its life as bad or worse.

She glanced over at the teen. The question was whether to make a decision now or wait and hope she didn't become irrational. Marnie had to get to the camp. She might make it on her own, but that would mean asking the girl to take care of Christine, one way or another. Christine couldn't do it. She couldn't force the girl to do that. But at the camp, there would be others. Adults. People that would know what had to be done. People that could do it. She had to make it that far. Maybe they had a doctor. Someone who could tell her whether it was just the baby or if Christine was infected. The thought made her shudder again. *No use waiting around,* she told herself, *if there's one more day, let's get it done. Just get it finished.* She sat up. Marnie looked over at her.

"Are you okay? You hurt your mouth."

Christine rubbed off the small crust of blood. "Fine," she said, "must have bit it in my sleep."

Marnie nodded and began sliding gear into her backpack. "We should get there this afternoon," she said. "Oh, found this in the bottom of my pack. It's not jerky, but—" she handed Christine a dented can of corned beef hash. "We can make a fire outside if you—"

Christine had already peeled back the tab and sunk her fingers into the cold mash. "I guess you can eat it that way," said Marnie. "Those cravings are no joke, huh?" She went back to packing.

Christine could feel the tiny bubbles of grease squish onto her tongue, mixing with the over-salted canned beef. She remembered her parents taking her to a restaurant when she was ten. It had been fancy. All she remembered was the steak tartare her father had ordered. He'd let her try it and it tasted like a fresher, cooler version of the hash. More squish. More liquid. *More blood,* she realized. She rolled the beef over her tongue, sucking the salt from it before she swallowed. It was too soft. She wanted something with more resistance. With more warmth. She slid her hand around the inside of the can, trying to scoop up the last shreds of meat. The sharp metal edge caught on her fingers and sliced them. Christine felt it but didn't stop. At last, she pulled her hand into her mouth, licking the little clumps of beef and potato, sucking on the slim flap of skin where her fingers were cut. She became more frantic and began to worry at the cut skin with her teeth, dropping the can to hold her injured hand still as she chewed.

Marnie turned as the can hit the floor with a thin ringing. The wrapper was covered with dark blood. She looked over at Christine, half her hand disappearing into her mouth. "What happened?" asked Marnie, already reaching for the first aid kit in Christine's pack. She didn't waste time waiting for an answer but began fumbling with the gauze pads and tape. She reached for Christine's hand but the other woman resisted.

"I'm just going to bandage it, Chris," said Marnie, pulling again, but Christine pulled back again. "I know you're the one with the training but you can't really do it yourself. Not with one hand. Just tell me what to do first, I can handle it."

Marnie pulled on Christine's arm once more. A deep, gurgling growl bubbled up from Christine's throat and Marnie shrank back. "You can't be," she said, scrambling backward. "You can't. Snap out of it Christine. Wake up."

Christine gradually realized what she was doing. She forced herself to put her wounded hand into her lap.

"I'm sorry," she mumbled, not looking at the girl. Marnie hesitantly knelt beside her again and began wrapping the bloodied hand in thick gauze. She handed Christine a disinfecting wipe for her face without looking. She didn't want to see.

"I thought you said—" she started. She sighed and stopped. "Maybe it's like a weird deficiency or something."

Christine didn't answer.

"Can you say something besides a growl so I know you're still you?"

"I'm still me."

"For how long?"

Christine snatched her hand back and began stuffing items into her bag. "Long enough to find your friend. Long enough to bring you home."

"And then?"

"I don't want to talk about 'and thens'. I just want to get through 'and now'."

Marnie was reluctant to drop the matter, but Christine turned away. Marnie got up and pulled the last of her things together. She regretted, again, having no weapon, but she wasn't sure she'd be able to do it if the worst happened anyway. She pushed out of the store's front door and waited for Christine on the already-baking tar.

TEN

The ring of falling metal woke Nella with a jolt. A seam of daylight flickered under the door turning the storeroom a deep brown. Voices began on the other side. She felt Frank sit up behind her. Her muscles pulsed with acid adrenaline but she stayed still, fighting the urge to burst out of the tiny closet to meet whatever was on the other side. There was a slow, ascending growl from the other side of the door and then a girl's voice sharpening in warning. Nella sat up, swinging her feet to brace the door, expecting someone to thunder through within seconds.

"We can't leave her," whispered Frank. "It'll kill her."

Nella was troubled. She wanted to open the door as much as he did. His stricken expression triggered an echo and she could hear him telling her the story of the boy in the bunker again. "I had to open the door. It was someone's baby. Someone's whole reason for being," he'd said, "Nella, how could I not open the door?"

She knew now, what he'd felt. She knew, also, if they opened the door and became infected, he'd never survive the guilt.

"She's already dead," she mouthed toward him, more to persuade herself than him, "We know for sure that they've been exposed."

Frank hovered on his knees, leaning toward the door. "It sounds like it's just a girl—" He reached toward the knob. Nella let her legs slide down to the floor and leaned in to stop him.

"You've been here before, Frank. For days, you've been begging me not to take any risks. We've gone to great lengths to stay safe." She put a hand to his cheek, turning his face toward her and away from the door. "We're in the bunker, Frank. We're safe and the little boy is knocking again."

Frank backed away as if she'd slapped him. "Why would you say that? Why now?"

She followed him, holding onto his hand as he tried to twist away. "Because I can't stand to see you that broken down again. You aren't blind. I know you realize that we probably aren't going to make it. Not both of us. Maybe neither of us. You knew it the minute Christine called us on the radio. That's why you begged me to stay away. We chose to come back anyway. *We* chose. If something happens— if I get sick and you don't— I can't let you blame yourself for it the way that you did with Sarah."

He shook his head. "Don't talk that way—"

"I *have* to. *We* have to. This whole mess, the false security of catching Dr. Pazzo, the reinfection of the City, Sevita's death— it's all because we met. I don't blame either of us, we tried to stop it. We failed, but we tried. And I don't think anyone else could have done any better. But I can't fail *you*. We've been happy, these few months, in spite of everything falling apart around us. This has been the very best part of my life, even if it came after the Plague. But now we have to decide how we live what's left of it. We have to decide who we're going to become."

Frank nodded but remained silent. The growl from beyond the door had grown.

"I can't bear to think of the memory of us being soured. I can't let you blame yourself for whatever comes next. So, here we are. We're somewhat safe in this storeroom. There's a child in danger that we might be able to save, for a day or two. But if we open the door, we're going to do it together. It isn't going to be anyone's fault if one of us gets sick. I want to open the door, Frank. Who wouldn't? You need to think for a moment. The moment is going to pass, like every other, and you've got to let it go, no matter what we decide. You can't carry it around forever."

She stopped talking and listened to the growl die away and their breath filled the space.

"Open the door, then," he whispered.

He was beside her as she unlocked the door with a soft click, and then twisted the knob. Cool air flooded into the store room and Nella squinted against the bright morning light streaming through the display windows. The store was empty. The only things left were a few drops of blood scattered over the dull epoxy floor and an empty can of breakfast hash lying on its side. There was no girl, no growler, no bodies.

Nella let out a shaky breath. "Maybe it wasn't a person with her. Maybe it was an animal."

"What about the blood? And why would it growl?"

"Maybe it smelled us."

"Maybe we waited too long," Frank frowned and crossed to the door. He looked down the road for some sign, but it was empty.

She curled a hand around his. "Maybe she was someone else's to rescue. Or maybe she just didn't need rescuing. Besides, we have other people to save."

He pulled her into a tight hug. "I don't want to die in the bunker, Nella.It gets in anyway. It always gets in. I don't want the rest of our lives to be a long, dragging dread. I mocked you once, when we were searching for the missing vials You were scared that we had reached the end, that we had missed some chance to stop the plague, that we were all doomed. And I told you not to worry, because I thought you were overreacting. That you were irrational. I'm sorry. Now I know what you were feeling. No matter how I try, I can't push that fear away. My mind is constantly screaming to turn around, to take you back to the boat and go. You said so yourself. You said we ought to go south, leave the City to take care of itself. Instead, we keep walking further and further from safety. And every choice is harder than the last, but we still keep going. And when we get there, what then? No one will know us. Nobody is expecting us. What can you and I do that will make any difference at all?"

"We can tell them what they don't know. And help them do what has to be done. We don't even know if they got Sevita's message. They may not even know that the Plague is loose. And even if they do, they may be expecting someone else to stop it. The City or some government army. You and I know that no help is coming. We've seen the capitol. We've seen most of the coast. We know there's nobody else out there big enough to stop this. We know that we can't wait. You and I know there's no cure waiting to be found. That there never was. Even after Sevita's message, people are going to be desperate enough to look and to hang on to their loved ones. Bottle them up, just like Juliana did, hoping. We know the truth, and we have to make them know it too. That every Infected is a carrier and a danger. That anything from the City is tainted. That it must all be wiped away if anyone is to be safe."

Frank shook his head. "Why should anyone believe *us*? We're the ones that failed to stop it in the first place."

"We're the only ones that *tried* to stop it. And because we saved these people before. They are going to remember us. They are going to remember *you*. You are the last thing they saw before waking up sane."

"You're assuming the same people that we cured are the ones who are in charge still."

"Yes. I have to assume there's some chance. The reason we keep going, though both of us have the urge to turn back, though both of us have terrible doubts, is that we have to *try*. When I worked in the Cure camps I watched people go through agony trying to accept what they'd done while they were ill. I watched you come apart because of what you couldn't control. You think you're alone in your guilt, because that's what the City *wanted* you to feel. They needed someone to blame, and the Cured were convenient. But the truth is, you may tear yourselves up about what you did, but the Immunes have to live with what they *didn't* do. What they didn't *try*. Certainly, it was hard to shoot a friend or a loved one, but soon it became normal. Nobody fought it, no one felt guilty after the first few. The Infected weren't people. They weren't even animals. They told us you couldn't be cured, so nobody *tried*. Nobody did what Juliana did. There were no people in the City that secretly held relatives in the closet or the basement. We didn't just kill to survive. We *hunted* the Infected. Took their resources, took their homes, claimed everything for the Immunes. And then, when you were cured, we still assumed you were less than human. We didn't try to make you feel welcome, we didn't return your goods or your families, we didn't try to make you feel human again.

"Frank, I can't tell you what keeps you going, when everything in you wants to turn around, but I can tell you why I keep going. It's because I have to make up for not trying. I have to make up for all the things I *didn't* do when I could have. For all the people I could have saved and didn't because I was scared. Because I ever let myself believe that the Infected were anything less than human. Less than you've turned out to be. I can't cure them now. But I can stop more from becoming Infected. And I can give the Infected the mercy I'd want. Not as threats, not as animals to be hunted, but as human beings that deserve better. That's why I have to *try*. But not without you. I'd leave it all and live with my own failures if it meant staying with you. If you turn back, then I will follow you."

"I'm not going to turn back. Not now. But we may get there and find out that the Colony is already infected.

Or that they won't listen. This whole thing might be pointless."

"Nothing we do is pointless, not even when we fail. We brought these people back. We dumped them into a bleak, foreign world with only a note to help them. I'm tied to them now. I have to try to make sure I didn't wake them up just to let them slide back into insanity and misery again. I have to make sure that curing them meant something besides the guilt and fear and grief it must have caused them."

"Then we'd better get on the road before someone else reaches them first." He let her go to pick up his pack. He watched her tie her sleeping bag back onto the pack frame, her hands working while her mind wandered miles ahead. The scar on her shoulder twitched and flashed at the edge of her shirt. He didn't want to revisit that place. They'd done what they could. He'd cured them. He'd dragged them one by one into the farmhouse, gathered wood, gathered food. Kept them warm when he could. What else could they have done? Nella had spent years helping the Cured, one by one. She'd listened to horrors nobody else wanted to hear. She'd accepted them as people when no one else would. He remembered the soft wince she'd fought to hide the first few times the scar on his hand had brushed her skin. Once, he'd thought it was revulsion. He'd realized long ago it was empathy instead. She didn't owe anyone either.

"Nella," he said, and she looked up from the latches on her pack, "you're a good person. Maybe nobody's told you in a while. You don't deserve the guilt you keep heaping onto yourself. We aren't doing this because we owe the world something. We're doing this because it's right. Because we're choosing to do good."

Nella smiled and stood up, strapping the heavy pack onto her shoulders. Her scar pulsed brightly under the weight. "You're lecturing me about guilt? That's a switch."

Frank traced the scar on her shoulder with a light finger. "It's just— if we're going to get sick, if— if I'm going to lose you— I don't want it to be for some imaginary debt, or to satisfy someone else's shallow judgment of us. You're— we're worth more than that. This is worth more than that. I can accept it if we are living the best we know how, if we die for something better in the future. But not for what happened in the past."

She pulled the left strap of his pack so he would bend closer. "We're going to be careful. If we get sick, you know I will take care of it. Don't think about it anymore. Try to imagine us being eaten alive by mosquitoes and hacking pineapples with dull machetes next year. This isn't the last day. This isn't the end. You told me once that the universe couldn't be that unjust. Where did that conviction go? Believe in me Frank."

She pulled him gently into a kiss. "Don't die," he whispered.

Everything dies, she thought. "I won't if you won't," was what she said instead.

ELEVEN

"You see them?" asked Amos, already reaching for his seat buckle.

"Yeah. I see 'em," said Rickey around a loose cigarette. "Should I stop?"

"Better, but not too close."

Rickey slowed to a crawl as Amos hoisted himself halfway through the open window to warn the group in the back of the truck. Rickey squinted at the two women who trudged slowly up the grassy path. The little one looked familiar, but Rickey couldn't place her. He pulled to a gentle stop as they turned to look at him. The older woman stumbled as she pressed the younger behind her.

"Shit," said Rickey, "I think she's sick."

"I knew we should have grabbed the extra cement yesterday when we had the chance. If they're this close we won't be able to travel again for weeks," muttered Amos. "Keep everyone in the truck. If they bolt for the truck or pull a weapon, don't wait for me, you got it? I can handle myself, but only if I know the rest of you are taken care of. You take off and don't stop for anything."

"Got it, boss," said Rickey, his knee bouncing nervously. Amos climbed out of the truck.

"Hello," he said, his voice rolling easily over the still, windless field. "You from the City?"

"Yes," shouted the older woman and took a few steps toward him. Amos held up his hand.

"Wait," he said, "don't come any closer yet— we'll help you, but we have to keep everyone safe."

The woman raised a hand to shade her eyes. "Amos? Issat you? It's me, Christine Das."

Amos was silent but Rickey saw him sag a little. "Don't you remember me?" she asked.

"Yeah, yeah of course I remember you, Christine. What are you doing way out here? I thought you'd be caring for people at the hospital."

"The City— there's an outbreak there."

"We know. We got Sevita's message."

"She— she sent a message?" She swayed a little, as if she were very tired or dizzy.

Amos crossed his arms. "Kinda thought you'd be with her," he said.

"She put me in the bomb shelter. Below the hospital. Tole me to stay 'side so I wouldn't get sick. She tole me to stay 'til someone came to help. She was already sick, she wouldn't come inside. I tried—" she took another step toward Amos but stopped as he held up his hand again. "I tried to persuade her, but she said I would be safe inside. And then she left. We waited—" she waved backward at the younger woman, "we waited several days, but she didn't come back. 'Nother group did, and threatened to break the door down. They had kids with 'em, needed the shelter more. An' Marnie—" she waved again at the other woman.

Rickey sat up straighter at the name. He shared a glance with Amos.

"Marnie said she had a friend here."

"Henry," offered Marnie, "He should be at the Colony."

"Yes, Henry. She said we could come and be safe, so we snuck out of the shelter to find the Colony."

"You've been in the shelter the whole time? You haven't been exposed?" asked Amos, his posture softening.

Christine hesitated. Rickey shook his head. "No. No, no, no. Amos, they have to go to quarantine, just like everyone else," said Rickey, opening his door.

"But if they haven't been exposed, it'll be like throwing one of us into a pen of Infected and hoping we make it out okay," said Amos.

"They have separate cells. They don't have to get

close enough to anyone to catch it."

"Except whoever is feeding them—"

Christine watched the two men arguing from each side of the truck. The people in the back began to stand as well.

"We have to take that risk. Amos, you *know* we have to. You promised Henry that we wouldn't bring any Infection back, that we'd be careful. Let them walk to quarantine. It's not that far. They'll be as safe there as at the Colony. If they are telling the truth, they'll just be uncomfortable for a few weeks. If they aren't—" Rickey looked up at the two women. "I'm sorry, we just can't chance it," he called. "You'll be safe in the quarantine. Henry can talk to you over the radio. It's quiet and clean and Vincent will make sure you have everything you need. Then, in a few weeks, we'll all be together again." He closed the truck door.

"Do you mind if we just get a ride on the back of the truck?" asked Christine, "We're just— we've been walking a long way—"

"No Christine," said Marnie, "it's not much farther. We can do it."

"I don't think I can," said Christine, sinking on her heels.

"It's less than a mile," said Amos, "I wish we could take you, but we have others in the back—"

"We'll be fine," called Marnie as Christine shook her head and began rocking back and forth.

"Get in the truck, Amos," said Rickey, suddenly uneasy at seeing Christine break down.

Amos hesitated. "I'll see if we can empty out the truck and come get you once we get back—"

Marnie shook her head. "We'll be okay. You should go. Now."

Christine was muttering something. Amos slid back

into the truck and Rickey didn't waste time, rolling quickly past the pair and holding his breath without even realizing it. He saw Christine stand up in the rear-view mirror. She flailed as if she were throwing something at the truck and Marnie stumbled backward. Rickey hit the gas, not wanting to see what happened next. *Hang on kid, I'm bringing help,* he willed toward Marnie.

"I'm pregnant!" shouted Christine. "I'm pregnant, bastars." She swiped angrily at a tear on her cheek. "Can't lea' me here. Jus' pregnant and tired. So tired."

"It's okay," said Marnie, helplessly, "We'll rest a few minutes. It's not far, we'll rest and when we're ready we'll take a little walk."

"Not okay. You should've tol' em I was pregnant. Would believe *you.* Everyone believes *you.*"

"What are you talking about? They didn't take me either. I'm in the same boat as you."

"You tol' em about this morning. You tol' em about the meat." She waved her bandaged hand in front of Marnie.

"Christine, calm down. You heard everything I told them. The meat is just a craving. Just a bad pregnancy craving. We're going to get you some, just as soon as we get—"

Christine ripped the bandage from her hand. "This look like a normal pregnant wom'n t'you? Hmm? You see lots of people eat themselfs? Should've gone with 'Vita. Should've left you in the bunker. She loved me. She loved me." She sank back down to the ground with a sob. "Now I'm going to die all alone. Or eat you and scrounge alone. Hurting people forever. Why didn't I stay with 'Vita? Why didn't I open the door?"

Marnie stood by, not knowing what to do. Part of her wanted to flee, to run to the Colony and make the men come back with guns. She couldn't do it, not while

Christine was crying. A flicker of shadow caught her eye as she feebly patted her companion's back. She glanced back the way they had come. The spindly silhouette of two people stretched against the bright, dry sky. Marnie stood up straight. She was torn between relief and panic.

"Christine," she said softly, but the other woman just continued to sob. "Christine, someone is coming." She shook her friend's shoulder. The silhouettes thickened into a very tall man and a smaller woman beside him. "Christine, we've got to go. We need to hide." She backed up a pace or two. The woman's silhouette raised a hand in greeting. It was too late. They'd been seen. Marnie scanned their surroundings for something, anything to protect them. There was nothing, and no close obstacles for cover. The couple stopped several paces from them. The man reached into his pocket and Marnie raised her hands.

"Please, we have nothing," she said. Christine just kept rocking and crying on the ground.

"We aren't going to hurt you," said the woman, "Are you from the Colony?"

The man pulled out a piece of cloth and handed it to the woman, who stretched it out and placed it over her face. A surgical mask, like at the hospital. Marnie relaxed a little as the man pulled out another and put it onto his own face.

"No— are you looking for the Colony too?"

"Yes, we're here to help. Are you from the City?"

Marnie hesitated, not sure what to say. "My friend is. There were some people from the Colony a few minutes ago. They said there's a quarantine camp less than a mile away." She leaned down and said, "Christine, c'mon, we have to move."

The woman looked startled and glanced at the man. "Did you say your friend's name was Christine?" She took a step forward, but the man touched her gently on the shoulder and she stopped.

"Yeah, she— she's not doing well."

"There are hundreds of Christines, Nella," warned the man.

"Do you— do you mind if I take a look at her? I'm — I was a doctor," said the woman.

Marnie hesitated. "I don't know if you should— I'm not sure what's wrong with her. She's pregnant but I think— there might be more."

She saw the woman give the man another quick glance. "I'll be careful," she said. Marnie wasn't certain if the woman was talking to her or the man. They came closer and the woman took off her pack and began searching inside. Marnie could see the shape of a gun in one of the side pockets. She backed up a little, still nervous.

"We aren't going to hurt you," said the woman. "I know that's hard to believe with what you've probably been through. My name is Nella and this is Frank—"

Christine looked up at the names and Nella stopped. "It *is* you. What happened? Where is Sevita?" Nella pulled on a pair of gloves and reached for Christine's wounded hand. Frank crouched beside them.

"She's gone. We had to go. Nobody lef'. The whole City sick. Now, me too. Me too. Should've gone with 'Vita."

"You said you were in the shelter. You said you weren't exposed."

"I was wrong. She was wrong. I wanted the baby to be okay. I wanted to believe we'd be okay. 'Sokay now. You found Ann?"

Nella felt the warmth of Frank's hand on her shoulder. "We found Ann," said Nella.

"So you have the Cure. 'Vita went away one day, but she might be— maybe the soldiers are protecting her."

"I'm sorry, Chris," Nella's voice cracked. "There's no cure this time."

"But there has to be. They made it, they have to know how to unmake it. You can find out. Jus' make her talk long enough. You'll find it."

Nella shook her head. "Ann's dead. They're all dead. Dr. Pazzo told us there was no cure."

"He's a liar. A LIAR."

She felt Frank stiffen as Christine raised her voice. Nella knew it wouldn't be long before she turned. She tried to stay calm. "I know. I know he was. You're right. But Dr. Carton said it was incurable too."

"So thass it? What do we do now?"

Nella tried to concentrate. "Let me see your hand. We'll get it bandaged up and then we'll go to the quarantine camp and get some dinner and a rest. We need to talk to the people in the Colony. Let them know how bad the City has become. You can tell them better than us. We'll see what they say."

Christine put her hand absently into Nella's gloved one. "You think they'll help? You think they can find the cure?"

A tear soaked into the flimsy paper mask that Nella was wearing. She tried to blink the rest away and concentrate on the ragged cut on her friend's hand.

"You're the people who were supposed to come get us," said Marnie, "We were supposed to wait until you came to help."

Frank nodded.

"I thought there were a bunch of you," said the girl. "I thought you had an army or something. Where've you been?"

"Trying to figure out how to get to you and what we were going to do when we found you," said Frank, a needle-thin tone of defensiveness creeping in. "We were going to the Colony to get help."

Nella finished cleaning the cut. "Why didn't you stay? Why didn't you wait for us? We wouldn't have left you."

"I know, I know," cried Christine, "but there were other people who wanted the shelter. They would have found a way in. We'd get sick if they broke in." Christine laughed. "Too late," she said. "Too late for 'Vita. Too late for me. Too late for the baby. But you aren't too late. You can take Marnie to her friend. You can stop me before I hurt someone."

"What?" said Marnie, "No, there's got to be something else we can try. You don't know for sure, yet. Maybe something's gone wrong with the pregnancy. Wait until we get to the Colony, they'll have doctors there."

Christine shook her head. "Two doctors here. Or close 'nuff. I knew long time ago. Didn't want to. Nella knows. She's seen it hun'ert times an' more."

Nella glanced over at Marnie. "Did she hit her head recently? Or eat something she shouldn't have or that was bad?"

"We— we were attacked in the tunnels when we left the City, maybe she hit her head then?"

Christine shook her head. "No, just my side. Besides, wouldn't explain this." She wiggled her wounded hand.

"Maybe it's just a craving. Maybe you just need more protein or something," said Marnie.

Christine shook her head. "Lots of wom'n had babies in the City. No more meat than me. Never ate their own hands."

The little group was silent for a moment as Nella played with the bandage on her lap, trying to decide whether or not to put it on Christine's hand. Did it even matter? Should she persuade her to go to the quarantine camp where she'd likely just turn into a threat to everyone there? Should she persuade her to turn back to the City and hope she didn't infect anyone on the way back? Christine knew what she was thinking about. She closed a hand around Nella's and squeezed.

"I know 'Vita was your best friend. I know I can never be what she was. But you're *my* best friend. I knew you'd find us. I just wish 'Vita were here, so we could go together. I don' want a stranger to do it, Nella. I don' want to starve in the woods or hur' anyone."

Nella cleared her throat and looked down at Christine's hand. "We went north, Frank and I. We found this place. This hospital. A woman was taking care of the Infected. For years. She didn't know about the Cure, maybe never expected one. But the people in her care were healthy and well fed."

Christine shook her head. "Not your burden, Nella. An' not your choice. *Mine.* I can still choose."

"But if there's a cure someday— if we could save the baby and you could see it someday—"

"We both know the baby won't make it. Not even if you tied me up. Too much adrenaline. Too little food and medicine now. It would be Infected too, probably. It'd die anyway from the infection. An' even if I could come back someday— would *you* want to?"

Nella shrugged as more tears dissolved into her mask.

"Frank," said Christine, "would you choose to come back, if you got sick again?"

They all looked at him. He glanced at Nella, his face drawn down into a deep, sad frown of sympathy. He slowly shook his head. Christine turned back to Nella. "Please. There's nobody else."

"I can't," said Nella. "What if Marnie is right? What if it's not the Plague?"

"If you belie'ed, could you do it? If you see, will you help me?"

She nodded.

"Then— will you stay until I turn? I'm afraid to turn alone. I don't want to be alone."

"I'll stay," said Nella. She pulled the small gun gently out of the side pocket of her bag and placed it carefully in her lap. Frank leaned over and kissed the top of Christine's head through his mask.

"I'm sorry," he said, and stood up. He picked up Nella's pack and turned to Marnie. "Let's go find your friend, okay?"

"You can't really mean to do this," said Marnie, "You can't expect me just to let you kill her."

"Marnie, you killed the man yesterday. Said it was mercy. Do I deserve less? What would you do with me?"

"We kept Henry safe. We kept him for years. We can keep you safe too."

Christine nodded. "Go with Frank then. Fin' Henry. Ask 'im. Ask 'im if it's worth it. You can come tell me what he says."

"*You* come find Henry. Come with us." Marnie gently pulled on Christine's arm.

"Too tired, too dizzy. Just going to sit with my friend a while."

"You can do it," cried Marnie, "it's not even a mile. Just across the field—" she pulled harder on Christine's arm. Frank put down the extra pack and put a hand on Marnie's shoulder.

"It's time to go now," he said calmly. "Let's go find Henry. Nella and Chris can catch up in a few minutes."

"No!" Marnie flung his hand away from her. Frank hesitated and then grabbed the girl around the waist. He pulled her away from Christine and lifted her, kicking at him, from the ground and began walking grimly toward the

Colony. Marnie twisted and yelled but he hung on until they were out of sight.

It was almost noon and a breeze sent the long grasses flashing white and gold as it passed over Christine and Nella and raced away toward the deep green woods at the edge of the field.

"Do you 'member the day we found that baseball field, Nella?" asked Christine, stretching out to lie on her back in the grass.

"You mean the one with the wild raspberries?"

"Yeah. It was like this. All overgrown and secret. I thought it was sad. The dugout all slumped and shadowy like an old woman's eye. And the fence all swallowed up by grass. Like we never were. Like all we ever leave behind are empty bases and ruined shacks. But 'Vita said I was wrong. There were swallows living in the dugouts. An' if you flipped over one of the rotten bases all those tiny gold snakes swam 'way. Even the fence helped the berries grow. She said if we left emptiness behind, it was only as growing space for something else. That if we all passed 'way, ev'ry lass one, the world would still 'member."

"Are you scared no one would remember you?" asked Nella.

Christine smiled. "Don' pull that psych stuff on me, Nella. You know me too well for that. I'm scared the world will 'member what people like Pazzo did. That it'll be a big empty scar. Where nothing grows back. But all the little things, all the tiny memories of love and kindness and mercy we add, those'll all be forgot. Swep' 'way in a quick breeze. They're so small against such big and terrible things we've done."

Nella sank down to lie in the grass beside her. "They're sticky though."

"Sticky?"

"Yeah. All those little things. They're sticky. Like

rain. They collect. They attract each other. By themselves, they seem so small. A raindrop never grew anything. But they keep collecting. First a puddle, then a stream and on to the river. Your quick breeze might evaporate one raindrop, but it can't hurt an ocean. World's full of ocean. Those little memories are what make up most of life. The bad stuff just looks flashier. But all scars fade eventually. Even big ones."

"Do it before I make a scar then."

"What?" asked Nella.

"I'm angry. I can feel it growing in my chest like water about to boil. I don't want to leave the world with my last feeling being hatred and rage." Christine rubbed her eyes with her hands. "It's not fair. We were good people, 'Vita an' I. We din't do anything bad. Tried to help people. But we're apart. Dying alone. That scum Pazzo got to see his revenge coming true."

"He died of it, Christine."

"He got to see that other scientist go first. Why should his wish come true? Why should anyone's? Why aren't you sick? Why isn't Frank? Frank killed people. Why does he get to live?"

Nella sat slowly up, her hand tightening around the gun. "Nobody deserves to get sick, Christine. Not you, not Sevita, not anyone. It just happened. It wouldn't make you feel better to see him sick, not really."

"It's this rage, Nella. It hurts. It hurts worse than the cravings. Don't let it change who I am. Don't let it devour me. Do it, Nella, please."

Nella shook her head and stood up.

"Please, Nella, before it's too late." Christine had gotten to her knees, her hands shaking by her side. She raised one of them to her mouth, frantically biting the nail of her index finger, not stopping as she reached the quick.

Nella cocked the gun and pointed it at her friend's

head. The metal just brushed Christine's skin and slid past. Nella steadied it with her other hand.

Christine shut her eyes. "Thank you," she said.

"I'll remember," said Nella and pulled the trigger.

TWELVE

They sat on the end of a rotting log pile just in sight of the quarantine camp. It was obvious they'd been spotted. A man was sitting in the road leading to the camp, waiting for them to approach. Frank wasn't willing to go farther without Nella. Marnie had struggled until they reached the pile and then the distant crack of a gun made her sag in Frank's arms. He set her gently on the pile and sat next to her without saying anything. Marnie curled herself inward and tried to pretend she didn't see the clean handkerchief Frank offered her.

"You were supposed to save us," spat Marnie at last.

"We tried," said Frank, pulling at the splintering wood beside him. "We were trying long before you ever went into that bunker."

"You could have stopped this. Even if it was a lie. She would have believed you if you lied."

"You mean about choosing to be cured."

"Yes."

"There's no cure, Marnie."

She sat up. "Then what was the harm in lying to her? What difference did it make?"

Frank stood up. "It made a *difference* to her. She got to choose while she still could. What *difference* would it have made for everyone else whether she died now or tomorrow or the next day? What difference does it make to *you*?"

"She was my friend!"

"Yeah, mine too. That's why I told her the truth, while it could still help her." Frank paced a little way back into the field, rubbing a nervous hand over his scalp, hoping to see Nella trudging up it. But nobody appeared. *There was only one shot,* he told himself, wandering back to the pile. Marnie was still glaring at him. "What did you think was going to happen when we got here?" he asked.

"They could have saved the baby. She said it wasn't infected yet, that's not how it works."

Frank shook his head. "It was too little, it couldn't be born yet."

"We could have tied her up. Kept her safe and fed until it was ready. She said the world needed babies. That people needed hope so they didn't just run down and die like old clocks."

"You can't just tie people up and keep them prisoner like that."

"Why not? She wouldn't be a person once she turned. And we could have got the baby in a few months."

Frank gripped the back of his neck with one hand, trying to remind himself that the girl had been a tiny child when the Plague first hit. That she didn't know better, couldn't know. He leaned toward her trying to catch her gaze. "Christine was a person. She would be a person whether she was still immune or she was infected or cured, like me. We're *real*. We aren't monsters, though some of the things we've done may seem monstrous. I'm a *human being*, Marnie, just like you. I hurt, just like you. I get scared and worry and grieve, just like you."

"But you didn't!" shouted the girl, standing on the pile so she could hover over him. "You didn't feel anything. Just hungry. Just angry. You were as bad as a sick dog, once. That's why you wouldn't want to come back, because then you finally have to feel what you did. Then you finally have to hurt like the rest of us have for *years*. At least Christine might have given the world a baby. Another chance. What have *you* done since you were cured? You didn't save us. You're just like Henry. You left us to rot until it was too late so you could spend months or years wallowing in self-pity while the rest of us struggled on."

Frank was very still and his face was almost as pale as the surgical mask that covered its bottom half. "You're on your own, which must mean your parents didn't make it. I'm sorry. I don't know what's happened to you, but I wish it hadn't. Nella would understand better. Maybe you should talk with her sometime. I hope someday you grow enough to be ashamed of your words, and when you do, I want you to remember that I forgive you. I'm not a monster. Henry is not a monster. Christine wasn't going to be one either. I knew, even during the infection, that what I was doing was *wrong*. I tried, we all tried, to stop. We failed, but that doesn't mean we didn't feel it. That we didn't or don't grieve. We're not dogs. We're not cattle or slaves or prey. We're not vending machines for babies. I did what was right for Christine, because I cared about her. I'm as sad as you are that she got sick and that she died, but that doesn't make what I've done wrong. Maybe someday, you'll understand. I hope not. I hope you never have to."

Frank fished a flattened mask from his bag and tossed it to Marnie, then turned back toward the field and began walking away.

"Where are you going?" shouted Marnie.

"To find Nella. I shouldn't have left her alone. I thought I was helping but you aren't the kid I thought you were. You have any trouble go find your friend Henry. Looks like someone's waiting for us anyway. Make sure you wear the mask. You've been exposed, he may not have been."

Marnie slumped down on the pile to wait as Frank disappeared over a gentle rise.

Nella crouched in the shallow trench of damp dirt, stabbing at the ground with a jagged stick. Her eyes kept blurring as sweat rolled into them. The filthy mask billowed in and out as she dug, her breath straining and

wheezing against the small square. She didn't look at
Christine or up at the field, only at the dark scrape of hard
earth beneath her. After a long while, the stick shattered
and she tossed it away, raking at the dirt with her bare
hands and pushing it to one side. The sky gradually
receded above her and the walls to either side began to
grow. The dirt was damp and smelled like spring, like the
Farm just tilled. Nella could almost hear the quiet chatter
and songs of the stone pickers who smoothed it out.

She heard her name being called but she didn't look
up. Frank's long hand was a ghostly white as it closed over
her mud-caked one. She stared at it, not quite knowing who
it belonged to. Then she sat up. "I can't leave her like
that," she said.

"We won't."

She was spattered with soil and blood, old leaves
caught in the gore and her hair, crusted with a second skin
except where the sweat had washed trails down her face
and neck. Frank slid down into the ditch in front of her. He
threaded a finger around one of the mask's loops from
behind her ear and gently pulled it off.

"I have to finish," she said, her voice hoarse and
thick.

"I'll help you. Have a drink." He held the canteen
to her lips. She expected the water to be metallic and
warm, an echo of the death beside her. But it was cool and
clean. He recapped the canteen and pulled a clean mask
from his pocket.

"I don't have a shovel," she said, and small sob
leaked out. She half reached for him and remembered she
was covered in infected blood and pulled back. He pulled
his own mask off and kissed her. Then he looped the new
mask over her ears and pressed it carefully into place.

"We'll get it done. We won't leave it this way," he
said and pulled his mask back over his face. "And then this

day will be over."

She nodded, but her shoulders curled around her and she cried anyway. Frank pulled her up to stand and waited until she had calmed down.

"I'm going to finish this, but it won't be deep enough. There is a pile of small rocks near the road. If you can get just a few—"

Nella walked toward the road, grateful to concentrate on something else, relieved that she didn't have to see Christine lying so still next to her any longer. She lost track of how many trips she took to the dusty pile of rubble, halfheartedly carrying stones back to the ditch. The sun was well behind the nearby trees when Frank carefully lifted Christine into the hole. They were kneeling beside the grave, carefully arranging the stones, as if they were a kind of puzzle, when Marnie found them, with an older man in tow. Frank thought it might be the man who had been waiting on the road, but he wasn't certain. Nella sat numbly beside him watching the girl and man approach. Frank ached to take her away, to shield her from the two strangers so she could grieve in peace.

"Is that her?" asked Marnie.

Nella nodded.

"I'm sorry to interrupt," said the man quietly. "I wanted to make sure you didn't get lost when it became dark.

Frank nodded and stood up. Nella touched one of the stones for a moment, her fingernail flaking off a bit of lichen, and stood up as well.

"That's it?" said Marnie, "You just stick her in the ground and walk away? You aren't going to say anything?"

Frank's jaw clenched but the sorrow in Nella's voice made his anger loosen and drift away. "We said goodbye already, Chris and I. She cannot hear us anymore. There's nothing left to say."

Frank reached for her hand but she drew away. "I'm covered in— in *her,*" she said.

"Nella," he whispered, his eyes filling, "Your gloves tore hours ago."

She looked down at the pale shreds of plastic that ringed her wrists. "I can still protect *you,*" she said.

Frank shook his head. "I don't want to be protected from you."

"Maybe I'm immune. Maybe— I don't think my hands are cut. I'll wash them, it'll be all right."

"Of course," he said with a small smile.

"Maybe I can help," offered the man who had come with Marnie.

"You're from the Colony?" asked Frank.

"Yes, my name is Vincent. We have water and food, a place to rest if you like."

"Have you— have you had many visitors from the City?"

"Some. Not as many as we expected."

Frank nodded slowly. "We're too late then."

"You mean to stop the disease? No. We knew. Are you ill? Did you come hoping for a cure?"

"No, we came back to help," said Nella.

"Came back? Who are you?" asked Vincent.

"Frank Courtlen, this is Nella and the girl who met you is Marnie. She says she has a friend here."

"Henry," said Vincent, fumbling with a radio, "He'll want to know. And you— you're the people that cured us. I knew you'd come. This changes everything."

Nella shook her head, "We've been exposed. Marnie and I, certainly. Maybe Frank too. We came to warn you. And to make sure it can't spread. If we came with you, we'd just infect you."

Vincent shook his head. "We have a quarantine camp. I've been exposed too. The Colony is free of infection. But I have to tell Henry—" He glanced at them as he fixed the radio. The girl was eager, but the adults were exhausted, hopeless. His mood collapsed. He was grateful to see them, as if Frank and Nella were the help he'd prayed for days before. But to see the people who had saved him, who had resurrected him from hell, to see them so beaten and depressed, made him ache to aid them instead. "We can wait, you need rest. Marnie and I can call Henry after we get you settled. Do you think you can go a little farther? The camp isn't far."

Nella nodded and picked up her pack. She stumbled a little as she pulled it on. Frank steadied her with a frown. She glanced up at him. "Just tired," she said, "it doesn't work that fast."

"You aren't infected," he said.

Vincent stood for a long moment at the graveside.

"What are you doing?" asked Marnie.

"Saying a prayer for her," he said.

"But you didn't know her."

Vincent smiled. "I don't need to. I can see she was important to you and your friends."

"Thank you," said Nella.

Vincent nodded and then turned toward the Colony. He took care to walk slowly, though the light had softened to a dull gold over the field and the breeze became swift and cool over the grass. There was no need to exhaust them further. He knew he was being irrational. They were just people. His heart made them into fierce angels, ones who would vanquish the delusions of Father Preston, ones who would save them all. But they were just humans who had been in the wrong place at the right time. He wasn't even certain that they'd cured him out of compassion rather than self-preservation. Still, he sent out a prayer of gratitude for their coming and hoped it was heard.

THIRTEEN

Marnie recoiled as the quarantine camp's fenced cages came into view. "You want us to stay in there? Locked away?"

"I know it doesn't look friendly," said Vincent, "but we really will take care of you. It's as much to keep you safe from the others as it is to keep the Colony safe from infection. It's just for a little while, until we're sure who is Immune or was unexposed. Then we'll go up to the Colony together. You can talk to Henry any time over the radio, he's been looking for you since we left the Lodge. He'll be happy that you're safe."

"How many are in there?" asked Frank.

"With you— it will be thirty-three. No, twenty-nine."

"They are turning already?" asked Nella.

"Most of them were exposed weeks ago, in the City. It won't be long, another week maybe, before we know who is Immune."

They approached the wire fence and Vincent unlocked the gate. He rolled the key in his hand and Nella had a dizzying sense of deja vu. "For me, another few weeks. And I'll pass the keys to someone Immune."

He opened the door and motioned them in.

"And the ones who aren't Immune?" asked Frank.

"I— didn't expect to see you. The message said there was no cure. I did what I had to."

Nella gently squeezed his elbow, careful to only touch cloth. "There was never a cure for this one. There is no return this time."

"We can't tell anyone, though. If there are stragglers, we have to persuade them to return to the City or gather them together somehow. We have to convince the Infected that the City has a cure," said Frank, his voice low.

"And then?" whispered Vincent.

Frank looked at him for a long moment. "And then we need to make sure there is nowhere for the bacteria to hide, that it can't survive to threaten the people who are left."

The light in Father Preston's tent turned on as the last glow of the day evaporated. Vincent didn't want them to meet yet. "We can discuss this later," he said, "we have time, and you need rest."

Marnie was hesitant to enter her small cage, but relaxed when Vincent promised to return with the radio. He didn't try to separate Frank and Nella, leaving them in the tent where the mother and boy had been and returning only to bring them water and food. The worry on their faces was too contagious.

Frank pushed their packs into a corner of the small tent. Nella was staring at her grimy hands, holding them near the lantern. He glanced back at the packs, wondering if either of them would ever pick them up again, or if they'd finally reached their final spot, destined to rot away for years and years. He pulled off his mask, crumpling it in one hand as he walked toward Nella, stooping under the sagging canvas.

Vincent had left a bucket of water. Frank dragged it over to the lantern and knelt beside it. "Let me see," he said, and pulled Nella down beside him.

"Maybe   maybe we can save them for last?" she asked, pulling her hands to her chest.

He dipped a clean handkerchief into the water. "Close your eyes," was all he said. She felt the cold cloth smooth over her forehead, break the tight shell of sweat and dirt that smeared her cheeks and the corner of her eyes. Then the soft chiming drip of the cloth being soaked again. He pulled the mask from her nose and mouth and the cool air was fresh and sweet with the smell of the crushed grass beneath them. The water dripped and curled down her neck, leaving a trail of relief behind. He reached for one of her hands and her eyes flew open.

"Not yet," she said, pulling back. "Not yet. Let me pretend a little longer."

He shook his head, his eyes already red with grief. "Why? What good will it do? Whether you know or not, the outcome is the same."

"Because if I'm infected, I'll go to another cell. We'll be apart. I just want to wait another minute. I won't touch you, I just want to wait a minute."

"You aren't leaving. Besides, I kissed you already."

"The gloves broke when I was getting the rocks. You aren't exposed. When I clean my hands, everything will change."

He pulled at her hand again. "It won't, Nella."

She let him pull the shredded plastic from her hand. The soft roll of water swallowed her hand as he submerged it in the bucket, gingerly scrubbing with the kerchief. She pulled it from the water and it shone in the lamplight. Her eyes were too full of tears to focus.

"See?" he said, kissing her palm, "all clean, not a scrape."

She sobbed as he moved to the other hand. "Everyone's gone," she said, "why would I be different? There's always a price, Frank. Always. I killed my friend. The world docsn't let that go for free."

"A disease killed Christine. A disease killed Sevita. Not you. Not me. You have to calm down. Whatever happens, it's going to be okay."

Nella shook her head, but he just pulled the plastic from her hand and pulled it into the water. The sting of her skin told her it was broken. She didn't even look as he pulled it back into the light.

She pulled her hand back and slid over toward the

packs. "You aren't leaving," he said.

"I have to. You're safe right now. If I cough, if I touch a cut on your skin, you'll get it too."

"Maybe you're immune. You couldn't carry it if you were immune, right?"

She tugged on one of the straps of her pack. "I don't think anyone's immune, Frank. They would have made sure. They would have tried to infect as many people as possible. That was the whole point, remember?"

"But there have to be *some*. A few."

"Why should I be immune?"

"Maybe I am then."

"We're not." She pulled the pack free. He yanked it away.

"You aren't leaving."

"Stop, Frank."

"I told you that it wasn't *me* turning that scared me most, it was watching you go through that misery. The worst has already happened. Either you are immune and we'll both be fine, or you're already infected and I'll take care of you as long as I am able. There's nothing left to be afraid of."

"You can *still* be fine."

He shook his head. "No, I can't be. Nothing will ever be okay without you."

"Don't make this harder—" she started, but he closed his long hands around her arms and kissed her hard enough to be painful. She tried to draw back, but he pulled her even tighter and she tasted salt as his bottom lip split with the pressure. She gasped in pain and he let go.

"What have you done?" she cried.

"There was no other way to convince you," he said, "I told you I didn't want to be protected from you. If you're infected, I'm infected. There's no way I'm reliving the hospital. We stay together until the end."

A dark spot of blood welled up where his lip had split. She wiped it away with one finger, still crying.

"I'm sorry if I hurt you," he said, but she wasn't certain he really meant it. He pulled her into a hug. "I didn't mean to. If there's another reason— if you want to go, I'll let you. But not to protect me."

She shook her head. "It's a waste of your life. You could have been safe."

"Safe for what? Nella, I was waiting to die before I met you. I was just plodding day to day waiting until my time was done. *You're* who I was saved for. Whatever is left, whatever time or sanity or life, it was meant to be with you. I'm happy to spend them all. There's nothing wasted about it."

Nella put a hand on his cheek. "Don't die, Frank," she said.

He kissed the scrape on her other hand and then smiled. "Everything dies, Nella. What is it you said? 'It's okay. The world will keep going'?"

"Mine won't," she said.

FOURTEEN

"When can I see Henry?" asked Marnie as Vincent closed the fence gate between them.

"I'm sure he'll want to at least talk to you as soon as he knows that you're here. I'm going to radio him right now. But he hasn't been exposed. So he won't be able to visit until you are out of quarantine."

"How long is that?"

"A little over a month."

"A month? What am I supposed to do for a month?" she asked, flopping onto the small grass patch in front of her tent.

"I can bring you some books if you like."

"Can't read," scowled Marnie, "I was in kindergarten when the Plague hit."

"But your mom tried to teach you at the Lodge. I heard her reading to you through your window every night for years."

Marnie looked up sharply. "How do you know?"

"I was with Henry at the Lodge. A few of us were. You'll meet Ricky and Melissa and Molly later."

She stood up and came back to the fence, squinting at him. "But you weren't in the same pen as Henry. You were in the front. I remember you before you lost the eye."

Vincent felt his heart sink. "Yes," he said quietly. "I was in the front pens."

"My mother tried to cure the front pens. She walked for days to get the Cure for you. Do you remember her?"

"I remember," said Vincent, trying to decide if he should say more.

"I can't remember what she looked like anymore."

"Very much like you, from what I recall."

Marnie was quiet for a moment. "Was it you?" she asked at last. "I— I know you didn't mean to. I know it was the sickness. But was it you? Did you kill her?"

"It was me. I'm sorry Marnie."

"But you *weren't* sorry," she said. "She was just food to you. I heard her crying for days. She asked my dad to shoot her, but he wouldn't. I wanted to help her, but she pushed me away."

Vincent crouched near the fence so that he could see her face. "She wasn't pushing you away to hurt you, Marnie. She was trying to protect you. She thought you'd get thrown into the pen with her. I fought it as long as I could. I remember her every day. I know it's too much to ask, but I hope you will think about forgiving me. For your sake, not mine. I will try to be your friend no matter what you decide to do."

Marnie nodded, though she wasn't certain that she could forgive him. Or that she should. She just wanted the conversation to end. "Can you find Henry for me? I'd really like to talk to him now."

"Of course," said Vincent and retreated to his own tent for the radio. He closed his eyes, fighting the picture of Elizabeth huddled against the splintery wooden palings weeping as she watched him and frantically turning her little girl away from the crack in the walls. She wasn't the first person he'd killed, but he remembered her best, because of Marnie. And now he had to hope she'd trust him to keep her safe for weeks. He needed Henry and dreaded telling him at the same time.

FIFTEEN

Henry stripped the last of the silk from the cob and dropped it into the fire where it sizzled and drooped. "How many for seed again?" he asked.

"At least two hundred. But we have to eat something. Remember, we want the biggest and sweetest for next year. No more labs to do it for us," said Amos, counting the cobs in his barrow. "We don't have to get it all from this batch though, plenty coming."

Molly sighed. "Plenty. That's a nice, comfortable word. Haven't heard that much lately."

"Wish I could say it was going to be a familiar word. There's just too many people relying on too small a garden."

Henry looked down the hill where the quarantine camp's lanterns glittered like a strange constellation. "Our numbers will go down, soon enough," he said.

"I hate to say it, but I'm glad it's the disease and not us that is doing the choosing," said Amos.

"That's only because it hasn't taken anyone we know yet. Vincent's still— himself, isn't he?" asked Molly, carefully spreading the husks to dry beside the fire.

"He's lost a few people down there. He's had to— he thinks he's a murderer. Father Preston apparently excommunicated him. But he's still Vincent. The longer this goes on, though, the more I regret setting up that quarantine camp to begin with. What if none of them are immune? We would have lost a good man for no reason." Henry tore at some corn silk.

"No Henry, don't regret it. Even if none of them are immune, that quarantine camp is what's saving the people up here. It gives the refugees some hope. Makes them less desperate. If it didn't exist, or if someone less kind and careful than Vincent were running it, the people fleeing the City would have attacked us just to be let in. They're so scared they don't even realize they brought the thing they were running from with them. They would have fought us and then people up here would have become infected. The whole Colony would have been lost. Vincent's not just saving the Immunes down in that camp, he's saving us *all*. The best thing for us to do is to honor that and help these people survive. We don't have an easy road ahead of us either."

The radio on Henry's belt crackled and startled them all. "Anyone home?" Vincent's voice was tight and strained. Amos stood up and looked toward the camp, as if expecting attack or fire. Henry held the radio up. "We're here, Vincent."

"The others are with you?"

"Molly and Amos are, do you want me to find the others?"

"N— yes, Henry, go find them. The people that cured us are here. They have— news. But give the radio to Amos first."

"I'm here," said Amos, after Henry handed him the set.

"Oh, good, well, we need to add a few numbers to the food delivery and we're getting low on lime."

Amos frowned. "He's gone, Vincent. What did you not want to tell him?"

"I'm not good at this."

Amos smiled. "I like you better for it," he said.

There was a long silence before Vincent sighed, "It was *his* Marnie. I'm certain of it. She's been exposed, the other woman turned just after you left them. What do I tell him?"

Molly sucked in a startled breath. Amos glanced at her. "Is she showing symptoms?"

"She's not sick yet, but the woman, Christine— they'd been in the same shelter for weeks."

Amos shook his head and looked at Molly. "If we tell him, he'll just go running down there. He'll feel like it's his obligation even though there's nothing he can do."

"If we don't tell him," said Molly, "he'll never forgive us. He'll leave anyway."

"Amos?" Vincent's voice stuttered over the radio.

Amos blew out a sigh and then spoke into the handset. "We have to tell him, Vincent."

"It's a death sentence."

"It's his choice. Maybe we can put him somewhere else to minimize the risk of exposure. Maybe she's immune. Maybe *he's* immune."

"But you need him there."

Amos nodded, though Vincent couldn't see him. "I do. *We* do. But we can't chain him up and force him to stay. He thinks Marnie is the reason he was cured, that protecting her is his entire purpose. I can't take that from him."

Molly stood up and put her good hand on Amos's arm. "Vincent, you said the people that cured us came in too. Maybe they brought another cure! Why else would they come back here?"

"I haven't asked them. They said they came to help — but I don't think they have a cure. I think one of them, Nella, might be infected. Besides, if they had a cure, why wouldn't they be in the City? No, Molly, I don't think there is one. And I think they came because they knew they were the only ones that *could* come. I'm sorry. I seem to be delivering only terrible news."

"What's terrible news?" interrupted Rickey. He yawned and tried to pat down his rumpled hair. "Henry said the people that cured us are here. They got to know something, right?"

"Henry's back," Amos warned Vincent. "Let me tell him. I'll call you soon." He snapped off the radio.

Melissa and Henry trailed behind Rickey and sat on the damp stumps next to the fire. Melissa picked an ear of corn out of the barrow and began shucking it as if it had been her task all along. Molly sat beside her and played nervously with the pile of drying husks.

"Well?" asked Rickey, crossing his arms.

Amos pocketed the radio. "The people who cured you are in the quarantine camp. They said they were here to help."

Rickey stretched. "We know that, that's why Henry woke me up."

Amos nodded. He lowered a hand onto Henry's shoulder. "They brought Marnie with them." He felt Henry start and tightened his grip to keep him seated. "They've all been exposed, Henry."

"Shit," muttered Melissa, tearing the husks from another ear.

"Maybe they brought a—" Henry started, but Amos shook his head.

"We don't know for sure," offered Molly, "Vincent was just guessing."

"I think he's right. There is no cure, Henry."

"I promised her mother I'd take care of her."

Rickey shook his head. "You tried. She refused. You've kept your promise. We *helped* you keep your promise. There's nothing you can do for her now, but wait. She's with Vincent. She's as safe there as anywhere else."

"What if some of them turn? What if they hurt her?"

"Some of them have already turned, remember? Vincent won't let them hurt each other."

"What about at the end, though?" asked Melissa. "You know what he's planning. He won't be there at the end, only the Immunes. Or whoever still appears immune by then, anyway. Are we just going to trust them to stay patiently in their cells until the fortieth day?"

"We have three weeks until then, maybe more. If Henry waits until Vincent leaves with the Infected, he may avoid exposure. If he goes now, all he can do is get sick. We need everyone we've got here," said Amos.

"Wait," said Rickey, "Why are we arguing about this? Vincent said the people that cured us came to help. He may *think* there's no cure, but has he asked? They must have come for a reason. Nobody would tromp all the way out here if they weren't sure it was necessary."

Melissa shrugged. "They're exposed. The City is at least cut off, maybe destroyed. They've nowhere to go. Maybe they are the ones that needed help, but they were afraid to say so."

Henry looked at his hands. "Except for you guys, there isn't another human being I'd rather help than those three. If that's what they came for, then that's what I'll give them."

Rickey twisted a husk between his fingers, automatically shaping it into the cigarette he was craving. "You so sure we all feel that way? I want to talk to them first. I want to know why they cured us. I want to know why they are back now. Are they just cashing in a favor? Cause I'm still not certain what they did was to our benefit."

"You can't really mean you'd rather still be wandering out there, eating people?" asked Molly.

Rickey shrugged. "I didn't know better. I didn't care. Now I'm a nervous wreck. You guys don't know, you've only seen me this way, not who I was Before. I spend my days terrified that I'll lose it again. Or that I'll starve or get some awful infection with no doctors around. Everything is scary now. Nothing's easy. Maybe I would have been better off. If nothing else, I wouldn't have dreaded dying."

"There must be *something* worth being sane for," said Melissa, "otherwise, you wouldn't be scared of losing it."

"You three can pretend all you like, but I'm not the only one who feels like this. Least I don't have to remember tearing my kid apart or slaughtering a friend. Turned too late for that. Some people might not have chosen to be cured, if anyone had asked."

Henry pushed Amos's hand from his shoulder and stood up. "You don't want this? There's your solution, down there. Why don't you go take a stroll? No one's going to bring you back this time," he yelled. "Nobody has to worry about coming back, ever again."

Rickey raised his hands. "Whoa Henry, I'm just saying, I want to talk with our 'saviors' before we bend over backward laying out the red carpet. It's practical to ask them what's in it for them. They are people, Henry, just like everyone here. Maybe they are saints. Or maybe they cured us so we wouldn't eat them. Or maybe they had darker reasons that we never heard about. I just want to hear from them. Why'd they come back? How did they find Marnie and how did they know you'd want her? Is that fair?"

"That's fair," said Amos. "We're going to talk with them. But we're going to calm down first. Nobody is going to make very good decisions tonight. Marnie is safe and fed, Henry. You're an adult, and as stubborn a person as I've ever met. I know you are just going to go do whatever it is you think is right, regardless of what I say. But I'm asking you to wait, even for only a few days, until we know more. You know how badly we need you up here. You know every hand is necessary if we're going to feed all the mouths depending on us. What can you do down there for Marnie except sit and wait with her? You can talk with her on the radio, you can check on her with the binoculars if you want. When she comes out of quarantine, don't you want to have a house and a school for her? Enough food and fuel to get her through the winter? If you're down there, you can't do any of it. And if you get sick, you'll be a threat to her instead."

Henry rubbed the back of his neck and nodded. He glanced over at Rickey. "If it matters," he said, "I'm glad you are sane instead of dead, even if you aren't."

Rickey blushed and waved him off. "Shut up, you know I didn't mean it. Not like that. I'm glad I didn't have to eat all of you either."

SIXTEEN

Henry sat in the silo, dangling his legs over the edge and watching the glowing line of lanterns in quarantine camp. "Hey kiddo," he said.

Marnie's voice was thin through the radio, as if she had been crying or sleeping. "I'm not five anymore," she said.

"Right, sorry."

"I'm sorry I left you at the Lodge. It was stupid."

"You didn't know the City was going to have another outbreak. Nobody did. If you were my kid, I'd be proud of you for not going with a stranger and seeking out a place where lots of people could help."

"Am I?"

Henry scratched his head. "Are you what?"

"Am I your kid? Is that why you are nice to me? Is that why you came back to find me?"

"I came back to find you because I made a promise. And because I didn't want to think of you being hurt. I care about what happens to you."

"My dad said my mother was in love with you once."

"No Marnie, your dad was the only one she ever loved. I was friends with both of your parents, but I'm not your father."

"So then— do you expect something else?"

"Something else? What are you talking about? I don't expect anything. I just want to make sure you're okay. I want to keep my promise."

"People don't do that out here. You don't get something for nothing. I'm not your daughter so you must want me to be something else in return for food and security."

"I'd like you to be my friend, but you don't have to be. I'll still take care of you the best I can."

Marnie snorted. "You sound like Vincent."

"Good, I'd like to be more like Vincent."

"I don't understand you. Any of you. You have all the food, all the people, most of what's left in the world but you're just letting anyone come in. You're safe, you just have to keep everyone out."

"I know it must look weird to someone that's grown up with Phil's way of thinking, but the world isn't always like that. It isn't always the strongest and meanest who win. Not even now. You'll see. Maybe not right now, maybe not for a while, but someday, you'll see."

"If I ever get out of here."

"You will, Marnie. It won't be long. It's not just the sickness, I'm still building the house and we'll be setting up a school next. In the meantime, Vincent's not such a terrible guy. And I'm only a radio call away."

"You aren't going to come down here?"

"When Vincent and the others go to the City, I'll come stay with you until the quarantine is up."

"What if— what if they start to turn down here?"

"They will, Marnie. But Vincent will protect you."

"He won't! He killed my mother," her voice broke.

"I know. But he was sick. Like me. Marnie, if your mom had been put in my pen instead of his, it would have been me that killed her. He never wanted to hurt her, or anyone else. He's a kind, good man."

"But he will get sick too."

"If he gets sick, it will be long after he's gone from the camp. I will be with you instead."

Marnie was silent.

"Please," said Henry, "try to be friends with Vincent. He hasn't forgotten your mom or forgiven himself. I know you are probably too young to understand, but he's not the same person you knew then. I'm not the same Henry I was before either. We have to learn to like each other again. Please try."

Marnie didn't answer.

"I've got to go," said Henry, "my watch is up. Think about what I've said. What I'm asking. I'll call you again as soon as I can. Goodnight." He clicked the set off and slowly climbed down the silo. He stood a long time looking at the quarantine camp fence, worrying.

SEVENTEEN

Thirty-five if I'm lucky. The sides of the thin tent trembled with warm water, condensed from their breath. *Maybe thirty-eight. Maybe twenty-three if I'm not.* Nella rubbed her eyes and tried to stop the countdown of days in her head. She turned to her side. The light through the canvas made Frank an amber statue. She touched the scar on his cheek. *Thirty-six for you. Oh, Frank, I'm so sorry. So sorry.* There was a clinking outside. It got closer and she sat up. She crawled out of the small tent to find a woman pushing a cart of plates down the grass lane between cells. She stopped at each wired gate and opened it to hand food through. Some of the occupants greeted her but most didn't come out of their tents. Behind her was a hooded man reading aloud from a thick book. Nella thought she caught some bible verses but they were still too far to hear clearly. Nella clung to the wire fence, trying to see if it was Vincent. There was an urgency now, a push to do what they had come for. She wasn't certain whether she feared that she would run away at the first chance, or the onset of madness from the disease.

The people slowly moved closer, one cell at a time until Nella was certain it wasn't Vincent. There *was* something familiar about the man, but his face was still mostly hidden by the shadow of the hood. *Maybe it's another of the Infected that Frank cured,* she thought, uncomfortable with her inability to remember him. His voice was loud, strident, as if he were trying to persuade not just the person he was preaching too, but himself and maybe God as well. His voice woke Frank long before he reached Nella.

"Who is that?" Frank asked, threading his fingers through the fence and squinting against the heavy glare of the sun.

"I'm not sure, I thought maybe it was one of the

people we cured."

Frank shook his head. "No, more recent than that."

"Someone from the City?"

He shrugged. "Not sure. We're about to find out, though. Why is he out of a cell?"

"Maybe he runs the camp, like Vincent. They're bringing food."

An arm shot out of a cell as the woman stopped in front of it. She stumbled back a step. The arm wriggled and clawed. The hooded man stood and raised his arms, reciting loudly. A scream ripped through the camp, overwhelming the man's voice.

"Someone's turned," said Frank, putting an arm around Nella as if he could shield her from it.

"What is he doing? Is he one of those faith healers?"

"I don't know."

"He's not— he's not going to let it out, do you think?" Nella pushed herself a few inches back from the fence.

Frank shook his head. "That other man, Vincent is coming. He has an ax."

They watched as the hooded man turned toward Vincent and shoved him away, turning to speak even more loudly. The woman was cowering against the door of an empty cell. Nella could see other people coming up to their wire doors and looking out toward the commotion.

Vincent picked himself up, but didn't interfere as the other man continued to compete with the screamer. The woman covered her ears as the shrieks grew more shrill and the man's strident voice tried to rumble over them, to squash them, to drown them. A stone came sailing from another cell and hit the hooded man in the chest. He paused for a moment but went on. A few moments later, another stone, and then a few more. The man fell silent for a second. "Unworthy! You are all unworthy of miracles," he shouted. "You've sunk into doubt, abandoned God!" A larger rock was flung this time and the man dodged it and walked away from the screamer's cell coming closer to Frank and Nella. The woman followed him. Vincent set his mouth in a grim gray line and opened the screamer's cage. He used the butt of the ax to push the screamer back.

"He's going to get bitten," cried Frank.

The woman with the cart had reached them. She shook her head. "No, we all knew it was coming. Yesterday, today, tomorrow. A few days ago, Walter asked to be restrained so that if Father Preston's healing didn't work, he couldn't hurt anyone. His hands are bound and he's tied to the back fence by the waist. That was the farthest he could reach."

Frank glanced over at the cage. The flicker of Vincent's ax shone above the top for a second and then disappeared, along with the screams.

"Father Preston?" Nella asked. The hooded man glanced back at them and turned to greet them. He removed the hood and Nella could see the livid purple scars where his face had been repeatedly bitten. "*You.* What are *you* doing here?" she asked.

Frank pulled Nella back from the fence as if Father Preston meant to strike her.

"I'm sorry," said Father Preston, "have we met?"

"Ruth told us what you did. You hung people in front of her hospital. You tortured Bernard for protecting them. And now you're here? I wish we'd let you get eaten," cried Nella. "How did you come among good people again? How did you fool them?"

"What do you mean?" asked the woman. "Father Preston saved us. He cured us in that hospital. Ruth and Juliana were kind but they kept us from Father Preston's miracle for years."

Vincent was walking toward them, drawn by the distress in the woman's voice. He'd left his ax and was wiping his shirt with a damp towel.

"You were in the hospital?" Frank asked.

"Yes, for years. My mother brought me when she couldn't find enough food for us both."

"I thought Ruth explained to all of you," said Frank, shaking his head, "This man didn't cure you. He had no miracle. He was trying to take you from the hospital. He wanted to use you. He wanted you to be a slave—"

"That isn't true," shouted Father Preston, "I was saving them from starvation. I was giving them purpose again—"

"He didn't cure you," said Nella, "we did."

"But— I remember biting him and then— and then I was me again."

"It's because there was a strong sedative in the Cure. You did bite him. I pulled you off myself," said Frank. "Don't you remember waking up again in one of the cells?"

"Y—yes, Gray let me out," said the woman, with a fierce blush. She turned toward Father Preston. "What he said was true? That dart was really the Cure?"

"No, no, it was just coincidence. I was cured without any medicine, years before. Remember? It was the same miracle that cured you."

Nella shook her head. "You're *wrong*. You got lucky. Your body fought it off. You have no special powers, no miracles. I could forgive you believing that. Anyone could. Everyone wants some hope—" Nella's voice caught and she stopped.

"But you were going to enslave those people," said Frank, continuing for her. "You murdered people that only wanted to show some mercy to the Infected they could no longer care for. You forced a pair of Infected to pull a car. You were going to do the same or worse when you got your hands on the others from the hospital."

"No, it was Gray," said Father Preston, "It was Gray who said they could be useful. Why shouldn't they be useful? Why shouldn't they help us do God's work rebuilding this world? To atone for—"

"Atone? For what, Brother Michael? Being ill?" Vincent folded his arms over his chest, his one eye squinting angrily at the other priest. "How could they atone if they had no choice? How could they atone for what wasn't a sin?"

"Don't speak to me," spat Father Preston, "You're a murderer."

"So are you," said Nella.

"So are we all," said Frank, resting his hand gently on Nella's back to recall her.

"I am no murderer," said Father Preston.

"The corpses hanging on iron beams in the hospital field would say different. How many were there? A dozen? More?"

"That wasn't murder. That was *justice*. Those people hired someone to kill their loved ones, people that depended upon them. People that might have been cured."

The woman with the cart shook her head. "You didn't kill those people for justice," she cried, "You killed them to force Juliana to give us up. To give us over into your hands where you could use us. But these people stopped you. How foolish were those of us who stayed? How stupid to fall into your trap again. You've been using us just the same for months. You let *him* touch me and you *knew*." She turned and pushing past Father Preston and Vincent and she cried, "No more, I won't let him use the rest of them a minute longer. They have to know." She ran for the tent at the far end of the camp. Father Preston's face was deep red, the scars a dark, bruised purple. Nella thought he might have a heart attack. Instead, he pulled the hood of his robe up and shoved Vincent out of the way to go after the woman. Frank caught Vincent as well as he could through the fence.

"Are you okay?" he asked.

Vincent recovered his balance. He looked at the two of them, the people who were supposed to be his answer, his angels, and felt ashamed of Father Preston's friendship. "I didn't know about the hospital until now. Henry told me he found a Cure dart a few days ago, but I didn't— we didn't know what he had intended or that he murdered people. The others still don't know. They have no idea how dangerous Gray is. We wouldn't have let them stay."

"How could you have known?" asked Nella, "He told you the story he wanted people to hear. He had no one to contradict him."

"I feel more and more, that we've wasted the chance you gave us. We left the City because we couldn't find a place in it. We let a pair of liars and murderers into our Colony and believed they were good people. We're barely keeping infection at bay with this little camp. I cannot keep the Infected, I don't have a hospital— or time enough."

Nella smiled. "We are not your judges. You aren't indebted to us. We happened to be here on the right day at the right time to help you. Just luck. I'm ashamed to admit it, but I thought about shooting you the next day while you slept. I thought it might be kinder. But Frank showed me there was more to the Cured than just stories of guilt and despair. If you've anyone to thank, it's him."

Frank shrugged and traced Nella's scar with one finger. "I was just trying to save her. We're just people like you. We've done bad things and stupid things and some good too. I'm glad we were here to help, but you don't owe us an explanation for your lives before or since."

Vincent glanced back at the large tent. He turned back to Frank. "You came— he's only been here a few weeks. His scars weren't even scabbed over by the time he got here. He didn't pass through the City."

"No," said Frank, "I think the City was already closed by the time he would have been near enough. We know the radio signal was already working by then, and we got there too late even though we left a few days before Preston did."

Vincent stared at them. "You were safe?" he asked. "You knew about the plague and you were safe? Where are your masks? You'll be exposed. I thought you came from the City. You didn't tell me—" He spun around as if there were a pile of surgical masks waiting behind him.

"Vincent," said Nella, holding up her hand, "It's done already. There's nothing to protect us from." The scratch on her hand glowed a fevered red.

"You were *safe*. Why did you come back? Why did you come here?" He was angry but he wasn't certain why.

"Because it's not enough to just be safe anymore," said Nella. "We spent six years just being safe. Nothing got better. People like you were abandoned, when you could have been cured years ago because we were all playing it safe. We hid behind walls and the world decayed around us because it was safer to ignore it, to pretend the Looters were gone, that the Infected had died out, that we could just wait for someone to come along and rescue us. Things don't fix themselves. Life doesn't get put back together by being safe. No one's coming, Vincent. We have to rescue ourselves instead of running and hoping it doesn't follow. Frank and I tried to stop it, before, but we failed. We have another chance to stop it now. We have a chance to be better than safe. To do something better than just barely exist."

Vincent squeezed Nella's hand through the fence wire. He shook his head. "I don't understand, how can you help? What is it you want to do?"

"The City is closed off," said Frank, "but not completely. There must be half a dozen exit points in the Barrier and who knows how many people got out before the Barrier collapsed? Some of them are here, most are probably scattered, hopefully too scared of being shot to join other groups. We have to find them before they turn. Most of them won't willingly submit to a quarantine like this, especially if they know they are sick. We'll never be able to track them all down in time. We have to find a way to reach them all and to convince them to come back on their own. Not here. They'd overwhelm the Colony. Maybe the City. You believed we had a cure, maybe others will as well."

"And then?" asked Vincent.

"There's no choice. We have to end the threat. I don't know how. A bomb maybe? A fire? We were hoping we weren't the only ones thinking this way. Neither of us are military geniuses, we don't know what would be best."

"The bacteria can last for weeks, months even, in cloth or on surfaces. We'd need something that would sterilize everything," said Nella.

"What if some of them are Immune?" asked Vincent.

"If they aren't showing symptoms by now and they are from the City, they probably *are*. But someone not showing symptoms isn't likely to look for a cure, are they? Your Colony is large enough that they can order the stragglers into the quarantine camp until they can prove they are immune." Nella squeezed his hand back through the fence. "Sometimes the wrong people die anyway," she added. "Nobody deserves this. We have to do what we can.

Even if it means we aren't part of what's saved."

"Will you help us?" asked Frank.

"We all will," said Vincent.

EIGHTEEN

Melissa held the radio as if she didn't know what to do with it. It had finally gone silent a few seconds ago, snapped off by someone arguing with the woman screaming into it. Melissa looked up to find a large group of people had surrounded her, abandoning the stone wall to listen. They were all silent now. Rickey was leaning on a shovel beside her. He reached for a cigarette, forgetting there were none in his pocket.

"I knew he was bad," he said, low enough so only she could hear, "but nothing like *this*."

Some of the people around them were muttering now. "We have to do something, before there's a riot," whispered Melissa.

Rickey shrugged. "Why? If what she says is true, if they were going to use them as slaves, why should we stop them?"

"Because he's lived with them for weeks after his plan backfired. He's obviously not scared of them—"

"Or us," offered Rickey.

"Or us. He'll fight back, someone else will get hurt."

There was a scraping noise as someone picked up the heavy dead blow hammer from the rock wall.

"Wait," yelled Melissa, holding up her hands. Rickey shrugged and held up his too, the shovel still clasped in one hand. "Remember that the people in the quarantine camp might not be— they might not be themselves. Maybe this woman— maybe she turned."

One of the men twirled a chisel on his palm. "Lisa's only been down there a few weeks. She wouldn't be sick yet."

"Maybe she's had to see things that upset her, gave her a bad scare or nightmares—"

"Well, let's go find out," said a woman from behind

Melissa.

There were murmurs of agreement. Melissa glanced at Rickey. He hesitated, then nodded slowly. "Yeah," he said, "why don't we do that. But let's leave the tools here, huh?" He chuckled as if it could break the tension. "Can't exactly replace them easily. That might be the last chisel in a hundred miles you know."

The man twirling the chisel looked down at it with a frown. He considered, then gently set the tool down into the grass. The shovels and hammers were quietly piled, one by one against the stone. "There," said Rickey quietly, "they can be reasonable."

Melissa's skin prickled. "I don't know if reasonable is the word for it. But at least there'll be less collateral damage this way. One of us needs to find Henry or Amos."

"If they decide to lynch him, I'm not going to stop them," whispered Rickey as the crowd pushed past them, "and you should know that Henry and Amos won't either."

She stared at him. "You've discussed this?"

"Not *this*. But him. We knew they were faking Father Preston's 'miracle'. But we didn't know he killed people. Or what he meant to do with the Infected if he gained control over them. We knew he had to go, but if we tried to expose him, who were Father Preston's people going to believe? We couldn't let him take them somewhere and keep manipulating them. So we pretended to be friendly. Now we can move against him. One thing's clear, he can't stay here. He's dangerous."

"The others should still know," she said.

"I think they are finishing the latrine sheds today," Rickey offered.

Melissa ran to find them.

Gray was in the garden with half a dozen of Father Preston's people. They were meant to be picking the last of

the beans for pickling, but he was dozing near the small
tool shed. The news was softly spread, but swiftly, like a
breeze across the field, and he didn't wake as the Cured
threaded their way toward him, slipping through the rows
of corn and stepping gingerly around the green potato tops,
knowing what each plant meant, even in their anger. They
moved like a single animal, like a snake coiling around its
prey, without speaking, without signals. They wrapped
around him, armed only with rage, but each of them knew
how much damage that alone could do. Most of them had
scars to remind them.

Rickey hung back, watching the others. It wasn't
his injury. Though he didn't like Gray and he'd make no
move to save him, it wasn't Rickey's vengeance to take.
There was a moment of stillness. A collective intake of
breath. Someone in the center of the circle kicked Gray's
leg. He sat up with a grunt, his face tightening with
surprised anger as he looked around him.

"What is this?" he snarled.

"We know," said the woman who had kicked him.

Gray stood up and took a step toward the woman,
towering over her. "What is it you *think* you know,
darlin'?" he sneered when she didn't back up.

"We know about the Cure," said a man behind him.

"And we know about the people you hung at the
hospital," said another.

"And about what you wanted us so badly for,"
finished the woman in front of him.

"Me?" Gray laughed. "What did I have to do with
anything? I was just being faithful. Just following Father
Preston. He said the people at the hospital were evil, that
they had to be punished, that God said so. I'm just a
humble man, who am I to argue with a priest? I just did as
I was told. It was *him* that wanted you, it was *him* that lied
to you. Not poor, guileless Gray."

A rumble rolled around him through the crowd.

Gray turned toward a few of Father Preston's people who were mixed in with the others. "I stuck with you. I stayed to care for you, keep you safe. But where's Father Preston? Off doing his medicine show bit for strangers. He doesn't care about you. You're old hat. Used up. He needs new people to con. But ol' Gray didn't leave you. No, I stayed cause I knew you were alone in the world. That you needed a friend to look after you. I've kept you fed, haven't I? Kept you from getting sold off to slavers or killed by bigger bands. Kept you from getting sick again."

"You knew about the Cure," shouted someone.

Gray put up his hand. "You're right. You're right, I knew. But I've made up for it, haven't I? That one teeny secret? Besides, I thought about telling you, I really did. You can ask Henry if you don't believe me." He pointed to Henry who had just come, panting, into the garden. "What good would it have done? Did it matter how you were cured? Nah. What mattered was that you *were* cured. If you wanted to believe in a miracle, it was harmless. Who was I to naysay it?"

"You used their belief to manipulate them, Gray. You've been acting the lord of the manor since you got here," shouted Rickey into the crowd. "You got the best food, the best bed, the women of your choice, because they thought you were part of the miracle. Because they didn't know you were *just like them.*"

Henry was still gasping to catch his breath as he pushed his way through the circle. He pulled the Cure dart from his pocket and threw it into the shed wall, where it stuck, the scarlet fronds trembling from its tail. "You didn't want us to tell them. You wanted to keep living with these people as your servants. And I almost fell for it. I almost bought that these people were so broken, they'd fall apart if they knew the truth. Look around you, Gray. These people aren't crumbling. They're reforged, sharp, dangerous. And they know a traitor when they see one."

"Then they should take care to point their anger in an appropriate direction," Gray spat. "I was only following orders, only carrying out Father Preston's requests."

Rickey caught sight of Amos crossing his arms over his chest, hovering behind the crowd.

"You sure worked hard to make certain no one questioned his version of things," said Henry.

There was a deep, throbbing rumble through the crowd again.

"Someone had to be in charge. Someone had to lead you out of that hospital so you'd survive. If you didn't believe Father Preston, you would have wandered off, starved, got shot. It would have been chaos."

"If you are so faithful to Father Preston," Amos said, his low voice slicing through the crowd's restlessness, "perhaps you should join him in his work at the quarantine camp."

"Now hold on, I've seen that Father Preston was wrong, we went separate ways long ago. You need me here." He looked around at the crowd, seeking out the familiar faces. "You don't know how it is out here. You've been locked away in that hospital all this time— I've been surviving out here. I can *help* you. These people— they seem nice, but everyone's out for themselves. We just don't know what they want yet, but rest assured, they want *something*." Gray stabbed a finger toward Henry and a few heads turned to follow. "They've done things— they haven't been kept safe in a hospital. They've *killed*. They've *slaughtered*. Maybe even after they were Cured. They aren't like you. They don't know how precious you are, you are *chosen*."

"They're Cured," said Rickey, "just like us. Not by

- 113 -

miracles. Not by Father Preston. And certainly not by you."

"It's true," called Melissa, holding up the radio, "the people that cured you are in the quarantine camp right now. The same people that cured us. You belong with us. Not with someone who wanted to use you like animals— who *still* uses you that way."

One of the men shoved Gray toward the edge of the garden. "Get out of here," the man growled. "Don't come back."

Amos flicked an uneasy glance toward Henry but didn't move.

"I'm not going anywhere," protested Gray, he pushed the man back, "I've as much right to be here as you."

"Do yourself a favor," said the man, "Go while you still can." The Cured pressed in behind him, a wall of restrained hate.

Gray laughed. "I *told* you, I'm not going anywhere." He punched the man in front of him, who crumpled under the blow. "Lesson one," Gray boomed, a greasy smile slithering over his face, his confidence back, "Might makes right now. I've got the brains and the strength to survive. *You* do not. I spent the past eight years learning how to thrive. *You* spent it being diapered and spoon fed. You want to survive out here? You do what *I* say."

Henry watched as a few of the crowd quailed, took a step or two back. He felt a passing wave of disgust at their weakness but he saw Amos look over at him. *The world needs innocence,* he'd told Henry, *These people aren't useless. They might be the most important ones here.* Henry strode through the crowd toward Gray. "They don't need you to survive anymore. They don't need to scrabble and fight and kill. They've got us. They've got this place.

Get out of here, Gray. Your kind doesn't belong here anymore."

"My kind?" shrieked Gray, "My kind? That's rich. You mean Immunes? You mean *humans*? Cause all I see in front of me is a pack of dogs. You want to know why I treat you like animals? Because that's what you are. You aren't *cured*, you're just as vicious as you were before. And you want to turn *me* out?"

"Actually," said Henry, "when I said 'your kind', I meant thugs, looters, murderers. And for the record, I don't trust you to leave. I'd rather kill you and be done with it, but these people seem to be kinder than I. If I were you, I'd take them up on their offer while it still stands. And if you ever come back, I'll rip out your throat with my own teeth and show you what a *real* animal can do." He said it coolly, the people around him falling silent as he spoke, but the pounding of his blood in his head, the sound of his own interior fury, was all that Henry could hear.

Gray must have heard it too, he understood Henry wasn't bluffing and stumbled toward the wall behind him. They watched him climb clumsily over the unfinished end and career down the field.

"He's not going to go that easy," said Rickey. "Tonight, tomorrow, next week, he'll try something. Heaven help us if he finds a few more desperate people to join him."

"We'll be ready," said Henry grimly.

NINETEEN

Father Preston's tent stood alone at the end of the wall, his followers having abandoned the isolated camp within hours. They'd mingled among the other half built houses and the barn, some re-pitching tents in the spaces between buildings, others invited in to share the buildings. Henry thought the large tent of the priest shone like a medal, the first trophy in the battle for the world. But he knew it ought to come down, it was a place to hide if Gray came back and they could use the canvas. It was after dark when he finally began pulling the stakes up, carefully scanning the wall, expecting a darker shadow to climb over it at any time. Molly joined him as the tent collapsed in a billow of air and dry leaves. She helped fold the cloth without comment. The grass crushing below their knees made a sweet green smell and the quiet murmur of the people in the tents around them reminded him of long ago concerts and evening football games. He had a sudden ache in his chest for everything and everyone he'd forgotten to miss.

"Any word from Vincent?" he asked, trying to brush the feeling aside.

"He's talking to Melissa. The people— the ones from before, they have a plan, but they need us. She went to get everyone. They'll be here in a minute."

Henry nodded.

"Are you still going to go?" asked Molly. "Even after what happened today?"

"You mean to the quarantine camp for Marnie?"

Molly nodded, her movement barely visible in the dusk.

"It would be okay. Everyone up here would be okay, if I did. You know how to plant now and keep watch and defend it. And the others are here. Marnie's got no one. Nobody she knows. She must be frightened. I was."

"I could go, instead, Henry."

"What? Why Molly?" He knelt beside her, pushing the air out of the folded cloth.

"People need you here. You're tough and you can fight and you and Amos are smart. I was just a grocery clerk. I was almost as young as Marnie, Before." She held up her scarred arm, the fingers of its hand gone, the skin shrunken almost to the bone, no muscle to pad it. "I'm not strong. I'll never plow a field or build a house or skin an animal. And there are a dozen others like me, who can't do those things either. We weren't meant for the world the way it is now. If that man, Gray, if he came back right now, I couldn't fight him, not like you or the others. But I can sit with Marnie, I can watch her for you. I can do something to help, have a purpose again."

Henry closed his hands gently around her shoulders, suddenly aware of how young she really was. "Molly, you *do* help. You already have a purpose. You *can* plow or build or fight if you want to, but you're important for all the things you already do. You're the best gardener we have, Amos told me. He would have pulled half the corn this year thinking they were too small but you tended each one until it caught up. Rickey says you are the most reliable on watch, that you never fall asleep like some of his guys or wander because you are restless. And since Vincent had to go, no one but you has been able to get the kids to pay attention to lessons. The Colony would *miss* you, Molly. It can spare me for a few weeks to keep Marnie company, but I don't think it will ever be able to spare you. Anybody can fight, in their way. It's not many people that can do what you can." He hugged her and realized how right Amos had been. It was people like Molly who were rebuilding the world. "I'm counting on you to stay, to look after this place. I trust you with it while I'm gone."

She nodded and he let her go. They finished folding the cloth as their friends gathered around them, lantern light bouncing across the grass.

"Okay," said Melissa, "we're all here."

"We're here too," Vincent's voice was thin, faded through the radio. Henry half expected it to pop like an old record. He wondered if Gray had tried to harass them or if there were a number of people who had just turned, to make Vincent sound so tired.

"How is— everyone down there?" asked Melissa, glancing at Henry. Molly slipped her hand into his and gave it a comforting squeeze.

Vincent sighed. "We had three more turn today, all from the early group. I think— Dr. Ryder thinks Father Preston's beginning to show symptoms. Paranoia, short temper, irrationality. Marnie is okay. No symptoms. She'd like to talk to Henry. Dr. Ryder and Mr. Courtlen are also showing no symptoms."

There was a pause.

"And him?" asked Molly.

"And you?" Melissa spoke into the radio.

"I'm— tired. But no stumbling or slurring. No cravings. Nothing that I can remember from last time."

"Maybe I should go down and help—" started Henry.

"But I don't want anyone to worry," continued Vincent, "we don't need anyone else exposing themselves. I'm still able and I have help now, with Nella and Frank. We have to decide how this ends, that's why we've called."

"How this ends? It ends when the forty days quarantine is up, doesn't it?" asked Melissa. "Then you come back with the Immunes."

"And if I get sick? How will they care for themselves?"

Melissa shook her head, though Vincent couldn't

see. "We'll deal with that when we get there."

"If that were the only danger—"

"May I?" a woman's voice broke in. Her voice was clearer as the radio was handed to her. "This is not the only place with Infected. Sevita tried to close off the City, but she may have been too late, and there are exits she missed. She stopped a flood of refugees from overwhelming this place but there will still be contagious people out there. That's to say nothing of the City itself. This bacteria can live for weeks in the open. People that know about the City will try to go there, thinking the sickness is over, thinking they can pick up what was left behind. We've either got to sanitize it or destroy it so that it won't be a temptation. And we have to draw the people that successfully fled back for — for the end."

"Give me that," scowled Rickey. Melissa handed him the radio. "You keep saying 'we', but why do 'we' have to do *anything?* Why not let the looters get sick if they rob a graveyard? The winter is coming, the Infected will just die off."

"But so will others. There are other groups, other settlements of *good* people that will take them in without knowing. The Plague has a long incubation, it can take its time to spread—"

"So go talk to those other good people then. Why's it got to be us?"

Nella's sigh was deep and shaky. Rickey felt an immediate slap of guilt in his gut. "It doesn't," said Nella, "We came here first because we knew where you were. Frank and I— we're not virologists or military experts. We're just— we're *what's left.* We came hoping someone here could tell us what to do to stop this thing. You have more people than anywhere else. We thought maybe someone there would know about a bomb or how to set a fire that would gut it or even just how to broadcast a signal that people can pick up to draw them back to the City."

Rickey glanced at the others, but was determined to have his say. "You came because you cured us. 'Cause you thought we owed you something."

There was a pause before the woman quietly answered, "I hoped you might be friendlier to us than a stranger, but I don't think you owe us anything."

"We never *asked* to be cured."

"I know."

"Maybe some of us would have preferred to die the way we were."

"I know. I'm sorry." Nella's voice had sunk to a shaky whisper.

"And you didn't even hang around afterward to explain things. Just left us a shitty 'Dear John' letter. Do you have any idea how terrifying it was to wake up like that? To find yourself older and injured and with memories worse than anything you'd imagined yourself capable of before. Why did you leave us like that? What was so important that you couldn't be there just to *explain*?"

It was a man's voice who answered him now, a calmer one than Rickey had expected after his prodding. "We left because we were trying to stop this. We were trying to find the bacteria that caused this before it could be released. We thought we had won. We thought he only had one opportunity. But we failed. So we're here asking for help to stop it for good. We're asking for help so we don't fail again. I *know* what you woke up to, who you saw in the mirror. We wanted to come back, we thought we could make it back before you woke up. We never meant for the letter to be it. But you were already gone when we returned. But if you are truly unhappy being Cured, you can come with us. Make this part of your life mean something besides guilt and misery. You can help us stop it this time, so nobody has to choose between death and the

Cure again."

"So what do you want us to do? I don't exactly have a nuke in my back pocket," said Rickey, his tone softening.

"A nuclear bomb won't work," rumbled Amos.

"You're far enough from the City," said Frank.

Amos took the radio. "If the weather holds, sure, we could use one. But a shift in the wind and it would wipe out our crops at the very least. Besides, like you said, there are smaller settlements that are way too close. And if a fire started who knows how far it could spread."

"Poison then? In the water. Even the people who have already turned would have to drink. We could make it painless."

"Still won't take care of the stuff people would want to loot," said Amos.

"What about the stuff from that seed store? You said it'd kill anything when we were looking for weed killer," said Henry.

"Chloropicrin," sighed Amos. "It will, it'll sterilize everything. But we'd need a lot. And it doesn't travel easy."

"Is there enough where you found it?" asked Frank.

"There is. But we can't just pile it in a corner, it's a fumigant. Someone has to spray it, over everything. We might be able to risk a sprayer truck but that would only get the streets. Someone would have to go door to door and spray every building. You'd never last that long. You'd be dead within an hour."

"There is more than one of us down here." His voice was gentle but he wasn't wavering.

"I don't suppose anyone knows how to fly?" asked Molly.

Amos shook his head. "Don't even know where we'd get the fuel." He spoke into the radio again. "Thing is, the dose could vary depending on the weather and where people were. It might take a few days to be sure. Or a few applications. Without masks, you'd never make it. And as soon as you drank or lay down to sleep, you'd be absorbing it anyway. You'd have to last long enough to be certain or the whole thing is useless. And that's assuming none of you are Immune."

"We'll find masks, then," said Frank. "And— there's a boat. Whoever is still able can stay on the boat, until this is done."

"And then?" asked Amos.

There was a silence. "And then we set out for open ocean. If anyone is still sane after forty days, they can return. Whoever isn't sane won't make it back to land to infect anyone else."

"You have enough water and food?" asked Amos.

Frank sighed. "We're putting the cart before the horse. If we make it that far, I'll worry about it. We've enough to do before then. Besides, we've yet to meet a single Immune. I don't think we'll be that lucky."

Rickey motioned for the radio. "Say we do this. Say we find this poison and the boat and the masks and somehow set up a signal, how do we know you'll follow through? How do we know you won't run at the last second."

"We weren't infected. We were safe, far up the coast. We came back knowing it was a risk. We've submitted to being in your quarantine cages without any protest. Nella has been exposed. There is no escape for us. If that isn't enough, we'll be with Vincent. You trust *him*, don't you? He won't run and he'll make sure we don't either."

Rickey was silent. Frank continued. "I know this is a lot to plan. We have some time, though it never seems like it. I'll— I'll give Marnie the radio so she can talk to her friend."

Rickey handed the radio to Henry. "Don't take too long," he said, "looks like we have a lot to do."

"Don't be so nasty," scolded Melissa, "They are trying to protect us, to help us."

"Yeah, well maybe I don't want to be protected," he grumbled, picking up the bundle of canvas that had been Father Preston's tent.

"You aren't the only person here," she chided and walked away with him, still arguing.

Amos helped Molly with the stakes and poles, drifting quietly back toward the village so Henry could listen to Marnie in peace.

TWENTY

Gray sat beneath the wall that had edged Father Preston's tent. He could hear Henry mumbling to the kid on the radio, but he mostly ignored it. He'd heard what he needed. They thought they could throw him out. *Fucking zombies,* he thought. They had no idea what he could do. He'd have left them alone, as soon as something better came along. But the truth was, he admitted to himself, he'd nowhere to go. No more favors to cash in, no more schemes to play out, no more suckers to wind around his fingers. So he sat there, becoming simultaneously more furious and more panicked with each passing moment. Until he heard about the boat. The boat was a way out. To somewhere better. To new schemes, to new suckers. A way out of this plagued, dying, used up place. All he had to do was wait. When Amos, Henry, and Rickey left, he'd hit them. He could handle a couple of dumb broads. The rest of them were practically helpless. Practically house pets who couldn't even feed themselves without the help of the leading five. And when they were good and distracted, he'd take the boat. He'd leave them all to rot, to turn, like the rabid beasts he knew they always were, that they were waiting to turn into. Gray stared down at the quarantine camp below him. He wondered if he could let a couple loose to wreak havoc. The camp was quiet. *Must be dealing with them when they turn,* he thought, *ah well, not worth risking catching it anyway.* He slunk back into the trees, careful to keep under the edge of the wall. One night of rough sleeping wouldn't kill him. Tomorrow he'd be headed for the sailboat. Maybe the tropics after that. Joe had said something about Florida years ago, long before he became the silent gardener Bernard. Gray hadn't listened then, but a sandy beach sounded pretty appealing these days. He flung himself onto the dirt, turning his face toward the dim lights of the Colony, keeping his watch as he imagined a new life, one with plenty of everything.

Molly climbed up to the top of the silo. It was late, even the watch fires at the ends of the wall were little more than coals. She liked the quiet and the soft blur of the mist rolling over the grass. The breeze mixed the smell of smoke and fresh sawdust and the sweet green smell of bruised corn leaves. It was comfortable. She didn't feel people watching her, she didn't feel "extra", apart. She wanted to believe Henry. She wanted to believe someone would miss her if she were gone. It made her happy to watch them like this, like a fairy godmother who'd sneak away before she was seen, but she sometimes wished she was caught at it. Not tonight, though, tonight she wanted to send a message without being overheard. She clicked the radio on. "Vincent?" she said softly into it. She winced as she watched a light turn on in the quarantine camp.

"Molly? Is everything all right?"

"I'm sorry to wake you. I wanted to tell the people that cured us— I didn't want them to think Rickey spoke for us all. Is the lady really infected?"

"I don't know. I hope not, but she buried her friend and was exposed to the blood. Unless she's immune, I don't know how she can avoid infection."

"Why is it people like them, Vincent? Why isn't it people like Gray or Phil? Why is it you?"

"It isn't a punishment, Molly."

"But everything happens for a reason right? So how come I'm up here, useless and protected while you're down there getting ready to die when so many people need you?"

She thought she heard Vincent laugh. "I'm glad you are safe up there. You are not useless, I miss you every day. One of these days even you will admit how heroic you are. Don't mourn for me, Molly. I don't know what the master plan is, but I know my part will help you, so I'm satisfied. And then I get to go home, when my work is done. Maybe Gray still has work to do, a chance to change. Maybe Nella and Frank have earned their rest. Maybe what's waiting for them is better than what they'd ever find here."

"But you'll leave us behind— just like all the rest of the world. We're just leftovers. Scraps."

"Not scraps, seeds. The hardiest of us, for a better garden."

"I'd rather come with you."

"No, Molly, they need you here. There are enough people following me back to the City. I will not be lonely."

"I will be. All of you with your roles, your quests. I'm just like the little boy who couldn't keep up with the Pied Piper."

"You think of your injury too much. How many others have a scar? How many are missing limbs or senses? I'm missing an eye, Molly, but it doesn't make me less. You can do more than you think. You aren't being left behind. You have your job to do too. You have to protect the Colony so the others have somewhere safe to come home to. You think Gray is going to stop because he's beyond the wall now? You think that when Melissa sets up the radio signal, no one will come looking for where it came from? We'll all be gone on our 'quests'," he paused to chuckle softly, "and the Colony will be at its most vulnerable. You have to rally the others, all those people from the City and from Father Preston's group. You have to defend it so that the others have somewhere safe to come home to. So that those quests have a purpose and a reward. You must be their King Arthur."

Molly laughed in spite of the grief sawing roughly at her chest.

"Do you want me to give the radio to Nella and Frank?" prodded Vincent gently.

She felt a blush rise in her face. "No, no, I'm afraid I wouldn't say it right. Will you tell them for me? Just tell them 'thank you'. I know it isn't enough. Tell them I'll remember them. I wasn't certain, at first whether I was grateful for the Cure. I didn't think I wanted to go on being me. I thought things would never be as good as they had been, before the plague. That my happiest days were behind me, so what was the point? Tell them I was wrong. I've never had friends like I do now, you and Henry, and the others. I was invisible Before, and I thought that was the best I could be. But now, after all the things I've done, with all the reasons we have to be jealous or fight each other, now I'm loved. And that's better. Will you tell them, Vincent?"

"I'll tell them. Goodnight, Molly."

"Goodnight."

Vincent clicked the radio off and scrubbed at his good eye. He didn't want to tell her, but her voice had made him the loneliest he'd ever been, even the solitude of the monastery couldn't match it. He had a need to be among other humans, even if they were strangers. He ducked out of the small tent, keeping his own night watch, checking the fences, listening for bad dreams. But the disease was merciful and nobody turned that night.

TWENTY-ONE

"I don't like leaving her alone while we do this," grumbled Amos.

"She's not alone. She's got the entire Colony with her. You should be more worried about Melissa and Rickey. Or me and you, when it comes to it." Henry glanced back in the side mirror, watching Molly carry a bucket of water as Amos pulled away.

"You can't really think Gray's just going to go away because we told him to, do you? What if he tries something before we get back?"

Henry's face paled, but he shook his head. "Not today, it's too soon. He knows we expect him to come back. He'll try something alright, but he's the type to wait until he thinks we aren't paying attention. He'll give it a few days." He paused for a moment. "Or he'll attack us for the truck, since we're on our own, or Rickey and Melissa for their gear," he added grimly. "But Melissa knows every footpath and street in the county, even after it's disappeared into weeds. She can outwit Gray. And as long as we stay alert, he shouldn't get the jump on us. And we should be back by tonight, right?"

"We'll make okay time there," said Amos, "we cleared it last trip. But I wasn't kidding when I said this stuff is hard to transport. You get a container of more than a dozen or so gallons and a little knock can make it explode. We're going to have to crawl back, especially if we can get a sprayer truck filled and working. And we have to. This plan isn't going to work without a sprayer truck." He was quiet for a moment. "Henry, you saw the cans in back? It's the last of the gasoline. All of it. I know you're looking at this week as a kind of endgame before you go into quarantine, and maybe you don't think— maybe you aren't planning for after. But I have to."

Henry scrubbed his face. "We checked all the

stations?"

"Everything in twenty-five miles. I knew it before we went anyway. Scavv teams have been out as far as a hundred."

"This is it then, isn't it? Either way, we're really on our own. Modern life is done."

"Until we can grow enough corn for ethanol. Assuming we could figure it out. It'll be a few years. It had to happen at some point right? Guess this is as good a reason for using what's left as I could ask for. Was kind of hoping to find a horse or cow first, though. Going to have to yoke me to the plow next year instead." He snorted and Henry laughed.

The truck kicked dust up into a cloud of gold around them and Henry stuck his arm out the open window, feeling the breeze, trying to hold the memory of movement close for when it wouldn't be there anymore. "I'm not planning on dying, if that's what you are asking," he said suddenly, grabbing a fistful of heavy goldenrod as they passed. The feathery blossoms broke off in his hand. "You were right, there's nothing I can do for Marnie right now, but when Vincent leaves, when he takes everyone with him, she'll stay because she's going to be an Immune. Then I'll go into quarantine with her. And when we're back in the fall, we'll find a library and start reading about ethanol. Next year will be better."

Amos nodded. "From your mouth to God's ear, Henry. Next year *will* be better. Amen to *that*." The truck bounced over a deep hole and Amos fell silent, gritting his teeth and concentrating on the miles left to go.

"Keep up," scolded Melissa, adjusting the heavy pack on her shoulders. "I don't want to get separated and have to come rescue you when Gray pops out of the bushes."

Rickey scowled. "I wouldn't need you to rescue me. Can rescue myself." But he picked up his pace. "Where's this place again?"

Melissa shaded her eyes. She pointed to a hazy point that poked against the horizon. "Top of that mountain."

Rickey groaned. "That's days away."

"Yeah, but it's the only one in range that has its own power source. Just hope nobody else is using it or we're going to have trouble."

He caught up to her and said in a low voice, as if afraid of being overheard, "It's not trouble ahead I'm worried about, it's the asshole we left behind us."

"Yeah, I'm worried about that too. But Molly's got almost a hundred people who can help her if he comes back. And Amos and Henry will be back tonight."

"What if he doesn't attack them? What if he does something to the quarantine camp? Molly will try to protect them and then the whole Colony will get exposed."

"Vincent won't let her. And that couple— the ones that cured us, they don't seem the type to roll over and die. They're tough and they've tangled with Gray before. I bet if they'd been with us, Gray wouldn't have been let go. I have a feeling he's done a lot more than we know about."

Rickey's thin face was still drawn in, all angle and nose as if he were consuming himself from the inside out, a vacuumed bottle of worry. Melissa glanced at him. "Stop it. We can't do anything about it. We're going to have to trust that the others are doing what they are supposed to, because we've got to do our job too. If we don't get this signal up in time, the whole thing's for nothing. And I'll feed you to the first Infected that shows up next spring."

Rickey glanced back once more, though the Colony had been out of sight a long while. He bounced the pack on his shoulders and then plunged into the thin woods behind

Melissa.

Nella paced the small square of their cage. She looked around her. Frank was fiddling with something inside the tent. She quickly stood on one foot and closing her eyes, began to mouth the alphabet in reverse order. *Still all there,* she thought with relief.

Frank's breath was warm in her ear. "You're still you," he said, and caught her as she lost balance and put her foot down. She gave him a sharp look, expecting that he was making fun of her, but his face was serious, sad even.

"I just thought you might want a second opinion, to make you feel better," he said.

Thirty-four, her brain said. He picked up the small bowls of oatmeal that had been left for them.

"You think it's safe?" he asked, "Father Preston was looking pretty murderous yesterday."

"Vincent brought those. He said that his friends have started their plans today. He'll let us know when they are back but we will still have to wait a few weeks for the signal to be heard. He says he and Preston should be at the end of their incubation periods by then—" she trailed off, thinking how close her own would be by then.

Frank folded himself onto the grass beside her. "It seems we are destined to spend month-long chunks of our time stuck in isolation together. Good thing you like me," he said with a smile, holding up her bowl, but lowered it again. "Stop that," he said and she glanced over at him.

"I can practically see you counting days in your head."

"I wasn't," she said, but felt her cheeks flush as if he'd seen more of her than she intended. "Well, what else is there to do?" she snapped, flustered, "They won't let us help them. They can't exactly let us go. There's no useful work we can do without contaminating their supplies. What should I be doing besides pacing this rut of panic in my head?"

"*You're* the head doctor. But if you are asking for suggestions, you could love me," he patted the grass next to him with a smile.

"I *do*. Which makes the panic worse and the time seem so short." She sat down beside him and wrapped herself around her own knees as if she didn't dare to touch him. "Every time I look at you, my brain tells me it's one less time that's left. Everything is finite. When— when I kissed you that first time, my life seemed to grow, everything expanded. Me, the City, the world— but now we're shrunken to a tiny cage and a handful of days. The more I try to slow it down, the faster and faster it whirls, sucking me toward the end. Of everything." She clutched her head in her arms, squeezing back the sob that threatened to spill out.

"Everything was always finite, Nella." He pulled her into his side. "You just didn't think about it constantly. I could have died in the bunker. You could have died from the Infected biting you. We could have sunk the sailboat. We could be hit by lightning. I could walk out in the street and—" he stopped and laughed. "Okay, maybe I can't get hit by a bus anymore." It won him a weak smile from Nella. "My point is, we can't constantly be living with a countdown. It ruins everything, even the moment you are trying so hard to keep hold of. Just be here, with me. The night you kissed me— it was one of the worst nights I'd had since being Cured. We had just talked to Dr. Carton and I knew we were in trouble. I knew we were talking about finishing off the rest of the world. And I told you the worst things about me— things I never thought I'd tell another soul. I was so miserable. And you were too. Worried and embarrassed because I was so clumsy—"

"You weren't," she protested.

"I was. But when you kissed me, it didn't matter. The minute before it didn't exist. The humiliation and depression, it was gone. And the minute after it didn't matter. The Plague didn't matter, Pazzo didn't matter. There was just you and me. And that's why it felt like the world grew. That's why it *felt* infinite. It passed, as this minute will pass, as tomorrow will pass, because it was always finite. But if we can let go, if we can stop the countdown and just be you and me, together, then that handful of days will mean more while they happen. Everything dies, Nella."

"It's not dying that frightens me," she said.

"What frightens you then? Why this panic?"

"Going mad. Hurting you. Making you hate me."

"I will never hate you, Nella. Not even if the worst happens. The person you are— the Nella I love, won't disappear when you turn. I know that you'll still be there, underneath. I'll love you until the day I die, even if it's you that causes it. But I won't let that happen. I won't make you carry the same guilt I have."

He sat with his arms around her for a moment, quietly. He stroked the puffy red scrape on her palm with one finger. "Besides," he said with a slow grin, "maybe it's tetanus instead. And in three weeks it'll surprise you by coming ahead of time."

She elbowed his ribs. "Thanks for that," she said.

He laughed and rubbed his chest. "My point is: stop thinking about it. Live in denial for a while. Let go. Just be here with me. Weeks of leisure with the person I love most in the world. Ten years ago people would have paid thousands for the opportunity to do this." He twisted to look at the small tent. "Well, maybe not *here,* but we have what we need. And it sure beats being separated from you by a glass wall. Let the others do their job. We've done ours. Let them worry about what comes next. Just stay with me, as long as you can."

She held his face between her hands and kissed him until the world slid away in bright, summery streamers.

The other occupants of the quarantine camp had no one to distract them from their own countdown. Most of them stayed calm for a while, cheerful even, for a week or so. But sooner or later, reality hit them all. Vincent tried to visit with each detainee every day, just to break up the monotony, for himself and for them. And of course, there were daily prayer sessions with Father Preston, but he rarely talked to anyone but God, instead standing in front of each cage muttering ominously for a few moments before moving away. And Lisa who brought them their meals. These were the only events that prevented the days from running into a long muddle of misery punctuated only by the shrieks of those who turned and the deep silence that followed Vincent's blade.

Marnie was playing War through the fence with Vincent with an old pack of cards she'd taken from the hospital. Christine had said it was a waste of space, but Marnie was glad she had taken them. They were doing her more good now than the heavy cans of food they'd shoved into the packs or the first aid kit Christine had insisted on. "Sorry for running when you came to help Henry at the Lodge," she offered, "I didn't know who you were then. I was scared. I— I should have given you a chance."

"Sorry I scared you," said Vincent. "Henry was convinced you were still there, but none of us believed him. Maybe if we had, we all would have come to the Lodge together and you would have seen we were safe."

"Did he really come back for *me*? He's not my dad. Why did he care so much about what happened to me?"

"He made a promise to your mom. And he felt

guilty about bringing Phil into your lives. You gave him a purpose after he woke up. A reason to try instead of just sink into despair about the things he did when he was sick. Pam had her family, Rickey had his tough persona, Henry had you."

"And you? What did you have?" asked Marnie.

He dogeared his cards without meaning to. "I had the others. And I had all the things I wanted to make up for. All the things I wanted to fix."

"Like what happened to my mom?"

"Yes. Among others."

Marnie shook her head. "But nothing can fix that."

He looked at her, his one eye searching her face calmly. "I know. But that doesn't mean I can't *try*."

Vincent looked up as Lisa approached them, wringing her hands. "What's wrong?" he asked.

"It's the man in cage six. He says it's coming and he wants you to— he doesn't want to wait until the turn. He asked me to talk to you. Father Preston is furious, but the man begged me to ask you."

He passed his set of cards through the fence to Marnie without speaking. He got up from the dirt and brushed himself off before heading slowly down the lane for the wheelbarrow. He left it in the lane in front of the cell. The blade rested inside it. He looked at it for a long moment and then picked it up. The cage door was already open. He'd have to talk to Father Preston about being more careful. Vincent ducked under the front tent flap. Father Preston and the man were both kneeling in the grass, the priest muttering feverishly, the man silent but beginning to rock on his knees.

"Colin? Lisa said you were asking for me."

Both men looked up. Father Preston's face immediately twisted into a scowl. "I asked for you both," said Colin, "Won' be long now. Want to be peaceful when I go. Not hungry an' raging like a starved wolf." He turned toward Father Preston. "Wanned your miracle to work, Father. Prayed on it every day. Prayed for *you* every day. I'm true believer. Never doubted you. Still don' doubt. Watched th'others go. That mother an' her boy. God forgive me, I thought she was unworthy because she din't tell us about him. I felt righteous when she went. Found reasons to justify the others too. Kep' right on praying. Never 'ccured to me, maybe I was unworthy of a miracle too. But 'ere I am. I was an Immune, last time. I was convinced it was only the wicked who grew ill, that they weren't human anymore. That they didn't deserve my mercy if they hadn't earned God's. I never did a kindness for a Cured. And now I'm an Infected. I see how wrong I've been. How gravely I've sinned against my fellows. I'm not worthy of your miracle Father Preston. That's why it isn't working. I pray for you and the others now, that you'll be able to save 'em, that your faith won't waiver. Faith made me hard an' mean. It burned me up, like a candle with too much wick. It was more important to show it on the outside than feel it on the inside. Wasn't meant to do that. Should have been kinder. Should have seen myself in them. All of 'em got a spark. Fell for a lot of flashy charlatans and missed a lot of true friends. Now I'm judged as I have judged them. Pray for me, Father."

"You can't do this," said Father Preston, "it's suicide. I can't allow it."

"You go on now, Father. There's a whole camp who need you and your miracle. You save it for them. Vincent and I, we're just going to make amends. I've not done right by him. Can't atone to everyone I've wronged, but I can ask his forgiveness."

Father Preston looked surprised. He got up, but hesitated to leave.

Colin nodded at him. "You got work to do, Father.

You've done your best here. It was me that was found wanting. Help someone more worthy than me. Someone kinder, who understands what faith really means."

Father Preston put a hand on Vincent's arm. His face was sunken, drooping. Defeated. "Please—" he started, but cut himself off. Vincent wasn't certain if Father Preston were begging for Colin or for himself. But the other priest just left the tent, closing the flap behind him. Colin was still on his knees. Vincent crouched in front of him.

"Are you certain?" asked Vincent.

"Been fighting it back for hours. Sometimes I forget why I'm here. Tried to pry the fence apart this morning." He lifted his hands to show Vincent a grid of thin cuts. "Didn't even notice it hurt. And then, when I bled and smelled it . . ." He shuddered. "Don't think I can come back again. I want to be me, at the end. Even a few seconds early. Father Preston thinks those seconds will damn me. Know you were a priest once too, Vincent. Don't mind admitting to you that those few seconds are probably the least sin on my tally. I'm certain."

Vincent stood up. "Forgive me," he said and circled behind Colin.

Colin nodded and began whispering. "...No evil. For you are with me." The blade whistled softly as Vincent raised it up to his ear. Colin was rocking on his knees, and Vincent dreaded missing. He wanted to ask Colin to stop, but he knew it was an unconscious tic of the disease. "Surely goodness and mercy shall follow me..." The blade flashed down. There was no scream, just the Colin's body slumping sideways as the head rolled upward, its lips still moving, "...house of the Lord forever."

"Amen," finished Vincent, before cradling the head in one arm and gently shutting its eyes.

TWENTY-TWO

The boat was a problem. He'd been too hasty, the night before. What if it needed a crew? Or fuel? And where in blazes was it? As far as he knew, there were only two people who knew for sure. And somehow, they'd known enough about what Father Preston had done to get Gray kicked out of the Colony. There was no way he could just saunter up and ask. He was certain there'd been more solid planning over the radio that morning, but he wasn't able to get close enough to the farmhouse to hear. Not without being spotted. Short of searching the farmhouse, he wasn't certain how he was going to find the one seaworthy boat between there and the City. He was going to have to get someone in the quarantine camp to help him, to ask for him. One more play then. One more scheme for one more sucker. Gray's stomach rumbled and cramped. If Father Preston wouldn't help him, he'd have to risk the farmhouse. It'd be better than starving anyway.

He watched the quarantine camp from the treeline. Father Preston's tent backed up to the fence and Gray slunk up behind it as he watched the priest fling himself out of a far cell and stride down the camp's lane toward the tent. Gray waited to see if Father Preston would say anything, in case Lisa or Vincent were inside. He could hear pacing footsteps but no one spoke. "Father?" he said in a hushed tone.

The pacing stopped.

"Father, it's me. It's Gray."

"*You?* What are *you* doing here?"

"I know, I know you're angry. You have every right to be," said Gray quickly, but his face wore the old greasy smile. Father Preston couldn't see it with the canvas between them. "The last time we spoke— I was harsh and I said things I didn't mean. I knew your temperament. I knew how self-sacrificing you are, and I didn't want to let you come here. I didn't want to risk you becoming infected, so I tried to make you angry with me. I tried to be angry and cold so that I could part from you easier. I know now, I was wrong. I was wrong to doubt your miracle and I was wrong to think that God wouldn't protect you. I've come to my senses, after some prayer and reflection—" he waited to see if Father Preston would object, would claim the ring of mounds at the end of the camp as his fault. When he didn't, Gray's smile widened. *Still too proud to admit you're a fraud, eh? I've got just the thing,* he thought. "But your people, the ones you led so faithfully from the hospital, they've betrayed you. Betrayed *us.* These people are unrepentant sinners. They aren't worthy of a miracle. That's why God withholds it, not to punish *you* but to punish *them.* There are other people that need us. People that need your healing, certainly, but people that also need to hear your preaching. We just have to get you out of there."

"Gray, *you* betrayed me. You awoke the anger of the woman who denounced us. You left the Cure dart as irrefutable proof that miracles don't happen—"

"I was wrong, and I'm so sorry. The Cure dart was mine. It was in my arm when I woke up. I wanted you to stay so I made you think it was yours. I want to atone for what I've done. I want to help you escape this wretched place, these undeserving animals. I can't undo the past, but I can help you save the future."

There was a short silence. "How?" asked Father Preston.

Gray knew he had won. "There's a boat. The others want to use it to kill the Infected. Wipe out the City with poison without even attempting to save any Immunes who might be inside. But we can save the innocents trapped there instead. We just need to know where it is. That couple— the ones that accused us, they know where it is.

Find out for me and we'll go together. I'll gather supplies for us and let you out of here. We can leave tonight, and save the Infected in the City before anyone knows we're gone."

There was a sigh. "I can't save the Infected. I can't save anyone Gray. And I'm not going to flee on a stolen boat and add to my crimes. I hope you are sincere, I hope you have found your faith at last and are becoming a better man. You should go. You should leave these people in peace. Find another settlement. Help them rebuild, be an example, but not mine. Go back, and seek forgiveness from Bernard. From Ruth if you can find her. I was wrong. I was proud and I let pride lead us instead of compassion. I knew who you were and what you really wanted, Gray, though you think you had me fooled. Maybe you still think you have me fooled. I thought I could change you. Make you a force for good. As if a person can ever force another to change. As if *I* could step in where God would not. Go, Gray. Don't return. The only help I can offer is my prayers."

There were footsteps and then a whipping snap as the canvas flapped back and Father Preston was gone. Gray swore and slunk back to the trees. *The hard way then,* he thought, though he admitted it would be more fun that way.

Father Preston walked down to the opposite end of the camp without looking back. Vincent was digging a new grave. He didn't look up from his shovel.

"I thought you were weak," said Father Preston, "I thought you lacked faith when you came back to the monastery. I thought you were— *bad.*"

"Maybe I was," said Vincent as he lifted another shovelful of soil. "I was certainly a younger, more questioning man. I blamed God for causing the misery I saw around me. For not stopping the famine. For not saving innocent children. I know better now."

"What do you know better? What is it, Vincent? Because I've tried everything. I pray without ceasing. I go back to the book. I observe the rites. Nothing is helping. Nothing changes. They are still turning. Why did He cure me if not to help them?"

Vincent stopped and leaned on the shovel. "So *help* them," he said.

"I *am.* I pray with them, I read to them, I ask for guidance on their behalf—"

Vincent shook his head and pushed the shovel down again with his foot. Father Preston stopped. "What?" he asked, "Is that not the duty of a priest?"

"Brother Michael," said Vincent, his voice warm and gentle, "how many years did you know the woman who ran the hospital?"

Father Preston shrugged. "Six or seven."

"What did she do there? How did she care for the Infected?"

"She— fed them, cleaned them, kept them warm. They were like infants. Or animals."

"And you too, before you were cured?"

"Yes, for a time."

"It must have been very hard taking care of all those people without electricity, without running water or an easy way to heat the place. And by herself too."

"She had people to help. Me, Bernard, Ruth. Some of the families."

Vincent paused and looked up at him. "Oh? What did you do to help?"

"I read a sermon every morning to the inmates. Took a few hours, we'd do a few cells at a time, and my congregation would pray for them."

"I see," said Vincent. "Did you ever stay to feed them? Do some of the laundry? Haul some water for baths?"

Father Preston grew red. "I was busy trying to save their souls. Their bodily wants were a distant concern that was being handled by others."

"Bread is the religion of a starving man, Brother Michael. You remember the hospital and see people that were cured by science. People that, for all your prayers and well wishing, not only weren't cured by your miracle but attacked you. You should have been the exception. They should have loved you enough to bypass you. After all, you were spared before. Singled out for a miracle cure. It infuriated you, so you were willing to believe they had to bite you to partake in the miracle. That a little dart couldn't possibly have saved your lives. That's how we got here. You know what I see when I look at those people?"

Father Preston made no move, so Vincent went on. "I see people not just cured by a miracle, but left almost unscarred by their time as Infected. Those people should have died years ago or wandered committing brutal acts of violence until they came to a Cure camp. But they didn't, because of one woman's faith. Seven years, Brother Michael, think of it. Day in, day out, all the time she was ill herself. She carried water, she split wood, she risked being bitten or killed, she changed their diapers and their bandages, made their food and went hungry or cold herself when there wasn't enough. Because she believed that one day, the Cure was coming. That one day, those people would be themselves again and that someone would want them. It doesn't matter that the medicine finally came in the shape of a tranquilizer dart or that it was made in a lab instead of a stroke of divine lightning. Juliana was the miracle. And her friends, that helped without hope of thanks or repayment or any advantage to themselves. You think they remember a single one of your shouted sermons? I guarantee they remember her. The times she bandaged their hurts when they couldn't tell her how much pain they were in, the warmth of new clothes in the winter."

"I can't be responsible for what they remember of me. I did my best."

"Did you? Maybe you were cured to help her. Maybe you were cured to give you a second chance at understanding faith. At understanding kindness. You came down here, and you didn't have to. You came down here though you knew, somewhere deep down, that you didn't cure those people. That you *couldn't* cure these. Some part of you wants to help them. Have you stopped to ask yourself why?"

Part of Father Preston wanted to lash out, humiliated at being questioned by someone he thought had a lesser faith, by a *murderer.* But he pushed it aside. Pride had helped no one. It had led him here. He was beaten. "I want to be *worthy*, Brother Vincent," he said, his voice breaking in the middle. "I want it to matter that I was cured."

Vincent put a dirty hand on the other man's shoulder. "Then *help* them."

"What do I do?" asked Father Preston. "Should I say a funeral service for Colin?" he looked down into the empty shallow grave.

Vincent shook his head. "I will care for Colin. I promised."

"What then?"

"It's time for the waste buckets to be emptied."

Father Preston just nodded and picked up an empty bucket before walking off. Vincent went back to shoveling, but a small hope gathered in his chest. Maybe Father Preston would make a miracle after all.

TWENTY-THREE

He'd considered waiting until night. It'd be easier to just climb over the wall without being seen in the dark. But the plan for the City had to be in the Farmhouse and too many people were still sleeping there at night. Over half the Colony still had unfinished or nonexistent houses and split their nights between the Farmhouse and the barn. During the day, it was all but deserted. Unless someone was injured or ill, they worked. And he wasn't certain Father Preston wouldn't blow his plan, given enough time. He had to move before they realized he was coming.

Getting into the Colony wasn't really a problem. They'd only built the wall on one side, expecting the thick forest that surrounded the other three sides to protect them from any serious assault. But the house was in the center of the Colony, a gray-shingled heart and everything radiated from it. There was no way he'd reach it unseen. Not without a distraction, anyway. He had to draw them all away long enough to find what he was looking for and get out. They'd all run to protect the garden, that was sure. But there were always people in it. They'd see Gray coming and drive him off before he could do anything. Besides, he'd no tools, only himself to cause damage. There was nothing in the garden that would help. He squatted in the deep shadow of the trees, scanning the small Colony as it began its day. The residents were scattered, their attention divided between many projects. Some worked on the unfinished cottages, their hammers a comforting, erratic series of thumps that quickly synchronized. Several carried water from the well or the shrinking pond for laundry or food. *Could hit the well,* Gray thought, looking around him for any plant he might recognize as poisonous. He quickly discarded the idea. It would take too long and wouldn't affect everyone all at once. He could see a few people checking the rickety drying racks near the barn. Without refrigeration, it had proved the easiest, most efficient way to store the Colony's excess crops for winter. Gray watched as they filled a barrow with dried corn and wheeled it into the barn. Once the barn caught his eye, Gray didn't even stop to plan. He kept to the woods, giving the little cottages and knots of people wide berth, though they weren't looking for him at all. He kept an eye open for Amos and Henry, but only saw Molly. *Did they leave this whole place to the cripple? Can't be.* He kept looking for the others. *Where's the loudmouth lady? And that smoker?* After a moment, he shrugged. The two most dangerous were definitely gone. He'd deal with the others if he had to. The barn was a good fifty yards from the tree line. The back door was open, but the interior was too dark to see if there was anyone inside. The people at the drying racks had moved on, but whether it was only to the barn or if they had gone to complete other tasks, Gray didn't know.

Fortune favors the bold, he thought. A stupid person would have sprinted. A less confident person. Gray strolled instead. As if he belonged there, as if he'd just stepped into the woods for a break and was returning to work. There were other people not very far away. Some of them must have seen him. But he hadn't mingled much with the people from the City. Only Father Preston's people really knew who he was, and Gray depended on the consistent divide between the two camps to protect him. Nobody stopped him. Nobody went running for the nearest guard. Nobody even stopped their work to look up at him. He slipped into the barn. It had been emptied months before and used as a place to house people. Now it was slowly filling up again as people moved into their own new homes and large wooden bins waiting for harvest lined the walls. A few were filled, and one wall shone with glass jars where they'd canned what they could not dry. It was a pitifully small amount for the number of people that would be relying on what was stored there. And they'd worked themselves ragged just to set that much by. For a short moment, even Gray hesitated. *What if the boat thing doesn't work? What if I need this food later?* He looked around at it. There was nobody in the barn. He could grab whatever he wanted. Enough for a few weeks if he was careful. Probably nobody would even notice. And it had been easy to get in here. He could do it again when he needed. Maybe he should just find a nearby farmhouse and hole up for the winter instead. Just until he found a new crew. And the whole plague-thing blew over.

It's easy until you get caught, old boy, he told himself, *they aren't going to toss you out the front door so easily next time. And they aren't going to care even if you come crawling on your knees begging. Next time they find you, they're going to kill you. And you know what that means, old boy. Got to hit them first, boat or no boat. So they know you mean business. So they know not to mess with you.* He didn't waste any more time with doubts. He looked around. A large barrel of diesel still sat in the corner, though the tractor it went to had been pushed out long ago. Gray dismissed it. Good to keep a fire going, but not so great at starting one. Same with the small shelf of motor oil bottles above it. He pushed aside a few crusty cans of house paint and found a small can of turpentine. He shook it and it still sloshed. He whistled an old tune as he climbed up into the loft. It had been swept clean when the colonists moved in to sleep, but Henry had stored most of the spare lumber and insulation now that people were moving out. *Oh yes, this is going to hurt them badly,* Gray thought, hunting around for some tinder. He swept together some small piles of sawdust where some of the lumber had been cut to length. An old paperback novel lay in the corner, forgotten by one of the colonists who'd moved out. Gray saw it and ripped the flimsy pages out in clumps, fanning them out over the sawdust. The turpentine came next, he splashed it over the paper and then as far as he could reach across the spare lumber. He pulled out his old flip lighter. Joe had given it to him, back when things had been better. Back before Gray had sliced his tongue out for betraying him. He looked down into the floor of the barn. Still empty. He was going to have to get back to the woods before they noticed the fire, otherwise, he'd be caught before he could reach the farmhouse. He took a deep breath and jogged a few steps in the loft, warming up. Then he bent down and held the lighter to a book page. The little pile went up with a whoosh and a little ball of flame that almost singed Gray's hand. He laughed nervously and then, seeing that the flames were spreading instead of going out, climbed down the ladder, slipped out the back and strolled just as casually back to the tree line. Then, he waited. His bladder squeezed painfully as the first shouts reached him. He hadn't been this excited in months. Years maybe. He grinned and relieved himself as he waited for the momentum to build, for the people to come running and gawking at what he'd done. He wanted to look for himself, to see the angry blades of flame piercing the roof of the barn, to watch the timbers slump and then cave in like ribs when you kicked them hard enough. He shook himself, forcing himself back to the task at hand. He slipped behind the stragglers to the farmhouse. They'd be back for pots and buckets in a few seconds. He didn't want to risk being found. He avoided the front door, shoving the living room window up in its peeling frame instead. He slithered through the window and let it crash down behind him as he bolted for the stairs. He wasn't certain where the papers he needed were, but he was going to start with the second floor until the firefighting was in full swing. He slunk into one of the bedrooms and carefully pulled back the curtain to look. The air was thick with dark smoke and the barn's open doors acted like wind tunnel whipping the flames into a massive twisted crown. The people below looked tiny and helpless. A few of them splashed water onto the barn, but they couldn't reach high enough to do much. He could see Molly stopping them, directing them to splash the nearby cottages. Then she ran inside the barn. He wanted to see if she'd come out again, but tore himself away. If she died, so much the better. He turned to the dresser and began yanking out drawers.

TWENTY-FOUR

She couldn't understand it. Amos had warned them about damp hay combusting, but she and Henry had swept out the entire barn together. Nothing had been left except bare wood and concrete. "Is anyone here?" she shouted. "Is anyone hurt, do you need help?" The loft was entirely ablaze. She hoped no one was up there and she glanced quickly around the bare bottom floor. Only food bins. They were too heavy to move by herself. She ran to the wall of canned goods. The glass jars were already warm, hot even, burning her arms as she gathered as many as she could carry and ran outside with them. She didn't know where to go. What was safe? If the wind changed, would the whole Colony burn? She wanted to cry. She ran toward the garden. That would be the last place to go. She'd make sure of it. She dumped the jars onto the soft dirt and turned back to get more. People were screaming, running past her. They needed someone to tell them what to do. So did Molly. She reached for the radio before she remembered they were all gone. Except Vincent. She could call him. He'd help her. How could he help her? He couldn't save her. He might as well be on the moon. It was *her* turn to save them. It was *Molly* who had to stop this. She stopped a few people running past.

"You, go get as many buckets and pots as you can. Grab as many people as you can. Meet us at the well." The woman's face was pale, but she nodded. Molly turned to the boy who was with her. "You go find as many blankets, towels, sheets as you can and come to the well. Tell everyone to come to the well!"

Molly spared one more desperate look at the open doors of the barn and turned back to the well. The food and lumber inside were already lost. She had to save the rest while she could. She found a man already pumping water into a bucket and others lining up behind him. She split them into two groups, sending one to the shallow pond. Rickey had said he expected the well to go dry if they didn't get some rain soon and she worried with every splash of water. But they needed it *now*, they'd worry about another well if the Colony survived. Soon, a bucket line had formed and she ran along it, directing the people to save the new cottages on either side of the barn. She had the kids pass out damp cloths to protect faces and lungs, knowing it would be a long time before they could stop.

She could hear people beginning to gasp and cough around her, her own chest rattled and burned, even with the wet scrap of sheet tied around her head. Nobody stopped or complained. Nobody spoke, just the coordinated movement of bucket or pot down the line.

It felt like hours, but Molly was certain it was closer to twenty minutes, when someone shouted, "Look out there, it's going down!"

Everybody stopped and looked up. Molly didn't dare to. *Don't lean,* she willed, *just collapse. Don't take anything else out.* There was a crash and a roar as a ball of smoke puffed up. The barn had crumpled inward, burning on its own footprint. Molly shook with relief. She redirected the bucket lines to put out the fire, urging them not to risk their lives by getting too close. Her radio crackled and she stumbled toward the garden to answer it.

"Molly?"

"I'm here Vincent. Everything is— every*one* is okay."

"What's happened? All we can see is smoke."

"It's the barn— all the winter stores, the spare lumber— it's all gone. There was— *is* a fire. I don't know what started it. I don't know if there was anyone inside the barn. I tried to help, I tried to find anyone—" She let the transmit button go and sobbed. She calmed herself down. "We saved the other houses. We're putting out the original fire now, but there was that big barrel of diesel in there, it's going to burn for a while, no matter what we do. And all the food— I only saved a handful of—" she turned and looked at the jars beside her. "A handful of pickled beans. A lot of good that will do us."

"You saved the people, Molly, that's what matters. Nobody is hurt and you did what you could. I wish that I could help somehow. But you don't need infection up there with everything else."

"But what *happened*? We didn't leave any hay in there. Everybody, even the kids know not to smoke in there. Even Rickey doesn't anymore."

There was a long silence. "Don't tell me it doesn't matter, Vincent," said Molly, "because it can't happen again. We have to figure out why it started."

"I wasn't going to say that." Vincent's voice was cautious, slow. "I don't want to frighten you, Molly, but maybe somebody started it on purpose."

Molly felt the hairs on her arms spike painfully. She didn't even bother to ask who Vincent meant. "Where would he— how would he have done it? He had nothing with him. Why? Why didn't he just steal?"

"I don't know. But if he wanted to hurt the Colony, he's done it. And he'll go for the garden or the well next."

Molly glanced around her and bent over to pick up a hoe. She was isolated, a little way from the well and everyone's attention was on the fire.

"I'm scared," she whispered into the radio.

"I'm coming," said Vincent, his voice hard and resolved.

"No! No, he'll know. It's what he wants maybe. For us to panic enough to wipe out the whole place. I'm going to find him. I'm going to finish this."

"Molly, don't go looking alone." But Molly switched off the radio. She wasn't going to risk anyone else. And she wasn't going to wait around for Gray to make the next move. She wished she had something more than a hoe, but she gripped it tightly and ran toward the woods, certain he was sitting there, watching them. A few colonists saw her and ran toward her. "Go back," she said, "Go back and guard the crops. This wasn't an accident. We can't let him get what's left." The people looked confused but ran back to the garden. Molly continued into the woods and stopped a few feet in. She had no idea how to find him. She wasn't a tracker or a warrior. She was a teenage grocery clerk that woke up one day ten years older in a world that didn't need her anymore. She spun around. *Stop thinking that,* she told herself, *You just saved the farm. Give yourself a little credit.* She looked back at the Colony, trying to see what he had seen. Where would he go if he were waiting for another chance to strike? Where would he wait if he were laughing at them? She crouched down and looked. The barn was still a ball of black and orange, the people's faces shiny and red as they doused it over and over. Her gaze flitted over the Colony, searching for the hiding places, the shadows between buildings, the spaces empty of people. He'd hit where it would hurt the most, maybe he hadn't hung around. The damage was done, wasn't it? But just as she thought it, the curtain in the living room window of the farmhouse flickered and swayed. A hand pushed up the pane as she watched. Molly started running even before Gray's face appeared in the open window. A scream of anger mixed with terror spilled from her as she ran and she saw him hesitate halfway out of the window to look up at her. He scrambled out of the frame, heading for the wall. But Molly was faster. She slammed the blade of the hoe down, catching the back of his calf. The impact shuddered up the pole, stinging and vibrating the stumps of her missing fingers and rattling her arm. Gray swore as he stumbled a few more steps. Molly lifted the hoe again, but Gray turned and hit the side of her head, knocking her backward onto her butt. The hoe clattered against the stone wall and out of Molly's hands.

"Fucking zombie!" he hissed as he tried to look at the deep slash in the back of his leg. He wound up for another punch. "Don't you know when to stay in your place?" He swung but Molly rolled out of the way, grabbing for the hoe. She would have grabbed it, had her hands still been whole. The stumps of her fingers brushed by the handle instead. She sprung up and darted around him.

"This *is* my place. It's *you* who don't belong here. Why couldn't you just leave us alone?" Molly demanded.

He swung again, this time connecting with her cheek and she fell backward into the wall.

"You're monsters. Vermin. Diseased rats that scrabble in the waste of normal people," he gasped with another tight jab, splitting her lip as his ragged thumbnail slammed into her mouth. Her head rocked backward and she struggled to keep it from smashing into the stone wall. A high buzz drowned out some of his words before dying away again "...cockroach-whore who should have died years ago. Practically ripped off your arm but still..." he grabbed her scarred arm and twisted it up over her head, driving her farther back into the wall. It ached as he pushed it farther behind her and she knew he meant to finish ripping it off, as if she really were a fly or a roach. She stood on tiptoe, her legs starting to slide up the wall as he pushed her arm up farther. Her other hand sought something, anything, grasping at the stones, reaching for the hoe. "You should all be extinct. Should be you that's homeless and hungry, not *me*. Survival of the fittest. Should have left *me*, me and the other Immunes. Then there'd be no new Plague, no ruined City."

Molly's hand yanked on stone after stone along the

top of the wall, finally finding one that wriggled a little as he shouted into her face, his breath damp and acid on her skin. The arm in his grip trembled as he tightened and pushed backward. She was no longer on her feet, pressed halfway up the wall by his body. She cried out in pain, but the other hand knew what it was doing, slowly working the stone back and forth, rocking it free of its mortar. "This isn't your place. You have no place." There was a sudden jerk and then searing pain spread from her shoulder. "It's *my* place. My world, all of it. And you don't have my permission to exist," he spat.

Molly took a deep breath and leaned into the pain to stop the waves of unconsciousness that threatened to crash down on her. The rock was free. She whipped it up over their heads. "You're not my God, nor my keeper. And we're starting to remember that it's our world too." She let the rock's momentum carry her down and forward. He let go of her arm to protect himself, but too late, the rock was already bashing the top of his head with a chalky clunk as if it had scraped the very bone of his skull. Molly's dislocated arm flopped next to her, useless and boiling with pain. She tried to slide free of him as he clutched his head, but he was too heavy, still using his weight to pin her against the wall. She kicked and he loosened, but not enough. He was distracted, though, and she managed to press herself farther up the wall, wiggling until she was perched on top and shoving him in the chest with the flat of her feet. She went backward over the top, landing in the tall grass on the other side, free. She lay for a second, gasping to recover the breath that had been knocked from her lungs. It was no good turning back to the Colony for help, they were out of sight now, the wall watchers all pulled back to fight the fire or guard the crops. She crawled toward the quarantine camp, no real plan except to be near someone, anyone before he came back. Vincent would help her. They'd stop Gray and the Colony would be okay until Amos and Henry got back. It was worth getting sick, she thought. But there was a thud and the ground under her knees shuddered. She looked back. Gray had jumped over, but the jump had been more than he bargained for, and he'd landed awkwardly on his wounded leg. Molly forced herself onto her feet and began running toward the wired cages. A hundred yards, that was all. She could hear the uneven thump of his limping run behind her. She yelled and saw someone come to the wire fence. Still too far to make out who it was. "Help!" she yelled again. The person at the fence began yelling, but between the harsh rasp of her breath and the deep thump that came from behind her, she couldn't make it out. He grabbed a fistful of hair and spun her in a painful circle. Before she could lose her balance and fall, he had a hand around her throat. He shoved her down and she kicked and clawed at him with her good hand. He punched the side of her head and she had a dizzy sense of tumbling though she was already on the ground. It was enough time for him to straddle her legs, making them useless. His other hand was closing around her neck when she heard a metallic rattle.

Thank you, thank you, she thought, still trying to shove Gray off, *Vincent's come to save me.*

Gray looked up for a second, squinting at the rattle. It was Father Preston. "Get off her!" he yelled, shaking the fence. Gray grinned. "Make me," he shouted back and then turned his attention back to Molly who was still flailing, trying to roll free. His hands clamped shut, the thin stream of breath she still had flowing and pulsing beneath his thumbs. It excited him.

"Could have prevented this, Father," he shouted, dodging another blow from Molly's good arm. "You could have helped me and none of this would have happened. Somebody's always got to pay the piper. So she's gonna do it for you."

"Stop Gray! I'll help you, let her go!" Father Preston rattled the fence again.

Gray pressed harder on Molly's throat, the stream of breath petered out, her chest beginning to sink. "Too late," he yelled, and his grin grew wider as he saw Vincent come running up to the fence. But Vincent didn't rattle the fence. He ran to the gate instead and Gray knew he was running out of time. He sank down, leaning into his forearms as they dug into Molly's chest. Her arm stopped flailing. She clutched the grass.

The sunny sky shrank to a small gray circle for Molly. Everything felt heavy, worn out. Gray's smile was too much. She closed her eyes so she wouldn't have to see. *Can't give up,* she told herself, *Vincent's coming. Hold on.*

The pressure on her chest was suddenly released and she opened her eyes. Gray's face was gone. His hands were gone. She tried to suck in more air, expecting a cool rush and a cough, but nothing happened. A thin wheeze, a trickling gasp was all. Then Vincent was leaning over her, his gray hair wild around him, his eye red and leaking. He gently tilted her head back. The trickle of air was steadier but still not enough.

"Get the doctor!" he yelled over her. She wanted to twist her head to look for Gray, but she knew she wouldn't breathe again if she did. The sky whirled as Vincent picked her up and ran to the wire cages.

"You can't bring her in here!" protested Father Preston.

Vincent ignored him and pushed past. "Keep still," he told Molly, "It'll help to stay still."

Her vision was getting foggy again and her chest ached as if it were snapping apart. She could hear others around her now. "He crushed her throat," she heard Vincent say.

"On the sleeping bag," said a woman's voice.

Molly felt the cool, slippery material on the backs of her arms. Hands on her face and then a gust of warm air in her mouth, but only a trickle made it into her throat. The deep, rhythmic ache of pressure on her chest again, where Gray had crushed her with his elbows. Everything radiated a tingling, tight pain. Another gust of warmth but no relief.

"Her windpipe is crushed," said the woman's voice.

"There must be something you can do," said Vincent.

"I'm not that kind of doctor. I wasn't trained to fix things like this."

"But you know what has to be done to fix it."

"It'd be like you trying to operate on her."

Vincent squeezed Molly's hand. She managed to squeeze back. "What are our choices?" He sounded worn out.

"We can try a tracheotomy and maybe save her, but it would kill her within seconds if I cut wrong, or we can sit here and wait until she chokes to death which could be days, but you'd get to say goodbye."

"Is she in pain?"

The woman sighed. "You mean from the suffocation or everything else he did? Yes, she's in pain." The woman's voice rose to an angry shout. "And there are no more *God damn* pain killers left!" There was a silence. "Sorry, Father," she mumbled.

"Then try. Either she'll pull through and make the suffering worth it, or it will end. Don't let her linger without reason."

There was a bustling around her, but Molly seemed to float through it. She felt a prick in her neck and then liquid heat. There were some shouts but it faded. And she thought, *Not King Arthur. Perceval instead. Wish I could tell him.*

TWENTY-FIVE

"So how do you know all this stuff about radios anyway?" asked Rickey, pretending he wasn't winded from Melissa's brisk pace.

"It was my boyfriend's fault."

"You had a boyfriend?"

Melissa rolled her eyes. "It's not really *that* hard to believe is it?"

Rickey blushed and stammered. "No, of course not, I didn't mean— you've just never mentioned him. Or much of anything else about yourself."

She shrugged. "It was Before. I don't like to think about Before very much. It just makes me sad or angry, and I can't fix it. No use dwelling on it you know? Anyway, Ben was my boyfriend. He used to fly those stupid planes. The ones with the radio remotes, you know?"

Rickey nodded.

"Most people break the plane by crashing it. But Ben was always breaking the radio. He used to joke that he was cursed, that any radio that touched him was doomed. So I eventually got curious and figured out how they worked. Found out how to fix them."

"But you're talking about little radios. Glorified walkie-talkies, that sort of thing."

"Yeah," said Melissa.

"You must have seen big towers too, right? I mean, we're not walking all this way to fix a radio tower because you patched together your boyfriend's toy right?"

She shrugged with a grin. "I fixed the Colony's radio, didn't I? I did a little more reading after I fixed his stuff, if it makes you feel better."

Rickey smacked at his bare arm, startling a horse

fly into buzzing lazy circles around his head. "You really think anyone's going to fall for this?"

Melissa shrugged. "If we sound official enough they will. Wouldn't you if you thought you were sick?" She stopped to roll up the cuffs of her pants again, flicking shreds of burdock from them.

"I guess, if I thought I was sick. What about the people that don't think they are, though? Aren't we worried about them?"

"Yeah," said Melissa, "at least, I am. Vincent's theory is that anyone that was infected in the City should be showing symptoms by now, so they'll know. We're just hoping they didn't infect anyone else, but that's why Vincent's waiting for a week or two, to make sure no one else starts turning. But I know how desperate people can be to avoid illness. They'll deny it until the bitter end. I saw it last time too."

"You saw it? Thought you were a mailman— lady. Mailperson."

"I was, had my own walking route for years."

"So how come you didn't get sick first? You talk to all those people every day, you'd think you'd catch it before anyone else. I was in prison, that's how I avoided it as long as I did."

Melissa sighed. "I don't think it had anything to do with what I did. In fact, I probably *caused* more infection than I prevented."

"How would you cause more infection?"

She shook her head. "It's a long story."

Rickey pointed up at the distant mountain. "We got time," he said.

"Why do we all have to trade sob stories, huh? Why do we need to know the dark, dirty past of everyone left?" she snapped.

Rickey held up his hands. "Whoa, I didn't mean to

pry. If you don't want to talk about it, you don't have to. I just thought that's what friends did, shared each other's lives. I don't know what you did Before and to be honest, I don't really care because I like who you are now. But I felt better after telling Henry what happened to me. I thought you might feel the same."

Melissa was quiet for a long moment. "I guess you're right. You really want to hear this?"

He nodded and watched her as the trail steepened and they began to climb.

"Honestly, I think it was just dumb luck that I didn't get sick very early. I had a pretty rural route. It didn't go quite as far as our farm, but I'd subbed that route before. It was close. Most of the people I delivered to were farmers or retired. They didn't go to town much and since it was winter, they didn't visit much either. If it had been summer, or even a few weeks closer to the holidays, things might have been much different. But nobody got sick at first. The office heard rumors from other branches of course, but they were confused, muddy. You see some weird things delivering mail, believe me."

Rickey snorted. "I bet," he said.

"So hearing that another postman got bit by a patron wasn't really that unusual. But it kept happening and by the time the fourth or fifth report came in, it was on the news too. I came in one morning, it was the day before the airport shut down."

Rickey shrugged. "I don't remember that part, but I wasn't watching the news at that point."

"It was late. When things started to fall apart and the hospitals started getting overrun. The national guard was already coming in. Anyway, I came in to the office to pick up the day's bins and the post master just had this little messenger bag filled with these bright yellow sheets of paper. They were evacuation orders, just photocopied, not even personalized. He said we were going to deliver them and we would be escorted by some soldiers. When we were done, we were to follow the order ourselves. They wanted us to report to the local high school. I told the postmaster that most of my route were stubborn old farmers. They'd never leave their homes. He told me that was what the soldiers were for. I think that's when I knew this was different. It wasn't just some riot on television or someone else's problem. It was real. Picking up that bag of evacuation orders was like stepping out of my life into someone else's."

"*You* were scared? I don't think I've ever seen you scared," said Rickey, serious for once.

"After that— I'm not certain what could be scary again. Not even waking up. Not even seeing the aftermath. It had all already happened in my head when I picked up that bag. Those soldiers were proof that everything I knew, everything I depended on, had failed. That order and civilization were over. Because I knew they'd shoot whoever didn't comply. And knowing they'd do it was as bad as seeing it done. But there was nothing else to do. I picked up the bag and got into the car. Three military trucks followed me. Any house that was empty, I left an order tacked to their door and an armed soldier stood there and waited. I don't know how long. Most people were home, though. Some of them cried. Some of them yelled. They all asked me what was going to happen and none of them believed me when I told them I didn't know any more than they did.

"There was this one woman, Judy. She used to bake me cookies every year as a Christmas present. She had dozens of grandkids. Her husband was out when we came, their heating oil had run out and he'd gone to get some kerosene to get them through until delivery. Fifteen, twenty minutes away at the most. She begged to wait for him, so they could go to the school together. She was afraid he'd worry or that if he came to the school he wouldn't be able to find her in the crowd. The soldiers wouldn't let her. She begged me for help, and I tried to talk to the sergeant but he said his orders were strict and they were for the sake of everyone. He promised to leave a soldier behind to bring her husband in, but she was inconsolable. I helped her write a note to him and tacked it to their door along with the order and got her into the truck. Each household was only allowed a few moments to pack up a change of clothes and lock their doors. The soldiers assured everyone they would be screened for the disease and then allowed to leave if they chose, so nobody packed for more than a few nights. Still, it took us hours to get through all the houses on my route. It was late evening by the time we pulled up to the school, and heavy snow was making it hard to drive by then. The lot was a slushy mess and there were trucks everywhere. People yelling and jostling each other. I wanted to hang back, wait for it to clear out a little, but a soldier walked up to my car and demanded the keys.

'I'm with the post office,' I said, 'I'm supposed to have it.'

'You aren't in trouble,' he said, though he sounded angry and tired, 'I'm just going to park it in the far lot so traffic doesn't get backed up in this one. You can go in with the others. Don't worry, it's only for a few hours.' He smiled as if it would make me feel better, but it was an automatic smile. A movement of muscles and nothing more. His eyes darted back and forth the whole time he was speaking to me, as if he were checking for danger everywhere and his hands never left his gun. I got out and gave him the keys. What could I do?"

"I would have expected you to slug him. Or plan a midnight escape," offered Rickey.

"I wasn't the same then. I believed they were there

to help. I *believed* them when they said it was just for an hour or two. I believed if you followed the rules and did what you were told, that's what kept us stuck together, what kept us all peaceful and friendly instead of crazed animals. I think *they* believed it too. We all know better now." Melissa fell silent as they wound through thick brush and small saplings began to crowd in around the dirt trail. The sun was beginning to set and Rickey glanced back toward the Cured Colony. All he could see was thick forest. A few hundred feet farther up, he might be able to see the small flickers of light, the thin gray line of the wall curling around the front like a shell. But they'd camp without those little reassurances, he knew. They reached the edge of a small pond. Little more than a puddle where the water of a stream hesitated before plunging into the rock below. The grass gave way to damp, dark moss and a few crab apple trees bent and twisted over their reflection. Rickey flopped down beside one without speaking, afraid Melissa would make them push farther if he asked. But she sat beside him, picking up a small pebble and flicking it over the water, her mind a decade away. "Well? What happened when you got to the school?"

Melissa roused herself and looked around at him. "I went with the people from my route, we were put into the shop classroom. The soldiers had pushed most of the tools aside to make room for cots but the drill press had been bolted to the floor, I remember it being right in the middle of the shop. It was cold because the floor was concrete and it was separated from the rest of the school in a kind of garage. But they set up large heaters and brought us sandwiches. There must have been hundreds of people, but they were all separated into different classrooms. They said we were scheduled to be tested in the morning. A simple blood test. They told us to get some sleep. Judy, the woman I told you about, she wasn't able to sleep. She'd wander to the windows every so often and then sit on her cot. I went and sat with her.

'They probably just let him sleep there tonight, he'll be here in the morning, I'm sure,' I told her, but the truth was, I had no idea what was happening. But that's how society's supposed to work, you know? You follow the rules, you pay your taxes, you work your shift and everything is supposed to turn out all right. She patted my hand and looked worried. I got her to lie down for a few moments and asked one of the soldiers if there was a way to give her a sedative. That was the one thing they had the whole time, plenty of sedatives. It should have scared me, that all they wanted was to keep us calm. But at the time, I thought they were just prepared. I went to sleep after a long while too, listening to people mumble around me. Every cough or sneeze made us all jump, we'd seen enough on the news to know it was an illness, but the symptoms weren't really agreed on yet. And it was December, almost everyone had a cold.

"Morning came at last, but there was no word about our testing and no move to send us home. Some cold cereal and fruit was brought in and the kids pushed the cots to the edges of the room so they could play games in the middle. The adults sat drinking cup after cup of coffee and looking out the window. The soldiers changed and they finally brought Judy's husband. But he was slow, clumsy. Almost like he was drunk. And there was some argument outside the shop before they brought him in. I didn't know it then, but I think they were arguing about whether we were already infected or if he'd infect us all. Finally, in the afternoon, they had us all line up and they walked us across the parking lot to the cafeteria. The sun was out and I remember it felt good to breathe the fresh air after being closed in the shop for so long. In the cafeteria, the mood was different. The soldiers there wore biosuits. They had big plastic masks, even the ones who were just standing guard. It took a long time, but they finally took my blood and then sent us all back to the shop.

"The soldiers who were with us apologized and said the lab was backed up and it was going to be a few days to get the results. People started to be upset. They wanted to call relatives, to watch the news. I wanted to call Ben, make sure he wasn't somewhere even worse. What harm would it do to let their loved ones know that they were okay? But all the requests were refused. We asked for someone in charge to come talk to us, to tell us what was going on. The soldiers said maybe someone would come talk to us that night. They changed again. This time, a few of the soldiers were slurring. I thought they were drinking too. But Judy's husband was still erratic, hours after he ought to have recovered. I didn't connect them at the time. I just thought they were cracking under pressure or something. There was nothing to do except wait and worry. Even the kids got tired as the novelty wore off. We all just kind of sat. Occasionally someone would ask a soldier for an update, but it was always the same. Someone would come to talk with us soon. We just had to be patient.

"Late in the afternoon, maybe three or four, one of the little boys stole a stuffed animal from another little girl. He wanted her to chase him, they were just playing. They were running in circles, both laughing, but the little boy accidentally bumped into one of the cots. It was the one Judy's husband was napping on. He sat up with this— this roar, as if he'd been injured, though nothing had hurt him. The kids ran back to their parents and Judy patted her husband on the shoulder, trying to calm him down. Everyone was so quiet, as if we'd been waiting for it. As if it were the first crack of thunder from a sky that had been darkening for hours. Judy's husband started swearing about the kids, getting more and more agitated. This was a man who had several of his own. Who'd played Santa for years at the town holiday parties. He *loved* kids. The boy that bumped into him had probably been to his house trick or treating for years. But he just kept yelling, getting louder and meaner. And his words were more and more indistinct. I could see some of the soldiers watching him. Finally, two of them walked over to him and tried to take him out of the shop. Judy started crying and a few of the other adults started asking where they were taking him, but the soldiers wouldn't answer. Then a man nudged me. He said I was the closest thing they had to an official representative. I guess because I'd delivered the evacuation orders, I don't know. He thought the soldiers would listen to me and asked me to talk to them. I told him I didn't know anything more than he did, but he insisted. So I approached the soldiers who were struggling with Judy's husband.

'Back off!' one of them yelled.

'Look,' I said, 'you'll get a lot more cooperation if you just tell us what's going on. Why don't you make everyone's life easier and just give us some information.'

The two soldiers exchanged glances over the back of the wriggling man between them.

'What are we going to do with it anyway? It's not like we can leave and go screaming it to the hills. We have no vehicles, it's freezing out there, and we're trapped in here. Nobody's going to care if you tell us, but it will make us more at ease," I said.

One of the soldiers nodded and reached down for his radio. I don't know if they'd encountered an Infected before, but Judy's husband felt the hold on him loosen and wrestled free. He turned on the soldier and tried to bite his arm through the heavy uniform sleeve of his jacket. The soldier shoved him off with the side of his weapon and Judy's husband growled and pivoted. Judy was standing next to him, still trying to calm him down. I was a few feet away. I saw him stumble a step toward her and lean in. I thought he was going to hug her, but he bit her neck instead. She screamed and the soldiers tried to pull him off. I saw a few of the other soldiers step forward. One of them began yelling for someone to shoot Judy's husband. But they were still trying to separate Judy from his mouth. She was bleeding everywhere and other people started screaming. More soldiers rushed in to help. I backed up, trying to get out of the way, but I backed into the drill press. It was cold. I remember thinking that. Really cold even through my clothes. There were four or five soldiers tackling Judy's husband and another trying to stop her bleeding. Another one was just standing there, watching me. Just staring. I stared back, not sure what he wanted. I shuffled around the edge of the drill press so it was between us. Almost everyone else was huddled in a far corner so there was nobody who could help. He kept staring and I could see him start to pant. His chest just kept heaving in and out. I knew what was coming. I don't know how I knew, but I did. Animal instinct maybe. I could tell I was prey. So I hit the button on the side of the drill press and it started to spin. The soldier jumped at me but a kept the press between us.

'What do you want?' I yelled.

The soldier opened his mouth as wide as it would go and shrieked. Just this shrill, unending yell. He reached for me and I froze for a second. Just froze, everything ached to run away but I couldn't. His hand closed on my arm and it was like a spell breaking. I didn't even think about it, I just yanked the arm that was grabbing me over the press. It had one of those big turning wheel things. It moved so easily. I spun it and held it as the press chewed through the man's uniform and into his arm. It whined and jerked but the bit tore through everything. I thought that would be it. That he'd yell louder and pull back or stop.

But it was like he didn't even feel it. He reached for me with his other arm. I jumped backward. He still tried to reach me, one arm still pinned in the press, the drill bit was buried and the motor was starting to slow down as bits of him splashed up into it and stuck. And then the shooting started. I crawled under one of the cots but there really was nowhere to hide. At first, it was just Judy's husband and the soldier in the drill press. But some of them thought Judy would turn and anyone else that had been bitten. They shot her too, and yanked me out from under the cot. I told them I hadn't been bitten but they didn't believe me. They made me strip to check.

"After several minutes another group of soldiers showed up, these ones in the biohazard suits. They'd heard the gunshots. I was allowed to get dressed again and we were all moved into the school. We were put in the gym with hundreds of others then and someone set up a mic at one end. I stayed near the back. I didn't want to be there anymore. Not if they were going to start shooting us. I could see some others had the same idea, a small knot of people was growing nearby. I could see a few lighters passing between hands and a few odd wrenches and hammers emerged from a tool box hidden near the bleachers. I should have volunteered, but I stayed separate. I just wanted to see what was going to happen. I still wasn't ready to break the rules. I still wasn't ready to fight the people who were supposed to protect me. Finally, someone appeared at the podium on the far side of the gym. The knot of people dissolved and inched their way forward into the crowd. I stayed on the edge, still trying to find a way to make a break for the door, but the soldiers filed in and surrounded us.

"I saw a kid slip behind the bleachers and I made my way over as quietly as I could. I don't know if any of the soldiers saw me, but nobody followed. There was very little room, but I managed to wriggle into the space behind the wood. It creaked with the weight of dozens of people. A few kids peeked out the other end. I stayed in the middle, watching the light shift through the cracks where feet shuffled. It was hot and the adrenaline from the fight in the shop was gone. The soldier at the front kept talking but I was too far to hear what he was saying. It didn't matter anyway, I was certain it was just the same spiel we'd heard before. I fell asleep for a little, waking up to more growling above me. There were a few bangs as things hit the boards above me and then a steady stream of dark blood that spattered onto the shining waxed floor. I shuffled myself sideways to avoid it, flinching as pounding footsteps converged above me. There were several gunshots and then a surge of voices mixed in. The kids at the end of the bleacher sprinted into the open, calling for their parents. It was pure chaos. Screaming and pounding and gunfire. I heard someone yelling 'cease fire' over and over but it didn't stop. Some of the boards over my head splintered as bullets tore them apart and the electric light of the gym poured through like an obscene mirror ball. I cowered there for several minutes. It felt like hours, but it couldn't have been long. Until it was quiet again. The air was smoky and smelled like fireworks. I wriggled out from behind the bleachers and stood up."

"They were all dead, weren't they?" asked Rickey.

Melissa shook her head. "I wish they were. Some of them were. There were people scattered everywhere. Mostly regular people like me, but a few soldiers were mixed in. The rest were gone. I didn't know where. But here and there someone would cry for help or just make a pained noise. If that were all— I would have stayed. I would have helped them. I'm not a cruel person, you know. I *do* care what happens to people—"

"I know," said Rickey, squeezing her hand.

"But there were Infected still walking and crawling around. I don't know how so many turned all at once. There weren't any that I could see when we got to the gym. I don't know if they came from other rooms where they were being kept, or if the violence that started in the gym made some of them who were barely holding on finally let go. But there had to be half a dozen that I could see. Every time someone cried out, one or two of the Infected would scramble toward them, crawling over other bodies to reach them and the person would scream and eventually fall silent again until the process repeated with someone else. I knew they'd find me sooner or later. The girls' locker room was just a few stairs away, but I didn't know what was inside or if there was another way out if I closed myself in. I wasn't even certain it was unlocked. I stood there, staring at the door, I don't know how long. I think I was in shock. Or maybe the disease was starting to set in. But eventually, I noticed an Infected looking at me. Her mouth was drooling thick, syrupy blood and her eyes were glazed over. She was probably full, but I didn't know how it worked then and I panicked. I bolted for the door and got lucky. It was open and I was able to lock it behind me. There was a small shower of pounding hands on the door afterward but the Infected gave up quickly. They had a whole gym of easy prey. It wasn't hard to find the back exit.

"It took me a while to realize I didn't know where to go. I didn't even know where my car was— and I didn't have the keys anymore anyway. If the military couldn't keep us safe, where was I supposed to go? Who was I supposed to trust? I wandered around the school, looking for anyone still sane. I found one of the military trucks and there was a radio set sitting in the front seat. I climbed in and listened all night as the world crumbled. In the morning, I climbed out, but I took the radio with me. And I just started walking. There were lots of cars that day, but nobody stopped. I didn't expect them to. I wouldn't have. It was very cold. Ben's apartment was the closest place I could think of, so I headed there. It took almost all day and I was headed in the opposite direction from most of the traffic. I was too upset to be scared. I'd killed all those people."

Rickey sat up from where he'd been lounging on the warm moss. "What? You didn't kill anyone. Well, maybe the soldier in the drill press, but he would have killed you if you hadn't."

"No, I killed all those people. They would have been safe, maybe for weeks, maybe for good, if they'd stayed in their homes. They were far apart, an Infected would probably die of exposure before it wandered to the next house to attack someone. They'd have been okay, except I had to follow the stupid rules. Never questioned, never argued, just did as I was told. And they paid for it."

"Hey," said Rickey leaning close to see her face as the sun drained into the dirt, "If it wasn't you, they would have found someone else to deliver the evacuation notices. Another mailperson, a soldier, it didn't matter. Maybe you saved some of them a few days because you convinced them to go instead of being shot in their homes. You don't know. It wasn't your fault, any of it. And if they were here, they'd tell you that."

Melissa shook her head. "That's easy for you to say. I can't believe it, even now, after everything. And even if I could— what I did to Ben is undeniable."

"Did you— were you in love?" asked Rickey, leaning back a little to give her room.

Melissa smiled. "I *thought* I was. I don't think he was. Not really. We were— we were comfortable. Friends, mostly. A compromise to keep both of us from being lonely. But nobody deserves what I did to him. Not even if we were mortal enemies. He shouldn't have let me in. His building was a mess. There was furniture strewn everywhere, poking out of doorways, flung across the lobby, like everyone had packed up and left. I was worried he had too, but you could hear the occasional radio or television on behind some of the doors so I knew *somebody* was still around. I got to his apartment and knocked. I had a key, but I always knocked first. I never wanted to be surprised by what I found him doing. I was such a fool. He wasn't sure about letting me in. He shouldn't have. I wish I'd turned around and walked away, but I called to him, told him it was me, that I wasn't sick but I needed help. He wasn't a bad guy, just scared. He let me in as soon as he knew it was me. The soldiers had already been there, but he said there'd been a fight in the streets and they'd left with the rioters filling their trucks. Nobody came back. I didn't tell him that the rioters were probably Infected. What was the point? We were safe. I told him what had happened but neither of us admitted that I might be sick, that I'd been exposed. We just pretended it was a close scare, that I was okay. We stayed quiet a few days, but Ben didn't keep his kitchen stocked very well. Neither of us did, really.

"We went to the grocery store on the third morning. I'd recovered enough to try, and things on his street had been quiet after the soldiers left. We thought maybe the worst was over. The streets were still pretty busy, but there were signs of things collapsing everywhere. Long before we reached the store. It was subtle at first. Unplowed side streets that had gotten slushy, or a car parked in a tow away zone. Here or there an object forgotten. A shoe, a hat, a suitcase or backpack. It got more obvious as we got closer. Shopping carts were abandoned on sidewalks and some of the smaller shops had broken windows. Alarms were left blatting in competing screams and people ran by us without paying any attention to them. There were even police, but they didn't seem to be stopping anyone from looting. I think they were looking for active Infected.

"We parked pretty far from the store, not wanting to risk it getting stolen or crashed into, and we sprinted into the store. There were no carts left, no baskets and we could hear a fist fight somewhere in the back. Other people skittered around the store like startled roaches, barely looking at us. Ben wanted to turn around, but we needed food. Most of the produce buckets were empty in their displays, so I took one and handed him one.

'Just get anything,' I told him, 'don't fight with anyone, it's not worth it. Just grab anything edible.' I didn't wait for him to agree, just ran down the aisles. It was a large store and I started to panic as aisle after aisle was just empty beige metal shelves. I didn't even look at what I was picking up, I just grabbed anything, any can or box that was left, anything that had rolled underneath the bottom shelf or been pushed back into a deep corner. There was nothing fresh left. No meat, no dairy, no fruit. I managed to fill my produce bucket and Ben was following close behind. There was nobody at the register. I was so stuck, so tied to the idea of the rules that I stopped anyway. I wrote down my name and address and made a list of what we took. Ben kept begging me to go, but I stopped and did it, and tucked it into the register.

"It was just long enough for another woman to come up and try to grab our baskets. Ben punched her in the face and she reeled back. I shouted at him, but he grabbed out buckets and pushed me toward the door. We ran out of the store with the woman yelling after us. We dodged a few more people in the parking lot, but they were still hopeful about the store and didn't make a real effort to take our food. I yelled at him the entire way back to the apartment. He told me things had changed and I needed to be realistic. I didn't listen. We holed up in the apartment again and pretended it had never happened.

"We were okay for another week, until the power went out. I was starting to feel slower, though, like I was moving through molasses or like I wasn't sleeping enough. I had trouble following the news reports before the power went out and Ben would have to repeat himself a few times for me to understand when he was talking to me. He thought it was just stress. I let him. But I should have known. It was almost night time when the power went out and it got cold really fast. We could hear people leaving around us. There couldn't have been that many left, but the people that were still sane enough were fleeing. 'We can't stay here,' said Ben, 'we'll freeze to death.'

'Where are we going to go?' I asked, but I'd started slurring and it was hard for him to understand me.

He shrugged. 'Maybe the fire department? Or the hospital? They must have generators. And if not, they can tell us where to go.'

I tried hard not to laugh at him, but I was already losing control. 'The hospital? Have you been watching the news? They were overrun days ago.'

He asked me what I suggested, but I had no answers for him. We held on for a few more hours, shivering under all the blankets he had in the place. Finally, I agreed that we'd have to try *something*. We sat in the car for a while, listening to the radio, trying to figure out where to go. The broadcasts were confused. The airport was out, we knew that. And the reports from other cities really weren't any better than what we were seeing. Finally, he just started driving. Said he was going to an old legion hall on the edge of town. Used to go there for boy scouts, when he was little. He said there was a wood stove, if nothing else. I was too slow to argue much and he thought I'd been drinking because of the slur. It was probably best he didn't rely on my judgment by then anyway. It was far away and it was easy for me to fall asleep. But Ben didn't have enough gas. He must have passed dozens of stations. I can only assume they were all out of gas in the panic. Or they just didn't have power to pump it. Either that or he just didn't realize how low he really was. He stopped at this big truck stop on the highway. Its lights were on and he figured they must have a generator and gas. But it turned out to be like a lone lighthouse, a giant flame to every moth in the area. I woke up as he parked in front of the pumps. I was groggy, and I remember being angry for no real reason. Frustrated that we had stopped maybe. Not happy to be with him, I guess. Really, for no reason. There were a lot of people milling around the front of the station. We thought they were just looking for supplies. He got out and swiped his card. I watched the people, bored and frustrated. The card beeped. He tried it again and I watched a few people turn their faces toward the car at the beep. It was too far to see details. The card beeped again. Ben swore and swiped it a third time. More people looked over. An electronic voice informed him loudly to come inside. It was the voice that did it. The people were like a herd of gazelles or something. They all turned at once. Ben wasn't paying attention. He opened the car door and told me he was going inside.

'Get in,' I told him.

He just laughed. 'It's okay,' he said, 'there's nothing wrong with the card. I'll just pay inside.'

People were shuffling toward us.

'Get in!' I wanted to yell, but I was so scared I just managed a squeak.

He shook his head. 'We need gas, Mel. We aren't going to make it another ten miles without—'

I grabbed his arm and yanked him inside. He fell

into his seat and I could tell it hurt. 'Shut the door!' this time, I *did* yell. The first Infected were only ten feet away or so. He slammed the door, still not understanding. 'What on earth is the matter—' he started.

I just banged my fist on the automatic door locks with one hand and pointed with the other. He finally looked and I saw his face go gray under the orange station lights. He started the car, but it was too late. We were surrounded and the Infected began pounding on the car, shaking it, rocking it back and forth.

'Shut it off,' I said, 'if we're very quiet maybe they'll forget we're here.'

'Sure, when the next poor sucker pulls up and they decide to eat him," said Ben, but I didn't care, as long as the next sucker wasn't us. I twisted the keys so hard they broke. He looked down at them in my hand. I apologized, but it frightened me. I hadn't realized I was so furious. I tried to calm down, but the shrieks from outside and the constant violent bumps just made it worse and worse.

Finally, Ben said, 'Look, Mel, we aren't going to make it if we stay here. I'll draw them away. It looks like most of them are right around the car now, and I can run fast. You get into that store and lock the door. Open it for me when I come back around. We can hole up there for a while.'

I told him no, that I was sick anyway, that it wasn't worth risking. I told him I'd draw them away for him, but he wasn't paying attention. It took a few minutes to force the door open against all those people. I could see his muscles straining to push them away.

'So stupid!' I yelled and he leaped out. He didn't even make it ten yards. I kept yelling, 'So stupid, stupid, stupid!' I started fighting the Infected around him, snarling and biting anything that I could reach. The other Infected were slow. I think they'd eaten recently. Most of them backed away rather than fight me and wandered toward the empty car. There was a small knot of them that fought each other over Ben and he pushed them off as best he could. His face when he saw me push through the crowd—" She stopped and sobbed into her hands. Rickey put an awkward arm around her shoulders and waited. "He thought I was coming to rescue him," she continued, "He was already bitten in several places, his face was bloody but he had this relieved smile as I bent over him, shoving aside the remaining Infected. He reached up an arm, thinking I was going to help him up. I leaned in further and bit down on his throat. I fought it to the end. Denied it until I felt him writhing underneath me, the bristle of his five-o-clock shadow scraping against my lips. There will be others who do the same. Even when they are stumbling. Even when they are slurring. Even when they get hunger pains and start chewing their own skin away. The radio isn't going to convince them. Nothing will."

Rickey looked up at the distant radio tower, its dull red light still blinking fitfully. "We have to try," he said.

Melissa wiped her face. "What happened to the guy that wanted to run away to the west, out into the empty country where something like a Plague could never reach him?"

Rickey smiled and squeezed the arm he'd draped around her shoulders. "The truth is, I'm too much of a coward to run away alone. Or I was when I originally threatened that."

"And now?"

His smile grew into a grin. "And now I have to stay because you have a crush on me and I'm too gentlemanly to break your heart."

She punched his arm gently and laughed. They watched the blinking red light for a few moments in silence.

"It's going to be okay, you know," he said.

Melissa sighed. "Maybe for you, you never even wanted to be cured. What do you care if you revert?"

"I care. I just don't like that everyone was treating the people that cured us like they were some kind of heroes. They were saving themselves. And even if they hadn't had to, wouldn't it be just common human decency? If you had the means to cure someone and didn't, that'd just mean you were rotten. It wouldn't make you their savior if you did decide to cure them. In the beginning, I was angry. I didn't want to face what I'd done. Why should I have to? It's not like I *chose* to do those things. It's not like I *chose* to get sick. I was busy pushing back against the guilt I could see weighing Henry and Vincent down. And against the City, treating us like animals instead of people. It's our world too. But I care. I don't want to go back. I'm here with you, trying to stop it aren't I?"

She nodded and returned his hug.

TWENTY-SIX

Amos backed into the loading bay of the large farm store. He leaned forward as he parked, squinting into the hazy horizon. "Is that smoke?" he asked, but the sky was a drained gray, a bleached bone and Henry couldn't pick out any smoke. Amos shook his head. "Just paranoid, I guess. Listen, I'll find the chemicals if you jump one of the sprayers. You'll need the gas, whatever's left in the tanks will be flat and useless after all this time. I'm not even sure any of the trucks will take a charge at this point, but I don't have another plan. We just have to get lucky this time."

He jumped out and Henry slid over into the driver's seat. "We'll find a way to make it work. Should have traded spots with Rickey though, he's made vehicles start that I thought were scrap."

Amos nodded. "Yeah, but Melissa's going to need that. Besides, I don't know if I'd trust Rickey to drive what's basically going to be a giant explosive back to the Colony without blowing himself up smoking a cigarette."

Henry grinned and pulled the truck out into the lot. Amos looked around. He'd been here before, for seeds and fertilizer. He'd noticed the chloropicrin the first time. Nobody else had reason to notice, but Amos knew what it was. What it could do, on a bad day. He'd thought about hiding it, but it was a huge shipment. Must have been for the entire county. He'd decided it would only draw curiosity if he tried to move it. Sometimes things hid best in plain sight. What were the chances an old soldier like him would stumble on this particular store anyway? It was even more remote that the soldier that did would want to use it as a weapon. Still, Amos breathed a little deeper when he found the canisters still stacked in the far corner, the dust settling in rings around them, untouched. They just had to get it all back safely. He glanced back toward the open bay door, shading his eyes for a moment, almost completely certain he could see smoke coming from the direction of the Colony.

Whatever is happening will happen without me, he told himself. He went into the dark store, hunting for pesticide spray suits. If they had the chemical, they'd have the gear, he reasoned. He concentrated on picking his way through the dark aisles so that he could let the unrest in his mind cool a little. It was all wrong. It had felt wrong since Vincent had volunteered to go into the quarantine camp, and it just kept getting worse. He'd had friends in the City. When Henry had asked him for help, Amos hadn't expected to stay separated from them forever. They were most likely dead. He'd left, not because he hated the City or the people in it, but because he *understood.* He knew how the Cured felt. He'd experienced it himself, Before. The Colony was meant to be a new start. A place without memory, without past. For Amos, too. He pulled the masks and suits from the rack, still smooth in their plastic bags, dumping them all into a bucket. He didn't bother counting. He'd let the others divide them. Let the others choose who lived an hour longer. Let them choose their own murderers. He'd put that part of his life away. This was a close as he was willing to get to picking it back up again.

You're just a farmer now, he told himself. Just a farmer that knew how to wipe out a city full of people and knew what men like Gray meant for what was left of the world.

"Amos?" Henry called.

"Yeah, in here." He shook himself and carried the suits back toward the loading bay.

"Sprayer is running. How do we fill it?"

"We need a standpipe or a well. I hope the pump on the truck is still working."

Henry shook his head. "We can't use the farm one. Not unless it rains. It's dangerously low on water."

- 180 -

"There's a fire station down the road, there must be a hydrant near it. We'll do that first. The longer we can avoid traveling with the chemical, the better. We can pour it in when we get back, that way we only need to worry about one truck exploding."

He loaded the suits into the pickup, keeping an eye on the horizon. The bulbous forms of smoke were plainly visible now. "We have to hurry, Henry," he said, pointing, "I think Gray made a move earlier than we expected."

Henry covered his forehead with one hand. "Alone? He can't be that stupid. What could he possibly gain by trying to hit us by himself? He wouldn't be able to steal much."

Amos shook his head. "Whatever is happening at home, they need help. I wish Vincent wasn't in that camp."

"We all do," said Henry, his gut clenching painfully. Who would they lose this time?

They didn't waste time discussing it, jumping into the sprayer's cabin and heading for the fire station before the clouds of smoke could spread even farther across the sky.

TWENTY-SEVEN

Gray's skull throbbed and blood spilled over his eyelashes as he limped to the tree line. He didn't stop, cursing under his breath instead, each step stretching the open flap of skin and muscle on his calf. He risked a glance behind him as the he reached the dim twilight of the thick woods. No one followed him. The priest must have stopped to pick up the girl. Gray sagged against the root system of a fallen tree. He wiped the blood from his forehead with the back of his arm and swore as he bent to look at his leg. *Fucking zombie,* he thought, *I shouldn't have bothered stopping to kill her. They're all dead already. No way they'll grow enough food now. And now I have to limp thirty fucking miles to the boat.* The leg was gushing with every step and he was dizzy from the blow to his head. He had to find somewhere to hole up and heal for a few days. Gray was in no hurry. He knew their plans now. He had weeks to spare before they'd move out. A small part of him worried that his attack on the Colony would speed up the timeline, but he relaxed into a nasty grin as he realized that nobody knew *why* he'd attacked. Nobody knew what he was after, except Father Preston. And now that Gray had acted, Father Preston would be too much of a coward to speak up until it was too late. They'd blame the priest for not warning them. He wouldn't risk it. Gray's secret was safe. For all the Colony knew, he would *keep* attacking. They'd tighten their defenses if anything, not risk more people in trying to get to the City. By the time they figured it out, Gray would have sailed halfway across the ocean.

But not if he bled to death. He hobbled farther into the woods, heading toward the City. There had to be something on the way. A house, a store, someplace he could stop and patch himself up. He hoped Molly was dead with every burning step. It was one thing to get beaten, he was no stranger to pain. It was another to be so wounded by a woman and a cripple. Humiliating.

He might be laid low, but he wasn't worried. This world was made for him, almost as if he'd shaped it that way himself. He'd waited, Before, his whole life. Biding his time behind a mask of polite civility until the Plague. When things like masks were worse than useless. When people like him, people that *faced* what the world really was, instead of pretending it would revert to what it had been, those people thrived. This world rewarded cunning and strength with power and ease where others scrambled to survive. Certainly, it was dangerous, but Gray wasn't relying on a barn of burnt vegetables either. And he'd yet to find anyone more cunning or stronger than himself. Even Father Preston had proved a dupe in the end. Gray had thought the religious act just a ruse, another mask, but, in the end, Gray had proven smarter and more practical. This place was used up. He'd never be a farmer. He'd never even be a good thief. Not really. Gray was a leader. A goader. An instigator. He needed people. He'd keep moving until he found some. Nice, gullible people. Who would farm for him and manufacture for him and be happy to do it.

No more Cured. They either collapsed under the weight of their own guilt or they turned out to be uppity and dangerous rivals. No, the further he went, the more likely it'd just be Immunes left. Frightened by the Infected, by the packs of wild animals, by the lack of everything, they'd thank him for saving them.

These are the things he repeated to himself, like a mantra as he stumbled through the woods. It was almost nightfall before he found the hunting shack. He'd lost a good deal of blood and become disoriented. He was farther from the road than when he had started the day, though he didn't know it. He dragged himself up to the porch. The door was locked and he flung himself at it, but was too weak to break it down. He stood a moment stupidly staring at the unyielding door. At last he looked around for a window and flung a stone through one nearby. He expected it to burst inward, but the crash was dull and the glass clung together in small shards. He used his shirt to carefully punch the glass loose and crawled through, swearing as his hand raked over a jagged piece he'd missed. He was in a small, unfinished bathroom and he pawed through the medicine cabinet for supplies. There was a collection of first aid kits, most were missing the band-aids but little else. He picked up three and walked out into the cabin. The tub that ought to have been in the bathroom was sitting in the middle of the living room floor, filled with packing peanuts and small plastic figurines. Glittering holiday ornaments hung from the unfinished rafters along with a pair of hammocks. Comic books were strewn over the floor. Gray smiled. It was little more than a tree house. Like one that had been in his backyard. He half expected to see a pack of partially smoked cigarettes or a dirty magazine tucked in one of the corners. He hoped the kids who'd been here had left him something to eat. He wouldn't have to worry about getting jumped and that was worth something. He sank down onto one of the hammocks and pulled open one of the first aid kits. The small hand mirror in the top of the kit showed him a crackled mask of deep rusty brown. He didn't bother to wipe it away. Instead, he attempted to see the cut on his head. He touched it carefully with one hand. Unlike his leg, it had already scabbed over. He rummaged through the box and found a few foil envelopes with pills. The labels were old and his eyes kept crossing as he tried to focus. He shrugged and downed a few of each, hoping something would help his headache. He opened the other first aid kits and swallowed the pills he found in them as well. Then he bent down to look at his leg. The sudden movement made him pitch forward onto the floor. He fought to stay conscious and a wave of nausea rolled through him. *Fucking zombie,* he thought again. He stayed on the floor for a moment, catching his breath and watching the glittering ornaments sway in and out of focus above him. *No passing out until it's stitched,* he told himself. He hauled himself up and propped the wounded leg on a nearby chair so he could reach his calf. He fumbled with the alcohol wipes and clumsily swept them one by one through the gash, hissing each time. It still looked red and puffy along the edges. He squinted at it for a while and then shrugged. He'd slap some antibiotic lotion on it after it was closed, he guessed. It wouldn't be the first time he'd had to sweat through an infection. He pawed through the kits again and swore. The suture kits were missing. He lay back down. He could wrap it in bandages but the bleeding wasn't going to stop. He stared at the ornaments above him. If he had to, he could use one of the wire hooks as a needle he supposed. The thought was as far as he got before losing consciousness.

TWENTY-EIGHT

Vincent pulled Nella gently away from Molly. Her lips were bloody where she'd been fighting the tide of Molly's pulse as she blew into the thin straw. Her hands shook, splattering blood across the sleeping bag as she backed away.

"I'm sorry," she said, sighing. Vincent nodded and sat down beside Molly's body and folded her hand into his own. Nella stumbled out of the tent into the sizzling summer light. The air was charred and gray ash sparkled in the sun, suspended in the windless day. Father Preston was waiting for her, wringing his hands.

She pushed past him. "She's dead," she said blankly. "I'm sorry," she added, but couldn't muster the same sympathy for him as she had for Vincent. She didn't know if he'd even known her.

"I have to talk to you," he said.

She kept walking. "I don't want to hear any of your lies."

"But it's my fault! And yours too—"

She wheeled around. "What's my fault?"

Father Preston pointed at the tent. "*Our* fault. The girl lying in there."

"*Our* fault? I did what I could. I'm not a surgeon. I warned him— the world is— is broken. Nothing *works* anymore. Even if I saved her, she'd have been infected. Everything is— everything is *wrong*." Her last word threatened to tumble into an angry sob and she pinched the bridge of her nose with two bloody fingers to stop herself from crying in front of him.

"Not that," said Father Preston, and his voice was softer than she'd ever heard it before. "I know you did everything you could. It's our fault that Gray attacked. I have to talk to you about him."

Nella shook her head. "*You* made him, not me. I'm

sorry, Father. A few years ago, maybe even a few months ago, you might have found a sympathetic ear with me. But I've seen your brand of fanaticism too many times. And there's barely anyone alive who isn't carrying some kind of guilt for what's happened. It's become the new norm. Besides, I'm dying. Office hours are over. I'm not your confessor and I'm not your therapist. Find someone else to dump your sermons on." She felt terrible almost as soon as the words left her lips.

"But you don't understand— I *must* speak to you —" he continued. She walked back to her tiny cell and slid into the tent, covering her head with one of the sleeping bags and burying her face in the crushed grass so she couldn't hear him. Startled, Frank met Father Preston at the fence.

"It's about—" he started.

Frank waved a hand. "She's upset. Let her calm down and we'll listen to what you have to say. Whatever it is, it can wait."

"No—" protested Father Preston.

Frank gripped the wire fence tightly. "Yes, Father, it *can*. We're trapped in here. Unless what you have to tell us can be solved inside this wire fence, then it can *wait*. It's just your bad conscience talking. I won't let you dump your guilt on to her. She's had more than her share of that. Leave her be. We'll speak later."

The priest backed away and Frank returned to Nella. She was crying and trying to wipe the blood from her mouth and hands.

"She didn't make it?" he asked, offering her a cup of cool water. She shook her head.

"There was nothing I could do."

"I know."

"I tried," she said.

"I know."

"It didn't even mean anything. It didn't even *count*. He got away. He'll come back, hurt some more people. And it won't mean anything either. And in a month, I'll die too and then you and then none of this will have mattered. None of *us* will have mattered. Because everything and everyone will be gone."

Frank shook his head. "That's not true. We know there are others out there. We've seen them. And even if they weren't— even if there were no more humans, it doesn't mean we didn't matter or that what we suffered made no difference. We are a handful of people, the leftovers of billions. We don't hold the memory of every person that lived and breathed before us. Not even in our modern age where everything seems to be recorded. How many millions and millions of people were born and lived and died without leaving a single trace in history? But they mattered. Their lives meant something. How many thousands just in the past few years, that were lost in the Plague, that have nobody left to remember them? But they still matter. So do you and I."

"To whom? When there is no one left, to whom will we matter?"

"To each other. To the people that lived with us, who knew us. To me, if you can't think of better. It matters that I met you. It matters that you loved me. Even if this is it. Even if it all stops when we do. You gave my life meaning. It means something that that girl existed. That she was loved by her friends. Even if they don't make it either. Besides, Gray isn't going to come back. You didn't see what she managed to do to him. I did. He's lucky he didn't lose his leg. He still might. He won't come back, not knowing they are ready for him this time. She *saved* them. Whether she saved them for an hour or a month or years, that means something. And you saved *her*, the first time around. Maybe so she could do this very thing. That meant something too."

"I didn't cure her, I just got bitten. You saved her."

Frank smiled. "Very well, I saved her. But you saved me. I don't know if I believe we are fated to do anything, or that we have a purpose outside of just existing. But if I were looking for a worthy one, I think helping these people would be a good one. And loving you would be the best one. I don't need any more than that."

Marnie slid her small fingers through the fence and fumbled with the latch on her lock. She unhooked it and slid out of her small cell, heading toward the tent where all the commotion had been. It was silent now, and she held up the flap to look inside. A girl was lying on the ground, pillowed by a few bloody sleeping bags. Vincent knelt beside her, brushing her hair from her forehead. He was quiet but the way he rocked slightly told Marnie he was crying. She sat down quietly beside him.

"What was her name?"

Vincent picked up the girl's hand. Marnie could see it was broken and scarred. "Molly," he said.

"Was she at the Lodge?" Marnie asked.

Vincent nodded.

"Did Phil do that to her arm?"

"No. It was one of our friends before they were cured."

"You're friends with people that tried to eat you?"

Vincent smiled. "I'm friends with whoever will have me as one. She and Henry were the best of them, though."

"What happened?"

Vincent's hand tightened over Molly's limp one. "Someone worse than Phil. Someone worse than all of us. Someone who enjoys being a monster."

"What will you do?"

He placed the hand across the girl's chest and then the other on top of it. "Say goodbye."

"What about the bad guy? Aren't you going to find him?"

Vincent shook his head. "If he comes back, I can't answer for what will happen to him. But I won't chase him. Molly died trying to protect this place. She'd want us to stay and protect it too."

TWENTY-NINE

Amos winced as the sprayer bounced violently over an unseen rut. He slowed down, glad he was the one driving with the chemicals. He eased the pickup over the dip, glancing at the dark truck bed as if he could will the box of pesticide containers not to move. The headlights swooped up to illuminate the back of the sprayer again, its tank still swaying slightly from the slosh of the water. He could hear crickets even over the rumble of the trucks and the wind blew a dry tang of smoke into the cab. Too heavy to be the campfires. They were still too distant for that to reach him. He was unsurprised to see the sprayer speed up. Henry was panicking. Amos had considered warning him, when he was certain the smoke had to be from the Colony. But there was nothing to be done. They had to trust Molly and Vincent to hold it together without them. Amos understood the impulse, but he kept his foot light on the gas pedal. It'd do no good to blow himself up. Then there'd be two fires instead of one. He'd kept his own panic in check as the day crawled on because the signs of smoke had diminished instead of grown. He knew they'd controlled it somehow. What he didn't know, was whether it was an accident. Had something truly ugly happened? He rubbed a rough hand over his face. He'd seen it before. Quarantines gone wrong. It didn't take much. A superstitious group, a collective fear, one person could set it off. It wasn't even hate, just sheer terror that would cause it. They'd certainly had enough of that.

Before, he'd been an outsider. He'd been trained. Grown up in a western world where things like witchcraft didn't cause disease. He'd looked down on the people he was trying to protect, even as he told himself he didn't. He practiced pretending they were equal, they were the same as him. But deep in his head, he looked down on their fear. Minimized it even as he tried to show that he cared, that they were there to help. Soldiers weren't built to fear, even when they did. He'd expected to be an outsider at the Colony too. As hard as Henry tried, as much as he liked the others, Amos really had been. The lone Immune. Nobody treated him badly, nobody pointed or stopped conversations when he came near. But he was still the outsider. Still the helper. Part of it was purely practical, he knew about farming. It was easy to fall into the role of teacher. And then leader. The others had been content to let him.

And then the radio message had changed everything. He understood the terror now. Now he wasn't the Immune. They were all vulnerable. And burning down the quarantine camp didn't seem as irrational anymore. It was *wrong*, but he could understand it now. He was one of them and he was afraid with them. For them. For himself. For the Infected.

He was a little ashamed of the sinking feeling he got when the sprayer pulled to a stop between the wire fence of the quarantine camp and the Colony's stone wall. The camp was still there, the tents a string of softened light in the dark. The Infected were safe. And still a threat.

What had burned? He parked beside the other truck and watched the people running toward the wall above them. Henry looked torn between running for the wire fence or racing up to the Colony.

"What's happened?" rumbled Amos toward the wall. "Where's Molly?"

The guard shook his head. "We don't know. She disappeared just after the fire was under control. We've been searching for hours. We think he must have dragged her off—"

"She's dead." Vincent's voice cut through behind them and Amos turned to see him leaning on the fence. Henry took a few steps toward the fence. "No," said

Vincent, holding up his hands, "Don't compound it by exposing yourself. You can't help her anymore. It's done. Dr. Ryder tried to save her but..." He ran a hand through his straggling gray hair. "There were no other casualties down here. I don't know what the state up there is, though."

"She— how? With all these people to protect her— how did she get hurt?" asked Henry, shaking his head.

"She was the one protecting them, Henry. Go and see. We will speak later. We still have many things to finish." Vincent let go of the fence and walked farther into the dark camp.

Amos didn't waste time, but raced up the hill. Henry sank down into the long grass. He sucked in the cindery air and sat in silence for a long time, staring into the dark woods. He looked up at the dark silo, expecting to see Molly's small form perched in the window, her head haloed by soft lantern light. But the window was dark and the side of the silo blackened with soot. Henry suddenly felt he had been gone for decades instead of a few hours. He climbed wearily up to the farmhouse, not even pausing at the wreckage of the barn where Amos was sifting through ash while others surrounded him, telling him the story. He found the spare handset and clicked it on.

"Vincent?"

"I'm here."

"I don't want to hear how it happened from anyone but you."

"Why did you let him go, Henry?" Vincent moaned, a sound of grief Henry had never heard from him before.

"I thought I was doing what was right. I thought I was keeping us from becoming like him. Or like Phil or all the others who used the situation as an excuse to shed their humanity. I can't say that I'm sorry for letting him go. I'm sorry for not staying today, though. For not being here, where I was needed."

"I could say the same. She said she was lonely, that we were all on 'quests' and she kept getting left behind. She saved the Colony today, Henry. It would have burned to the foundations without her. When he comes back—"

"When he comes back," said Henry, his voice lowering to a sharp growl, "My face will be the last thing he sees."

THIRTY

Rickey stumbled over a thick cable. He caught himself on the half buried arm of a lift chair. "Watch out," he called to Melissa. "There's a lot of metal lying around."

"We must have hit the resort. We aren't far now," she said, carefully picking her way around the tangled cable.

Rickey kicked at it. "Hope the radio equipment is in better shape than this."

"That's why I've got you along."

Rickey scratched at a thin patch of hair. "I can fix some things, but I don't know much about radios. How do we even know anyone will be listening? What's the damn thing broadcasting anyway?"

Melissa shrugged. "Probably the message from the City, unless someone's stopped it. It was still broadcasting that message when we left. It would have been broadcasting the last emergency message before that."

"For eight years? Why would anyone tune in now? Who even has a radio anymore or anything to power it? You know, I didn't want to say anything before we left, but we're down to the last few gallons of gas ourselves, let alone batteries."

"Look, I know it's a long shot, okay? This whole plan is insane. But I'm hoping we can do what the lady in the City did. If I can figure out how to trigger the emergency broadcast, maybe other stations will pick it up too. We were listening, maybe others are too. Maybe they'll spread the word. We have to try. Otherwise, we just have to shoot anyone that approaches the Colony for a year in case they're sick."

"Sounds like we're going to have to do that anyway," he grumbled.

Melissa nodded. "Probably, but maybe the other groups out there will be protected if they don't make the same choice."

"How many people could have gotten out?"

She sighed. "I hope this is as pointless as you are making it out to be Rickey, I really do. If there's nobody listening or nobody infected then we made a six-day hike for nothing. It's not really a big loss, is it?"

Rickey grinned. "I dunno, six days alone with you might ruin my reputation. People might talk."

She rolled her eyes.

The trees fell away and brush took over, green melting into scarlet and purple of high blueberry barrens clinging to the thin dirt and cracked stone at the top of the mountain. The station was a lone spike in a sea of twisted branches that sighed and flashed at its knees as the breeze swept through. Rickey stooped to pull a few berries.

"We should come back here. If we're alive next summer. There's enough for the entire Colony. And Amos and Molly could probably transplant a few." He popped a few into his mouth and made a face. "Yech. Needs sugar."

A shadow peeled itself away from the station's tower. Melissa froze beside him and put a hand on his arm. "Shh," was all she said. The bulky shadow lumbered slowly toward them.

"Shit," whispered Rickey. "Is that a bear?"

"Lie down."

He didn't argue. They sank into the brush, the sharp twigs pricking them and held their breaths listening. The animal was still too far from them to hear. "Maybe if we go back to the woods—" Rickey whispered.

Melissa shook her head. "There's no shelter back there. It can climb."

"We can't stay *here*," he hissed, "all I've got is a little pocket knife and a lighter that doesn't work half the time. I'm not exactly intimidating."

"If we play dead, it won't be interested."

"Bullshit. It'll just bat us around a little, right? So I'll be mauled instead of chewed. We're going for the station."

"No! If you run, it will chase you and it can run faster."

"Not going to run. We're going to crawl. Then we can be dead if it finds us like you want, okay?"

"If we just leave it alone, it'll go away. It probably just wants us gone."

He started pulling her arm and inching forward. "Melissa, you were a mailperson. What did dogs do when they wanted you gone?"

"What?"

He pulled her up onto her knees and peered over the top of a bush. The bear was sniffing around, still walking toward them. "You ever see a strange dog quietly amble up to you? Animals make noise when they want you gone. They let you know. That bear isn't defending itself. That bear is hunting. And it's hunting us. No more deer, no more cattle, just a hell of a lot of blueberries and us, a couple of sticks of tasty turkey jerky in its field. No more debate. Let's go."

He sank back into the bushes and pulled her forward again, their bodies making soft slithering whooshes through the bracken. She tried not to notice that his hand around her wrist was shaking. She didn't dare crawl, fearing the pack on her shoulders would stick above the branches and the movement would catch the bear's attention. Instead, she slid on her belly, trying to pull herself along beside him over the rocky gravel. They were blind, the gold-red flash of the blueberry bushes swallowing the edge of the hill, the station ahead, everything but the startling blue of the sky above. She hoped they were headed the right way. The swoosh of their bodies through the leaves fell into a rhythm and Melissa began to let it lull her into a hesitant calm. Surely, it would have attacked if it was going to. A low snuffle near her foot made her freeze and adrenaline tore painfully up her sore muscles. Rickey squeezed her wrist painfully tight. He looked over at her and his eyes were wide, his breath made little puffs in the dust below the bushes. "Don't. Run." She mouthed at him. She wasn't sure he really saw her until his chin dipped in a slight nod.

Another snort and then a weight came crashing down onto her pack. Her breath puffed out in a dusty plume. Rickey sprang up.

Don't run, she willed at him.

He started yelling and waving his arms. She felt the weight lift from her back. She scrambled to her feet. Rickey was clapping his hands and shouting. She turned to look at the bear. It began to circle, still making no noise, a massive shadow pacing past, threatening to come between them and the station. Melissa swung her pack down from her shoulder. Her mind raced. There were tools in there, things to fix the radio if necessary. No good if they were dead. She pulled it back and hurled it. It knocked into the bear's flank with a metallic clank as the tools smashed into each other. The bear drifted sideways, surprised. It stopped to sniff the pack, and she grabbed Rickey's arm pulling him steadily back toward the station. He stopped yelling and they backed steadily away. She glanced behind them. They were closer than she'd expected. "You got food in that pack?" he asked.

"No, it's all in yours, remember?"

The bear abandoned her pack and turned back toward them. It broke into a run. "Shit," swore Rickey, fumbling with his own pack. The bear stopped just shy of them. Rickey threw the pack over its head. It turned its head but then refocused. After a throaty bark, it moved to circle them again. Melissa looked around. Nothing but flimsy branches and pebbles.

"I'll pull it away," said Rickey softly, "you get to the station. See if there's a gun or a flare or something."

"No."

"We have to. It's coming and it's hungry. It's going to get one of us." He was pressing her behind him, still backing toward the station. Two dozen yards. A sprint.

"We'll run together."

The bear was closing in, snuffling and slapping at the ground as it came.

"No. You can fix the radio. I can't. If one of us is getting hurt, maybe we have a chance to determine which. Just play it safe—"

"Fuck that," said Melissa. She yanked him backward as the bear charged and shoved him toward the station. She squared her shoulders and turned back to the bear, planting her feet on the uneven ground. The bear closed in on her, its shoulders bouncing, its top lip folding back. The teeth were dull yellow and thick, its tongue lolled, drooling as it sniffed the air. It was easy once she let go, falling back into the primal instincts that had governed her life for the past several years. Falling back into that guttural shriek that meant she was about to attack. About to feed. Rickey's skin crawled as he watched. He began to salivate at the familiar sound, even as he held up his hands to block it. The bear stopped just short of her. It reached a massive claw toward Melissa, intending to knock her sideways. She darted in toward it instead and closed her teeth around its wet nose, biting until her jaw ached with the pressure. The bear's nose squished between her teeth and it yelped and shook its head. She let go, falling backward into the brush, its massive paw batting her backward and slicing her shirt and skin. The bear took off, bounding toward the trees, the crimson field rustling and parting in a clumsy wedge behind it. Rickey ran to pick her up. She was laughing.

"Are you okay?" he asked, his legs still shaking and his hand searching for a cigarette that he didn't have. He didn't wait for an answer. "You're fucking crazy. Why didn't you listen?"

She wiped her eyes as the laughing faded. "Tired of listening. Tired of playing it safe. That's how we got here."

"What on earth were you thinking?" he asked, helping her up and checking the shallow scratches that the bear had left on her stomach.

"I was thinking that I'm sick of cowering and waiting to get eaten. For a decade, I've been sitting around waiting to get eaten. And then I remembered that *I* did the eating. I was a zombie, what's scarier than that? It's *my* world too. They used to be scared of *us*. Bears, dogs, other people. We used to be predators. *I* was a predator. I can be dangerous too."

Rickey ran a hand through the wild tangle of hair on his head. "The bear agrees. Me too. You scared the crap out of me." He retrieved the packs, jogging gently back toward the station. "If it's all the same to you, though," he said when he reached her again, "let's not do that again anytime soon."

"Don't worry," she said spitting into the bushes. "I don't want seconds. Bear tastes awful."

THIRTY-ONE

Vincent was standing in front of the fence. Frank had seen his shadow through the tent flap as he woke. He pressed a hand to his bleary eyes and slowly pulled his arm from underneath Nella's shoulder, careful not to wake her. He glanced up, but the shadow was still there, waiting. He wondered why it didn't call him. Frank stretched and pressed himself up, flipping the tent flap back as he rose.

"Father?" he said, blinking in the early sunlight. "Do you need Nella?"

Vincent shook his head. He had tried to clean himself up, his hair was neatly tied back and he had shaved, but Frank thought he looked ten years older and ten pounds thinner than he had the day before. It was a long moment before he said anything.

"No, thank you. She did her best yesterday for me — for Molly. I've come to ask a favor."

"Of course, whatever we can do."

"We are burying her today. I'd like to give her a real service— I mean, I've given them all real services, but she has friends that want to say goodbye. If I wear a mask, maybe they can be there. Outside the fence, of course. Maybe it would be safe. Do you think?"

"Yes— that should— I think we've got some in the pack. One minute."

Nella sat up sleepily as he pushed back into the small tent. *Thirty-three,* her mind murmured rebelliously. "What'sit? What's happened?" she asked.

Frank paused to smooth her hair away from her face. "Nothing's happened. It's okay." He turned away, his face falling into a frown at the slur. *It's just from waking up,* he told himself, but his own mind echoed hers, *thirty-three,* it hissed.

"Here we go," he said with a tight smile, holding up the flimsy yellow masks. "Do you need more than one? Is

Father Preston going too?"

Vincent looked lost.

Frank took his hand through the fence, pressing three masks into it. "This should be enough. Don't worry, we have a few more."

The priest nodded and turned to walk away.

"Vincent—" called Frank in a low voice. "How many days do you have left?"

Vincent shook his head. "I'm not certain. Ten? Twelve? We'll leave when Rickey and Melissa return. That should give us enough time. We just wanted to make sure the broadcast was heard by as many as possible."

"Won't that make it dangerous to be on the road?"

He shrugged. "Isn't dying the entire point? I hope healthy people will be too frightened to get near enough to hurt us. And we'll take nothing of value. I don't want to tempt grave robbers either."

Frank nodded.

"What did you really want to ask?" said Vincent.

Frank hesitated and glanced over his shoulder. "The slurring and stumbling— when should we see it?"

Vincent shook his head. "I don't think you will. It's only been the last few days for the people who have turned here. It starts with fatigue a few weeks before. Fatigue and not being able to say what you really want. Don't you remember?"

"I remember, I just wasn't sure I remembered right. It's so easy to see it in every little action."

"Is she—"

Frank shook his head. "I just— I don't want us to wait too long."

"You won't. I promise. Not even love can disguise it when it comes."

"Thank you," said Frank, though he wasn't certain what for.

"And thank you," replied Vincent, holding up the masks before turning to walk away.

The tents around them flapped suddenly in a quick, forceful breeze. Frank looked up to see clouds deepening on the horizon as they crashed into each other and piled.

"That's going to be a bad thunderstorm," said Nella, coming up to the fence. She curled her fingers around the wire. "Makes me a little nervous, being in this giant grid of metal with nothing else around."

"It's still pretty far. Maybe it'll blow itself out by the time it gets here." Frank shivered though and pulled her away from the fence. The morning was quiet except for the wind snapping the canvas at intervals and the steady thud of Vincent digging at the end of the rows of cells. There was movement up in the Colony, but it was too far to hear.

Frank frowned as he looked up at the wall.

"What's wrong?" asked Nella.

"Just— She hurt Gray, pretty badly. But if he doesn't die— I hope they are ready."

"It's beyond our help, Frank. We don't get to see that part of the story. Believe in the happy ending and be at peace with it."

He turned to face her. "That's the hardest part, isn't it? Never getting to find out how it turns out. We try all our lives to make it better, to make sure the ending is happy, but we'll never know for sure."

"That's why they call it 'having faith'," interrupted Father Preston as he approached their cell.

Frank tried to push Nella gently behind him, as if he could shield her from him. She held his arm, but stayed close to the fence.

"I have to talk to you," said Father Preston.

Nella sighed. "I'm sorry for what I said yesterday. It was— unkind."

"I can't say it wasn't deserved," said Father Preston, looking at his feet.

Frank was surprised at the change in the man. His confidence was utterly gone. Had someone convinced him at last, that he was not a miracle worker?

"It was unfair, regardless. I was angry and I took it out on you. What is it that you wanted to tell me?" asked Nella. Her face had reddened with discomfort and Frank was certain she wasn't entirely over her dislike of the man.

"It's about Gray. He came to me, a few nights ago. After he'd been kicked out. He sat outside the fence and listened to you making plans. He— he knew about the boat. Wanted me to get its location from you. I— he said we'd start over, go somewhere more worthy."

"What did you do?" snapped Frank. The scar on his cheek pulsed and he took a step toward the fence, towering over the older man.

"I refused!" cried Father Preston, holding up his arms as if Frank were going to strike him. "I refused. I knew better. I've been a fool. I know. I've— I've ruined so much. I know I can't heal them. I know now. But I'm trying to *help*. I refused and he attacked the Colony to find it instead. Did you tell the others where the boat was? Did he find out from— from *her*? He choked her a long time."

Nella bit back a groan. "He could have," said Frank, "but he'll never make it. I saw his wound. It's days away, he'll die of an infection or blood loss before then. And even if he gets there, we've got the keys, he won't be able to make it out of the bay without the engine."

"He could destroy it," said Nella.

Frank nodded. "He could. But we'd have the lifeboat we came in on, if we had to."

"All these people are not going to fit on the lifeboat, Frank!"

He took a deep breath, hoping she'd mirror him. He

squeezed her hand. "All these people aren't going to make it to the lifeboat. Most won't even make it to the City. We aren't planning a big trip, Nella. You understand? We don't have to come back. We don't have to save anything for later. We just have to make it to the finish line."

Father Preston sobbed and sank onto his knees outside the fence. "It wasn't supposed to be this way. It wasn't supposed to end like this. I was meant to save them. Every life is sacred. That's the rule. And now I'm expected to walk them all to their deaths. As if they are nothing. As if— as if I were *Ruth*. Vincent says I was cured to get a second chance. A second chance at what? I can't save them. Any of them. Can't change them. Can't even ease the ones that don't already believe. What was the point?"

Nella exchanged a glance with Frank and then knelt on her side of the fence. She pushed her hand through a gap in the wire to clasp Father Preston's shoulder. "We aren't saving the Infected. We can't. Not even ourselves. That's out of our hands. We can't do what Juliana did. The Plague would spread until there was no one left to take care of the Infected and then they would die anyway. But we can save the others. That's the point. That's the happy ending that we don't get to see. We're protecting this place, so it can go on. Whatever happens in the next few weeks— whether we make it to the City or turn before then, whether Gray steals the boat and we have to build a raft to sleep on until the poison is finished, you have to believe it's going to go on. Without us seeing it. Without us having a hand in it. You told Frank that was what having faith was about. We do what we can, and then we must let go. Like Juliana. And Sevita. And all the others that have died to get us this far. Like Molly."

Vincent cleared his throat as he walked back toward them. He was covered in dust and the ominous yellow light of the storm clouds made him seem more like an old, worn photo than a man. "Lisa is preparing the body," he said stiffly to Father Preston, "Can I trust you to watch the camp during the service?"

Father Preston stood up. Vincent pulled a long blade from his belt, the same one Father Preston had watched him use on Colin. He offered it to the other priest. Father Preston hesitated.

"I'll do it," said Frank heavily.

Vincent began unlocking the cell.

"No," said Father Preston. "I said I wanted to help. I meant it. In whatever form. God forgive me for making you bear the whole burden until now." He held his hand out. It was shaking. Vincent handed him the blade.

"Thank you," said Vincent.

THIRTY-TWO

Gray came to with a groan. The wood under him was sticky with drying blood. It took him a moment to remember that it was from his leg. He'd let himself go without stitching it. Now he was in trouble. He gathered himself for a moment, knowing he'd be dizzy as soon as he moved. He turned his head. There was a table a few steps from him, a ball of fishing twine lay on it. There was no way he'd get that lucky with a needle. He sighed and resigned himself to using an ornament hook. He heaved himself up halfway, his upper body swaying. His head almost cleared, except for an insistent buzzing sound. The wound ripped open again as he peeled his legs from the pool of blood that had dried underneath him. The pain seared up his leg and back and he shouted, but he was more conscious than he had been a moment before. Hobbling to the table, he reached up and yanked an ornament from above. The fine glass shattered into little more than glitter between his fingers but he caught the thick wire hanger. He sat heavily down at the table, fighting nausea as the room dipped and rolled around him. He straightened the hook as well as he could, pulling the back into a small loop. It still looked massive and thick. *Don't be a pussy,* he told himself. *You want to die to save a little bit of pain? Fucking coward.* He reached for the ball of fishing line and cut a generous piece with his knife. His fingers were shaking as he squinted at the homemade needle. He swiped at a trickle of sweat to clear his eyes and then swore as the fishing line missed the needle's head. And again. He took a deep breath, threading it on the third attempt.

He leaned over. The world grew clearer. He poked the wire into the puffy red skin at the edge of the wound in his calf. It wasn't as awful as he thought. A sting and then a dull throb. He took a deep breath and pulled the fishing line through. And screamed. He had to stop. Tears streamed from his eyes without him even realizing it. He panted for a moment. Two. *Best get it over quick,* he told himself. *Nobody's going to come do it for you. Got to rescue yourself.* He plunged the needle into the other side of the wound and vomited as he pulled the stitch tight.

It didn't get better, but he had nothing left to vomit and the agony kept him from drifting off again. The biggest problem was his shaking hand. He stabbed himself a half dozen times in the wrong spot before he was finished. But finish, he did, tying off the last stitch and throwing the wire needle across the room. He rolled himself into the hammock and let the dizziness take him. He'd deal with the infection tomorrow. *If it comes,* he told himself.

Rickey cleared the last of the massive nest from the top of the radio tower and tightened the bolt holding the last dish. He looked out over the top of the mountain and swore as a dark shadow lumbered at the edge of the field. He climbed down toward the ranger station's roof.

"Bear's back, Mel," he called. She was already locking the door as he tumbled through the skylight onto the table.

"Probably won't come up all these stairs anyway," she said.

"Better safe than sorry," said Rickey. "The tower's cleaned up, should send a clearer signal now. One of the dishes was twisted and hanging by a thread. Did you get everything in here working?"

"I think so, but I can't tell. I'm not receiving anything. I don't know if something's broken or there's just nobody broadcasting." She shrugged and then sighed. "It also means that maybe nobody's listening."

Rickey scratched his head. "We all knew it was a long shot. This whole thing. Even if it's working and there are people listening we don't know if they'll believe us. Or if they'll think they're healthy and not go anyway. We're doing what we said we would. We just have to hope for the best. And try not to get eaten…" he glanced out the window trying to spot the bear but the sky was beginning to darken with thunderclouds and the field, dappled with shifting shadows ate up any definite shapes below. They'd found a few cans of bear spray in the supplies at the station but neither of them was certain if the stuff had an expiration date and Rickey wasn't comfortable relying on it if he didn't have to. He wasn't looking forward to the trip back.

"Looks like there's a storm coming. We'll have to stay here tonight anyway."

Melissa tinkered with the transmitter a little. "It's okay, I really haven't figured out what I'm going to say yet anyway. I need some time to figure it out."

Rickey nodded. "Will they hear us at the Colony when you do?"

"The Colony and much further I hope. This station is connected to a few others, I'm hoping it will just pick up like the emergency broadcast from the City did. At least, that way, healthy people will know to be cautious, even if I can't convince the Infected to turn around."

"Feels weird to be on this side of it," said Rickey, "making these decisions about who is okay and who's not."

"You still wish you'd never been cured?"

He shook his head. "Never really meant that. I mean, it would be easier. No big moral dilemmas. Infected don't worry about lying or about hurting innocent people or about what happens tomorrow. But there was no joy in it. It was misery and rage for years and years. It's not that I didn't want to be cured. It's more that maybe it'd be better if it had just— ended. No more pain, no more guilt, no worry to wake up to. Just done. These Infected will have that comfort at any rate. They never have to wake up and see what they've done. Never have to wake up and decide whether to keep on going or not."

"Is it really a hard decision for you?" she asked.

He sat down on the sagging couch. "Some days it's a harder decision than others. But not since I decided to go with Vincent. Now I've got a purpose."

"Go with Vincent? Are you mad? Why would you go with Vincent? I love him too, but he's got people with him. He doesn't need to take you too."

Rickey snorted. "Who? Father Preston? I don't trust him. And the others will have turned by the time he gets there."

"He's got the people that cured us. They won't turn before then. And why you?"

"Why *not* me? I hardly have a handful of survival skills. Hell, I don't even know what to do about a bear. I certainly didn't think to scream at it and try to eat it." He grinned, trying to sidetrack her, but Melissa was angry.

"You're the only one who knows how to fix the electrical stuff. What are we going to do without a mechanic?"

Rickey blushed but then looked serious. "Amos didn't tell you?"

"Tell me what?"

"We're down to our last few gallons of gas. No more vehicles, no more generators. What good is a mechanic?"

"We'll get more, we'll *make* more. Maybe we can figure out how to get the electric plant back online and running out that far. Or we'll take solar panels from places like this. It's not a reason to give up. None of us were equipped for this when we woke up, but we're learning. You don't have to stay what you were."

Rickey shook his head. "Aw Mel, I'm never going to be a good farmer like Molly's turned out to be. And I don't have the guts to be a serious soldier like Henry and Amos. I'll just be deadweight. If I go with Vincent, I can do some good, maybe. Make you all safe."

"We're going to need more than soldiers and farmers to survive, Rickey. We're going to need plumbers and electricians and artists and even a mechanic or two."

He snorted. "What I know could be learned in a month or two by anyone else."

"Maybe, in the world Before. When it didn't really cost anything to learn. But everything is irreplaceable now. It's expensive to experiment. You could teach people without destroying things. We're going to need you." She was quiet for a moment. "We would— *I* would *miss* you."

He looked startled, as if he hadn't considered it before. He shook it off. "Nah. I'm just a guy that woke up with you. An extra. The ex-con comic relief. Disposable for the greater good. Like Pam and Vincent."

"Pam made her choice," said Melissa sadly, "We understood it. Vincent too. I love him. I'll miss him, but he had to do what he thought was right. I still hope he'll make it through somehow. That he'll come back when this is done. But neither of them were disposable. And Vincent chose to do what he is doing because nobody else did. Because somebody had to and so none of the rest of us would. You included. And you aren't the comic relief. This group would be lost without you. We might drift along in Henry's wake for a while, but it wasn't him that led us out to the Colony. Or Vincent. Wasn't him that started the wall or decided we would welcome anyone that decided they wanted to join us. Henry took care of our past. Righted the wrongs done to us. He's a good protector. He has a strong sense of justice. But he's not a planner. His whole life's going to be about fixing what happened. To us or by us. And Amos is a great leader. He sees what has to be done for us to survive. There's so much, though, and so many people, he'll never get us past our basic needs. It's people like you and me and Molly, we're the ones who will get the lights turned back on and the water running. We're the ones who are going to finally bring us from survival back to civilization. If you go— it might be another twenty years before someone else comes along or grows up with a knack for machinery and knows how to work with other people—"

A crack of thunder shattered over them and she jumped.

"You really think I'm that important?" Rickey asked after a moment.

Melissa smirked. "Now you're just fishing for compliments."

Rickey shook his head. "I shouldn't have doubted you. Whatever you broadcast, you'll definitely convince them."

Melissa laughed but her smile faded. "I really *would* miss you, Rickey."

He avoided her gaze, blinking back his own tears. "*Why?*"

"Because you're funny and smart, although you try really hard to hide it. Because you're kind and passionate about justice where other people give up and accept the way things are. Because I— I *like* you."

Rickey's face snapped back to look at her, to see if she was teasing. "I like you too," he said at last.

So you'll stay?" she asked.

"If you protect me from the bear," he said.

THIRTY-THREE

"Am I going to be down here alone?" Marnie's voice was worried, stripped of its complexity, as if she were terribly young. Which, she was, Henry realized.

"No, of course not," he said, keeping his voice light. "You see that truck they're putting chemicals in?"

"Sure."

"When it's full, or in the morning if it gets too late, Vincent and anyone who feels sick will go. After they are gone, I'll come down there to be with you until it's time to come back to camp."

"What if I'm sick too?"

"Do you feel sick?"

"No— but nobody else did either, until the end. Even the doctor, she says she feels fine, but she knows she's dying anyway. I was with Christine a lot longer than the doctor was. I'm going to get sick too, and— and you'll chain me to a pole." The transmit cut out, but Henry knew she was crying.

"No Marnie, never. I'll never do that to you. I promised your mom I would take care of you. I promised *you* I'd take care of you. I'll never chain you up. You're going to be okay. You're immune, I know it. Like you said, you were with Christine a lot longer. You'd be starting to show signs now. We're just going to play cards and be bored for a few more weeks, then we'll come back up here, you'll see."

"What if you get sick? From touching things? From being where they were?"

"Vincent is burning the empty tents. The only things that will be left will be what you or anyone else that isn't sick has touched."

"There's only one other woman. She's the only one not going. She's not stumbling or anything. She wants to go with Vincent, but he won't let her. She wants to get the miracle cure, but he says she isn't sick, she's just scared."

Two out of thirty-five, Henry thought to himself, his heart sinking. He hoped the radio broadcast worked. They had to keep this plague out of the Colony.

"The others— could Christine have gone with them? Could she have turned back?"

Henry closed his eyes, the realization of what they were doing stabbing at his chest, not for the first time. "No, Marnie. There was nothing that could be done for Christine." *Or any of the rest,* he thought, *sending them on a death march. With Vincent at their lead. How can we do this? What kind of people have we become?*

The top of the water truck closed with a bang as Amos climbed down with the last empty cannister, his face hidden by the thick gas mask. Henry watched as the larger man's shoulders sagged and he brought one hand to his forehead. And for a moment, Henry let the despair overwhelm him. This was no better than simply shooting them. It was worse. It was lying. How was he better than Phil? Even Gray would have given them a better chance at surviving. It was no use arguing that he wasn't making them miserable while they *were* alive. Dead was dead. And he was driving them there. He watched Amos lift his head and the mask turned toward him, a rubber death's head looking to him, to Henry, for comfort he didn't have to give.

He thumbed the radio's transmit button again. "I'll see you tonight, Marnie. Can you find Vincent for me?"

"Is it time?" she asked.

"Almost."

"He isn't coming back, is he?" She didn't pause long enough for him to answer. "I should have come with you, when you both came to the Lodge. Maybe it would be different then."

Henry shook his head. "Vincent chose to do what

was right. He would have done the same whether you came with us or not. There was no talking him out of it."

Rickey was packing a box of plastic suits into the cabin of the sprayer truck. On top, several more canisters of poison were carefully cradled, waiting to be used by hand where the sprayer couldn't go. The quarantine camp was shuffling and rippling with movement as people prepared to leave. The bonfire where Father Preston's tent had been was dying down now, Henry could see someone flinging clothing or debris in occasionally, but it was mostly left to smolder. The radio crackled in his hand and Henry looked down.

"I'm here," said Vincent, his voice already far away, as if he'd been walking for hours before calling. "Is everything ready?"

"Yes, we've found everything you will need. There are a few hazmat suits to make certain someone will last long enough to complete the— the spraying. There is roughly enough food and clean water for three or four days, though if you pick anyone up on the way— they will have to fend for themselves. I wanted to send more— enough so that— but the fire…"

"Henry, it's okay. We don't need it."

Henry slid down the ragged stone wall, his t-shirt catching on the irregular lumps. "I can't do this, Vincent. I can't let you do this either. How could we live with ourselves if I did?"

"We all have our tasks, Henry. It's always hard to be left behind, I know. But someone has to help these people keep going. Someone's got to show them there's some hope left. I don't know anyone who is better at that than you."

"Me? Vincent, I—"

"You kept us going when we woke up. When we wished we had just stayed sick. You persuaded Rickey to stay with us, even when he wanted to break away, to be responsible for no one but himself. You kept Molly alive after she wanted to give up, after everything that she'd done, after she realized she would probably lose her arm, after all that came crashing down on her, you persuaded her to stay with us. To save us, in the end. Your hope for us made dozens of people follow you out here, without enough supplies, without a secure home, nothing but each other to depend on. *You* did that, Henry. And now, you must do it again. Don't feel bad for me. I just have to walk a few more miles, and then my job is done. I've got the easy part."

"But the others— I know that you know what's coming, but the others, I'm sending them to die."

"You are only sending them home. They were already dying."

"Even worse. I should be caring for them, not banishing them."

Vincent sighed heavily. "I am caring for them. You must *trust* me, Henry. You already carry so much. Guilt from the past, worry for the future, let me carry this part. Let me *help*." Vincent laughed and then continued, "It's my turn to save the world, Henry. Let me."

"You have been one of my best friends," said Henry, helplessly.

"And you have been one of the best human beings I've ever met. I spent years among good, religious men. People who spent their entire lives trying to be the best, kindest versions of themselves. I don't know that a single one of them would have had the strength to let Phil go after what he did to us. You asked me once about how much of what we'd done could ever be forgiven. But *you*, Henry, have been my example on that front. You give me hope. Now you must give it to others. Goodbye, my friend."

"Goodbye, Father," said Henry, giving Vincent the

title he knew he'd wanted most.

He clicked the radio off and watched Father Preston get into the cab of the sprayer. They'd told the quarantined that the truck was to put out any remaining fires in the City. Only the two priests, Lisa, Nella, and Frank knew what it really was. The lie pinched at Henry's chest. He watched the small line of stumbling people clustering around the truck and wondered how many of them knew what this really was. Undoubtedly a few must know. The ones that were still sane enough to put it together. Amos sank down next to him, the gas mask long abandoned in the truck. He scrubbed at his face as they watched Vincent hand out packages of food that they carried in packs.

"He's going to have to kill at least a dozen on the road. If they don't all turn at once and overwhelm him," said Amos. "He's already had to put over a dozen down since the quarantine started."

"He has help."

Amos shook his head and Henry heard his breath hitch. He turned his face toward Amos and was startled to see the large man shaking with a suppressed sob.

"What is it?" he asked, alarmed.

"I'm not an angel. I've done things I'm not proud of in my life. Before the Plague and since. But I always *tried* to be a good person. I always *tried* to own my mistakes and make amends. But this— I know Frank Courtlen. I know Dr. Ryder. And most of the others down there. They are decent people. People that tried to make the world better, most of them. They don't deserve this. Nobody does. And we're pushing them out. Like they're garbage. Sending them away to kill each other or choke to death in some lonely corner of that empty City.

I was able to pretend before this. I was able to pretend I didn't bear the same load of guilt that the

Infected did. I didn't kill anyone except when I had to. When they were going to kill me. Not even— not even when I should have. I lied to myself. Told myself I was a good soldier, not a barbarian like the Infected. Like some of the Immunes. I pretended you were equal to me, that I believed you couldn't help yourselves, because of my wife. She was Infected, too. And what she did— I knew she couldn't have done it if there was anything left of her inside. But— you started coming *back*. You weren't supposed to come *back*, Henry. You weren't supposed to be human anymore. So deep down, I never—" Amos shook with another sob, covering his face with his hands. He took a deep breath and watched the sprayer truck start up. "I never really believed you *were* human anymore. Not like me. Not equal. It was just a front.

My dad was a vet for a city zoo. He used to bring me to work with him when I was little. I loved the big cats. He'd let me touch them when they were sedated. Always warned me, though, they might seem quiet. They might *seem* like they loved you sometimes. Like they'd make good pets. But underneath, they were just the same wild, hungry beasts they'd always been. 'They're just waiting, Amos,' he'd say, 'They just bide their time until they think they've got you fooled. It's not the growlers you need to watch out for. There's nothing so dangerous as a purring lion.' And that's what I thought of you. All this time, you were just quiet lions. That you were pleasant enough, but I shouldn't expect anything but a bite if I trusted you. And I'd only have myself to blame for it.

But I know better. I've always known better. It was easier to pretend. So much easier. Because how could she have hurt our little girl if there'd been anything left? How could I have stopped her the way I did, if she wasn't just a husk? And it didn't matter until now. My pretending didn't hurt anyone. Nobody knew. Even after I came here to help,

I reasoned that we don't let beasts starve. But now— I can't pretend anymore. How could I watch you day in and day out working yourself to the bone to feed a few dozen strangers and think you weren't a decent man? And poor, sweet Molly, giving everything to save them from a *real* monster, all alone fighting to rescue a handful of crops. Or Vincent who walked into that quarantine camp with his eyes wide open to nurse people he owed nothing to, people he'd never met and who'd likely have treated him like scum if they had? How could I think you were less? These people we are turning away, they are *real*. They had families once. People they loved as much as I loved my girl. They didn't ask for this and some of them tried to stop it. And we're pushing them out, not even hoping they'll go somewhere else. We're pushing them out, hoping they'll die. *We're* the bad guys, Henry. We're the villains. No matter what happens, even if we save the people here, even if there was no other way to stop the disease, we can't undo this. I'll never be able to justify it to myself. Not really. I'm *bad*. Deep down evil."

The truck pulled away, trailing its train of stumbling people. Henry saw Vincent raise one long arm and returned the gesture. "Vincent said that we all have our tasks to do. Maybe yours and mine are to accept the roles of villains so that other heroes can save them all. So other stories can survive. What we're doing— everything we've done so far, is to keep going, so that something, some*one* will survive to make the world better than it was. Better than the world Before, better than the shell-shocked scrabble for survival after the plague, better than *us*. Because that's the choice, Amos. We turn them away and the Colony survives. Or we welcome them as part of us and we all die together. If your daughter were here— if she and Marnie could both know the whole story, maybe it wouldn't matter so much how they remembered us, if it meant that they were still alive to do the remembering. Maybe I'm okay with being evil if it means Marnie won't be. If it means these people won't make the same mistakes we did. Or don't have to make the same choices that we do."

They sat watching as the train of people was swallowed by the bright summer grass swaying gold against the blue sky and the rumble of the sprayer truck faded into the distant thunder of a faraway storm.

THIRTY-FOUR

It was good to be moving at last. Nella felt the old familiar tug of excitement as they packed up, as if they were going on a pleasant day trip rather than the City at the end of the world. She found she didn't much care, the anxiety of waiting now finally relieved. They were doing *something*. The morning was warm and fresh after several days of heavy thunderstorms. They'd not discussed Gray or the boat and the countdown kept getting muddled in her head. She knew she was in denial, but she didn't try to fight it. What good would it do now? It would only distress her and destroy Frank. He kept reaching for her hand, rubbing his finger over the scratch that had already healed, as if it were a magic crystal that could tell him how much time they had left. She let him do it without comment. He made her read aloud to him at night, telling her he was finding his eyesight weaker these days, though she knew he was counting the pronunciation mistakes and unintentional slurring she might be doing as she read. She let that go too, trying to let him accept what she couldn't yet.

She watched the other cells empty, the people in various states of clumsiness and exhaustion ambling out of the fence. Every face was etched with terror, hardened with despair. They were all going to die alone, and they knew it. Alone and surrounded by strangers. Her chest tightened and twisted as a wave of gratitude overwhelmed her. Whatever happened, whether it was a few hours away or years, she and Frank didn't have to worry about being alone at the end. She looked away from the cluster of people emptying out of the quarantine camp toward him as he folded the canvas that had been their tent as tightly as he could, tucking it into a corner of his pack. The deep stain of his scars on his bare arms made him seem frail, and worry had drawn his face thin and taut. Almost a reflection of the misery around them. She knew he was fighting to pretend the days weren't winding down, the summer wasn't draining away. *Their* summer. The one that should have lasted fifty more years. But he'd stopped planning sailing trips the day they'd found Christine. He no longer talked about building a farm or exploring forgotten islands. He didn't talk about the future at all, unless it was to plan their part in finishing the City. Her chest twisted again, this time with grief. Was it just that he didn't see a future with her anymore? Or was it that he couldn't see one for himself either?

She knelt beside him as he clipped the last buckle on his pack. She brushed her fingers over the edge of the scar on his cheek and he glanced over at her, startled. She kissed him, a reverse of their first kiss. This time, it was her seeking his forgiveness.

"What was that for?" he asked, smiling.

"These people— don't become like them. After. Promise me you'll find a farm. Let me imagine you on a sunny beach, happy."

He brushed the tears from her face but shook his head.

"I don't want to leave you, Frank. I'm *sorry.* Let me go believing you're going to find something better."

He pulled her into his chest. "There's nothing better than you've been," he said. "If you're infected then I am too. Whatever happens, it'll happen together. Just—" he stopped and kissed the top of her head. "*Hold on,* Nella," he begged.

The sprayer truck rumbled to life and they looked up to find themselves almost alone in the camp. He pulled her up with him and slung his pack over his shoulders. A lone woman watched them pass her cell without speaking. Across the way, Marnie offered a weak wave to them.

"I'm glad you're staying," said Frank with a gentle

smile.

Nella nodded and held up her hand as well. "Good luck," she said, "Remember Christine. She deserves to be remembered well."

Marnie nodded. She clung to the fence. They passed out of the gate, closing it gently behind them. Nella gave a last glance toward the people who were watching at the wall. She knew they were all strangers, but still, her gaze clung to them. She hoped they'd thrive, that they'd remake the world someday, into something better. Happier. More just.

Frank looked back at them as well. His only hope was that they were worthy of the people who were sacrificing everything for them, most of all, the woman at his side and the priest walking somewhere ahead. He reached for her hand and curled his fingers around hers, grateful for the warm pulse in her wrist. *Hold on, Nella,* he thought, *just wait for me.*

They weren't able to stay together for long. The sprayer truck rumbled along quickly, leaving the group behind relatively early. It waited where Vincent had chosen to camp for the night, but the trek took longer than anyone had calculated. Of the nineteen left of the quarantined, twelve were in the end stages of the disease and had to be helped up from repeated stumbles or redirected as their attention wandered. Only Vincent, Nella, and Frank were willing to extend a hand to help. The others were too frightened to get close and were content to let the stumblers stay where they had fallen. So they reached the camp in two packs, the healthiest arriving first. Vincent kept a nervous eye on the sicker members, but nobody turned that day. The exhaustion from the walk didn't do them any favors, though, the slurs and clumsiness becoming more and more pronounced as the afternoon drew on. Nella half dragged an older woman into the parking lot of an empty furniture store just after sunset. The sprayer's form hulked against the remaining gold and purple light and a small fire sparked and popped on the tar several yards from it. She was the last one in and she could already hear raised voices. She helped the woman to sit down near the others.

"— can't expect us to *sleep* like this. We should— we should tie em up or something. Look, that one could barely walk," yelled one of the men around the fire, pointing toward Nella and the woman she'd been helping. She saw Frank's thin silhouette straighten suddenly as the man pointed and he darted over to her silently, pulling her away from the group of people sitting on the tar.

"They've done nothing wrong," rumbled Father Preston's voice, "you can't expect us to tie them up when they are just sick—"

Nella was surprised to hear him speak up for the Infected.

"It's not a matter of right or wrong," broke in someone else, "be practical. What if one or more of them turn overnight, while we're sleeping? This miracle cure isn't going to help us if we've been eaten alive—"

Frank whispered a swear. "I thought that story was just for the radio," he hissed.

Nella shook her head. "Some part of them *must* know— Vincent has been taking care of the people that have turned for weeks. They've all seen it. They must know, deep down, he wouldn't do that if there really was a cure," she whispered.

"I don't like that the Colony didn't tell them the truth. Even if they ought to know better."

Nella sighed. "How else would they have got all these people to just peacefully leave?"

"And when we get there and they find out for sure?" asked Frank.

"They must have some kind of plan," said Nella, "it's beyond our help anyway. We turn off tomorrow night for the boat. Vincent and Father Preston must have some kind of idea of what they are going to do. They wouldn't be able to— to fumigate the whole City themselves anyway. Some of the healthier ones must be in on it."

"Lock em in the store," shouted a woman. Her face was half illuminated by the small fire, her anger and the orange glow creating a snarling gargoyle. "We'll stand guard. If they want to rip each other apart, let them. They won't get the rest of us."

"Surprised atchu Joanne," muttered a slumped shadow from the tar. "Known you 'mos ten years. Someday, soon, you'll be where I am. Soon. Miracle we've lasted this long. Should have turned weeks ago with the others. Jus' luck. Jus' luck now too. You wan' me to stay 'way. Okay. I'll stay in the store. 'Cause we're friends. But soon, you'll think 's not enough. Soon you'll want to kill me before I turn. Put me out of my misery. Jus' remember, when you think you're doing a mercy, jus' remember you'll be here too, someday."

The woman shook her head. "We're going to get the Cure before then. We'll be okay. You aren't going to make it. You'll be crazy by then. Sorry George, that's just how it is. It's too late for you. I can still make it."

Frank watched Vincent for his reaction. The priest covered his face with one hand, but didn't interrupt. The woman that Nella had helped began laughing. It started low and throaty and grew as she rocked back and forth on the tar. Everyone scattered, thinking she'd turned. Her laugh dwindled and she said, "You don' buy that horseshit do you? *We* don't. *We* know. No cure, none. We been cast out. We're goin' to walk until we die. Right, Father? They kep' telling us the priest was going to cure us. That he had a miracle. How many died in the past few weeks? Time's running out. The Colony don't want us. Can't blame 'em, we did the same, and worse. Sending us home, to the madhouse, so we all go together. So we can't infect anybody else. This is what they want. We'll eat each other, until we're all gone. You go 'head and lock me away, none of you looks particular tasty anyhow. Let me die sane. Let me die as myself. I'll welcome the priest's knife when it comes. You can scrabble for the scraps of minutes that are left, all of you. Waste the seconds fighting. It's endless war when you turn anyway, might as well practice."

The woman fell silent and nobody else offered an argument. Lisa passed out a small packet of food to each and they ate near the fire, nobody speaking. There was no more mention of the furniture store or of guards and one by one, the people crept into their sleeping bags, most turning away from all the others.

Nella and Frank sank down next to the fire near Vincent. "I don't know if I can do this," he said softly, "Not when it comes down to it."

Nella nodded. "This isn't like before. There's no urgency to it. It isn't self-defense."

"It will be," rumbled Frank, "if we wait a few more days."

Vincent sighed and squinted out into the dark lot. Frank squeezed his shoulder. "Don't you remember?" he asked softly, "what it was like? These people don't know. They were all immune last time. But *you* know what's coming. They don't have to feel that. They don't have to do what we did, not if we stop it."

"It would have been kinder to do it at the camp, before they were turned out. Before they were rejected by everyone," said Vincent.

Frank shook his head. "Some of them are holding on. Some of them still have reasons to hang on. We shouldn't rob them of whatever sanity they have left. Not until we must." Nella reached out to clasp Frank's hand, her breath suddenly tight and painful in her chest.

"What will you do, after we leave for the boat?" she asked in a whisper. "I thought more were coming with us. How will you manage?"

Vincent glanced around at the sleeping forms. "Our story is more transparent than I originally thought. There will be a few who accept the end. A few who will help those that can't. Amos says that it is quick, if the amount is enough. Like drowning, he said. The people that have turned won't even realize what has happened. Those that haven't—" he stopped for a moment. "It will be frightening, and for that I am sorry." His voice cracked. "God, forgive me," he whispered.

"Forgive us all," said Nella, leaning past Frank to hug Vincent.

THIRTY-FIVE

He squeezed the puckered edge of the stitched skin. Yellow fluid dribbled over his dirty hand, gassy and fetid. He wiped it away with his sleeve and stood up. The pressure was better, but now it throbbed from his touch. *The boat will have better stuff. Good drugs. Alcohol maybe.* The woman was a doctor, wasn't she? She probably had things he could only dream of. He limped along the road. It had cracked and washed away in places, a patchwork of tar islands floating over gravel. He'd fallen into deep potholes more than once already, but the weeds growing in the bottom had cushioned him, preventing any serious damage. But the girl, the one-armed zombie scarecrow, had made sure that he was in trouble anyway.

His head buzzed as if it were filled with the horseflies that kept tangling in his hair and biting him. He wanted to vomit, but there wasn't anything left in his stomach except a slosh or two of water that threatened to slide up and out every other step. He'd been more aware in the morning, catching the right road before he slipped down into the fever. Everything was too bright, too heavy with heat. He gasped to breathe though he wasn't going much faster than a shuffle. He wanted to lie down in the cool moss at the edge of the road, the thick shadows of the trees promising relief from the buzzing and dizziness. But he couldn't remember how much time had passed. He had to get to the boat before the others. He had to be long gone, uncatchable, by the time they arrived. So he kept going, licking his lips to cool them and thinking longingly of the deep purple damp of evening that seemed to creep further and further away.

He thought he was dreaming the bite of the salt air until he stumbled into the water and felt the chill of the ocean lap over his toes, splash up his leg and sting with an unholy sparkle of salt in his wound. The heaving gray-green hypnotized him as he looked up, making him forget for a few moments why he was there. The glare of the sun was even worse here and he squinted and stumbled backward onto the rocky beach, turning his face away. He sat for a while until his head stopped spinning quite so hard. He looked out over the water again, seeing the dark shadow of the sailboat. He was here first. He'd won. He glanced around for a rowboat, but gave up quickly. It was only a few hundred yards. He could swim it if he had to, wounded leg and all. He just had to have a little rest first. Just a nap on the chilled stones of the beach and then he'd be ready.

They started picking up stragglers the next morning. Never more than one or two at a time. Some had come willingly, hearing the broadcast and hoping to receive the Cure, they'd changed course, returning home. Others had been turned away from group after group and realizing they had nowhere else to go, had turned around again. It troubled Vincent that he couldn't tell if there were Immunes among them. He couldn't turn them away if they were. If he told them of the quarantine camp, he risked the Colony again and undermined the story of having found a cure even more than it already was. He hoped they were all sick, for their own sakes, but few were showing symptoms. His own group wasn't so lucky, three more had started stumbling after breakfast. Father Preston had disappeared with the sprayer again, early that morning and collected a few more travelers, squeezing them into the cab or perched on the top of the sprayer, so that when they finally reached camp, they numbered almost thirty again, and Vincent began to have doubts about being able to control them. They were still two days away from the City and Frank and Nella would be slipping away that night. He'd be alone again.

The day was hot and dry, the cicadas song throbbed in the air around them. It was not a good day for the weaker set. It wasn't even noon before the first attack. The camp had separated again, the healthy quickly outpacing the others again, except for the few that stayed to aid their fellows. More stopped to help than the day before, the sad confrontation at the camp having had some effect on the conscience of a few. Vincent was kneeling next to a man who had fallen, feeding him a few sips of water when it happened. The tail of the group had almost passed them, when one of the women stopped. She stood in the center of the road, swaying slightly. Vincent looked up at her. "Are you all right?" he asked. She didn't answer, turning slowly in a circle as if looking for something. "Wendy? Did you lose something?" Something sparked as he called her by name. She stopped and turned slowly toward him. Vincent helped the other man to his feet.

"Are you thirsty, Wendy?" he asked holding the water bottle out hesitantly. The other man shambled slowly away toward the others as Wendy just stared at him. Vincent took a step toward her. "Is it the sun? We can walk in the shade in a moment or two, there's a little wooded area ahead. It will be nice and cool." He reached for her hand to lead her, and that's when she snapped. There was no warning growl or shriek, no snarling expression, she just sprang at him, knocking him flat on his back in the dusty road. The water bottle skittered away as it flew from his hand. The woman scraped at his face with her fingers as her mouth opened. He could hear the muscles in her jaw creak as she opened wider and wider and pushed down toward him.

"Remember yourself," he begged, holding her arms back with his hands, her face still darting perilously close to his. She drooled with a gurgle in her throat. "Wendy, fight it," he said. She lunged forward, closing her teeth on his ear. Vincent shouted and shoved her to the side. She rolled off him and he leapt up, but she followed close behind. He fumbled with the blade in his belt, the side of his face splattered with blood and collecting dust. He could hear footsteps running toward them. She'd attack whatever she could reach. Whoever was coming didn't know what they were running into. He flung up an arm as she sprang at him again and her teeth tore into the tough skin of his forearm. His other hand freed the blade. He shook her off and held the large knife in front of him. "Please, Wendy, don't make me—" but she leaped at him again, and the knife crunched through her ribs with a jarring thud as her momentum carried her farther and farther onto it. Vincent tried to take a step back but it was too late. Wendy was still flailing, grabbing for him even as she panted, her chest gaping and clenching around the blade.

"Forgive me," said Vincent, and felt a hand on the hilt of the blade. Nella took it gently from him, holding Wendy's shoulder, she twisted and then pulled, leaving a large hole that quickly foamed with a pink froth. Wendy staggered backward, gasping faster as she did, stumbling until she fell into the dirt. Nella knelt beside her and covered her nose and mouth with both of her hands, pressing even as she whipped her head sideways.

"Don't—" cried Vincent.

Nella gritted her teeth for a second before speaking. "If I don't it will take her another ten minutes to suffocate on her own blood. Terrified and in pain." Wendy's thrashing became frenzied and she tried to pull Nella's arm away. She kicked and then slowed. she kept her hands over Wendy's face until several seconds after she'd stopped and the foam on her chest started sinking away. "She won't wake up now," Nella said grimly, "she won't feel it anymore."

"Thank you," said Vincent, but his voice was

emotionless. Nella rose and began digging in her pack.

"We need to take care of those wounds," she said, pulling out what was left of their first aid kit. They sat in the grass on the side of the road while Nella cleaned the bites. Vincent watched a dark stream of Wendy's blood roll down the gravel and sink into the dust.

"What do we do with her?" he asked.

"If we stop to bury her, the others will turn back to see what's happened to us," said Nella.

"We can't leave her here. It's not right."

"No, it's not. Her body would also be contagious for a while. We'll have to carry her to camp. We can bury her or cremate her when we get there."

"Is anyone else— close?"

Nella shook her head. "I don't think so, not any closer than this morning. But it's hard to tell. Frank is with them, though. He knows what has to be done. I will carry her for a while. You need to let your wounds start to heal."

Vincent shook his head. "It's my fault she's dead. I will carry my own burdens."

Nella took his hand in hers. "Father, you didn't kill her. A bacteria did. We were just witnesses."

"But—"

"If it wasn't the knife," said Nella, "It would have been exposure in a few nights or thirst or starvation or falling off something high— she couldn't take care of herself. It's not your fault, and it's not your burden. And if we don't start sharing our troubles, *none* of us are going to make it to the City and none of the people we left behind will be safe. Let us help you, while we can."

Vincent nodded slowly and they got to their feet. Nella picked up the woman's body and draped it over her shoulders, thanking her luck that the road was relatively flat. She was relieved when they finally caught up to Frank and he lifted the woman from her for a turn. The expressions of the others upon seeing the woman's body ranged from dull acceptance to fear but nobody asked about her or what happened, they just trudged along, sweating and stumbling in the afternoon sun. Nella kept an eye on Vincent, but except for an occasional itch at a bandage, he seemed okay.

She took the body back just before they reached the camp, the air finally cooling as the sun rolled behind the trees. She and Frank came over a small ridge, the last of the travelers and down into the same gas station where they had slept twice before. She was surprised to see how many extra people had gathered around the sprayer, but she didn't have long to stare. Some of them challenged her, told her to drop the body, demanded that she find a place to wash before coming near them. Frank pulled her in close to him and walked her through the camp. She could feel his arms tighten and the scar on his cheek pulsed. She knew he was ready for a fight. But they drew close to the tire pit and the others let them pass. Together, they found the spot where they had buried three other Infected beneath the tires. Vincent brought them a soup can of gas he'd taken from the sprayer's supply. Frank dumped it over the tires and lit it.

"Meant to do this months ago," he said grimly. He looked up and found the pit surrounded by the others. "Most of you were Immune before," he said loudly, "didn't care what happened to the Infected outside the Barrier. Didn't much care what happened to 'em inside the Barrier either. But you're starting to know now, what happened to us. Who we were. Why we should have mattered more to you. I wouldn't have wished this on my worst enemy. We tried to stop it, Nella and I. We *tried* and we failed. I'm sorry this is happening to you. To *us*. This woman's life mattered to someone. The people we buried here this spring mattered to someone. *You* matter to someone.

Fighting each other is only going to make you turn faster. Show some compassion. We're *all* dying. Every one of us. It isn't a race. Help each other reach the— the Cure. That's the only way you'll get there."

Nella pulled him gently away from the smoky flames and they helped Vincent back up the steep slope to the store. There was no talk of separation that night. The smoke was heavy and oily and foul, a thick recrimination with every breath. They had no energy to argue and Vincent sat with Nella and Frank in the shadow of the empty gas pumps watching them.

"More will turn. Tonight and tomorrow. The next day too, before we reach the boat. How will you manage?" asked Frank.

Vincent shook his head. "I'm not even certain how I would have managed today. I will be ready, next time."

Nella opened her pack. She pulled out the pistol and a box of bullets. "Maybe this would be easier," she said, placing them in front of his bent knees.

"I don't know anything about guns," he said. "With a knife I can't miss. Not really. And what if you needed it? I don't know what you will face once you get to the City docks. No, I have trusted in the goodness of people so far, I will continue to believe in that until I no longer can. If the worst happens— Father Preston knows what the sprayer can do. If we don't meet you at the docks, you will know that we had to do it early." He handed Nella a large pack instead. "There are two suits in here and two cans of the pesticide. In case. I hope we will be able to do it all, but Amos thought it would take more than us. I will find you if I am able." He stopped and Nella repacked the pistol and arranged the suits and cans within her pack.

Vincent put a hand on each of their shoulders. "I just want to thank you again for curing me. Us. From where you're sitting it must seem pretty pointless now. I wanted you to know that every day of sanity I've had since you found us has been a gift. Even ending the way it will. I'd do it all over again if I had the choice."

"I wish we'd been friends long before now," whispered Nella.

"Isn't there anything we can do to help? Anything we can leave with you to make it easier? Maybe we should stay. Find another way," said Frank.

Vincent shook his head. "This way is best. We need you there at the docks to make sure we finish. And to carry any Immunes away. There must be a few. They need an escape. Someplace safe they can wait out quarantine. Your job is to give us hope. It's more important than you know."

Nella shouldered her pack. "We *will* see you at the dock, Father. Three days."

Frank stood up. "Good luck," he said sticking out his hand. Vincent shook it.

"To you as well." He hesitated a moment before adding, "I hope that Gray is long gone, but if you should see him— Molly was dear to me. They all are, back there. Don't let him hurt any more of them."

Frank nodded. He slid an arm around Nella's waist and they slipped through the shadows into the forest across the road, seen only by Vincent in the cloudy, moonless night.

THIRTY-SIX

Nella clung to Frank in the dark, the heavy pack overwhelming her balance and the roots underfoot threatening to send her flying every third step.

"I know you hate this," he whispered. "Just a few more minutes and we'll turn on the lantern. I just want to be sure we're out of sight."

"I'm okay," she lied. Her hands were sweating and she knew he could tell that she was nervous.

"In a few days, we'll be back at the boat with the stars all around us."

She smiled. It was the closest thing to a plan he'd said in weeks. She tripped and went sprawling into the dirt. He groped for her in the dark and helped her sit up.

"Are you all right?"

"Fine," she said spitting a pine needle from her lips. "But I can't see anything."

He reached over her back and pulled out the lantern lighting it between them. She brushed off her hands in the bright electric glow and gently picked crumbling leaves from her hair. The harsh light drew deep shadows in his eye sockets and etched lines into his gaunt cheeks. She cupped his chin in her hands. "You haven't been sleeping," she said.

"I can't. How could I? I'd miss time with you. Time I'll never have again."

"You *must* sleep. It will only bring the disease on faster if you don't."

He pulled her into a clumsy hug, trying to hold her around the massive pack. "It isn't fair. Any of it."

"No, but it's happening anyway. And we have to get through it. As well as we can. So you must sleep."

"A few more feet, we're almost to the Barrier. It'll be cleared for a way around it." He picked her up and then the lantern.

They walked on for a while, the silence heavy and unbroken except for the soft hum of the electric lantern. Then a breeze rippled through the trees around them and a flickering shower of early gold leaves fluttered around them. Frank plucked one from his shoulder and stopped to look at it. "There were so many things I wanted to share with you," he said, his voice hoarse and quiet. He crushed the leaf in his fist. "I should have known that jeweler was lying. I should have known he would fall for whatever lie Pazzo told him. I fell for them too. How could I expect anyone else not to?"

"I don't think he knew what was going to happen. We couldn't exactly tell him either. Not then. It was an accident, Frank."

"It *wasn't*. It was because of *him*."

She wrapped her hands around the fist clenching the leaf. "We also met because of *him*. Do you want to give him credit for that too?" His fist loosened and the leaf fell. "We can't undo either event. Vincent said he'd do it all again, if he had the choice. I would too, even if I couldn't change how it's going to end. If it hadn't been us— if it had been another lawyer or if he hadn't pushed to hire me — we wouldn't have even had the few months that we did. Nobody else would have stopped him. We would all have been dead by May. And no one would have introduced us either. I've been happy, Frank. No matter how long we had. Haven't you? Isn't that worth whatever price we have to pay now?"

"It's not what *I* need to sacrifice that bothers me. It's what it has taken from you."

Nella shrugged her pack from her shoulders, unwilling to walk farther in the dark. She pushed his gently off too. She stood on her toes and slid her arms around his neck, waiting until he was staring at her to speak. "Before you came along," she said, "I didn't know my neighbors. I hated my job. I hated myself for the things I'd done. Christine and Sevita were the only people who I could stand to be around for any length of time. My entire world was that closed in, small minded City. Meeting you has taken *nothing* from me. You've made me a better, happier person. I'm kinder, more patient, less judgmental because of *you*." She kissed him as the breeze shook more leaves around them, flickering in the lantern light. But in her heart, she understood his disappointment and anger, and for a second she gave thanks that she would go before him, that she wouldn't have to be the one to carry on without him.

The sun was cresting over his bare shoulder when she woke. He was watching her and tracing the jagged outline of a half-turned leaf on the skin of her hip.

"Shh," he whispered, "if we pretend it isn't here yet, we can stay a minute longer like this. Close your eyes, go back to sleep."

"Have *you* slept?" she asked rubbing his eyelids gently as he closed them.

"Yes, I slept. I only woke a second or two ago." He pulled her tighter, the rough starburst scar on his chest pressing into her skin, familiar and comforting. "Stay just a little longer," he said. *Hang on, stay with me,* he willed her.

He was able to push aside what was coming for most of the day. It slid by cool and windy, if quiet. He found they had little to speak about. Everything seemed either unimportant or too close to the coming grief to say. Frank didn't want to think past the boat and though he tried, he couldn't convince himself there'd be an "after" with her. So he didn't make plans. They couldn't speak of friends, because they were either long gone or in trouble. Even Ruth and Bernard were hard to think about. The walk, though beautiful, seemed too trivial, too fleeting to talk about. So they walked side by side, both in a sort of suspended misery for the other. Until Nella fell. The road was uneven, gravel and tar, broken and eroded. Nella was right beside him when she tripped at the top of a small hill. The weight of her pack was enough to throw off her balance as she tried to recover and she rolled, hitting a half dozen jagged lumps of tar that jutted up along the way. For a moment, Frank's only thought was that he was glad he'd switched the pesticide to his own pack or the explosion might have killed them both instantly. Then he was running down the small hill to help her.

"How many days?" he was muttering to himself, "how many days left?"

She heard him mumbling as he ran. He stopped when he reached her, helping her up. "I'm okay," she said as he checked, "Just a few bruises. It's okay."

His hands were shaking as he touched the scrape on her elbow. "Frank," she said, pulling his chin up until his eyes focused on her face. "It's not time yet. I'm still me. No slurring. I tripped over a piece of rubble. Plenty of days left. It's not time."

He nodded and folded her into him. She could feel his chest shudder as he tried to hide his sob. "It's okay," she said again, "I'm still here."

But he couldn't let go for several minutes.

Henry was absorbed in an old battered copy of The Guide to Gay Gardening, studying edible insects, when the radio crackled to life. "These two hunters got lost and were wandering in the woods and got captured by cannibals. They were tied up and put into an enormous pot of water. A large bonfire was lit underneath them and things were really starting to heat up. All of a sudden one of the hunters starts giggling uncontrollably. 'What's so funny?' asked the other, thinking his friend had finally snapped. 'I peed in the soup!' said the first one."

Henry rolled his eyes. "Hi, Rickey."

"C'mon, that deserved a chuckle. Let me tell it to Marnie, she'll laugh."

"Is everyone okay up there?" Henry asked.

"Yeah, but worried about you. We finished repairing everything but the barn. I think it's a total teardown, sorry Henry. At least the foundation's poured. We can get some kind of structure up before the snow. Amos thinks it should be a school instead of a barn. He says we could use it for meetings too. Wanted to know what you thought."

"What do *you* think?"

There was a pause. "Without Vincent— I miss him, Henry. I should have gone with him. I let Melissa persuade me to stay."

"He would have wanted you to stay. There must be other teachers— if not, we could take turns. You could teach mechanical stuff. We need more people with that knowledge. Amos and Moll— Amos could teach farming. We'll make a list."

"She saved this place, you know. The others say the whole place would have burnt if she hadn't been here. Who would have thought? She was always so quiet. They say Gray will never be able to walk properly again, after what she did."

"I hope he dies of it," snapped Henry suddenly. "Shouldn't have been here alone. I should have stayed. It was stupid to go the next day."

"She wasn't alone, Henry. And I think she'd be proud. She'd want you to be proud too. She loved you, you know. She never would have said anything, but anyone with eyes could see it."

"That doesn't make me feel better."

"It should."

Henry was silent.

"You want anything down there? How is Marnie and the other survivor?"

"Her name is Nancy. They're both still fine, but Vincent said to expect that, mostly. They were the only two who weren't failing the coordination tests, but that doesn't mean they won't in a week or two. I think we're safe, though. They are almost through the incubation period. We could use more books down here, if you have any to spare. Marnie's a little sick of cards but we could all use some distraction. If Amos has any work we can do..."

"No dice, Henry. Sorry. Anything you touch could be contaminated and then we couldn't use it. He said the best thing you can do is use the time to build skills. Read books, practice survival junk. All that boy scout stuff we never did."

Henry laughed. "I'm trying."

There was a long pause. "Hey Rickey," said Henry, at last.

"Yeah?"

"Any news from the City?"

"Nothing yet. Melissa has been sweeping the channels, but we might *never* know."

"I know. Thought I'd ask, in case."

"If he *can* come back, he will. Or he'll send word. I know it."

"Yeah," said Henry. "I know you're right. It's just hard to be the one left behind."

Vincent woke to a chorus of screams. His hand went immediately for the blade at his hip. He was up and running toward the sound before he'd even rubbed the sleep from his eye. Father Preston was struggling with a larger man near a small crowd of people huddled near the tire pit. The grave still smoldered and stank, coating them with black smoke. A figure at the bottom of the pit was aflame, stumbling in a slow, agonized circle. Vincent bypassed the other priest and his opponent, plunging down the ramped side of the pit. He ripped his shirt off and shoved the burning figure down into the dirt, slapping it with the cloth, trying to put it out. The skin bubbled and peeled and a long, drawn shriek peeled out of it, stopping only when the thing was out of breath and paused to take another. Its arms and legs shriveled in towards its stomach, curling it like an unborn child. Vincent knew he was too late. "I'm sorry," he said. "I'm so sorry. I'll fix it now. No more pain." He slid the knife out brought it down on the thing's neck. It was done. His shirt caught the flames and the body blazed up again. He turned back to Father Preston who was shouting.

"I won't let you, you can't do this, they haven't turned. They're still human."

The man grunted. "How long father? Ten minutes, another day? I'm not risking it. That thing almost ate one of us. Would have if I didn't put it down. These people need to be taken care of. You don't have to do it, Father. Just stand aside. It'll be a mercy to us all."

"No!" cried Father Preston, driving at the other man.

Vincent heard a few growls echoing from the small, huddled group. A few of the people were rocking back and forth, chewing on their fingernails nervously.

"Calm down, now," warned Vincent carefully.

But Father Preston and the man didn't hear him. They kept shoving each other, grappling at the edge of the pit. One of the growls grew louder, stretched out. Vincent began walking toward the little crowd, afraid to attract attention by running, but unwilling to wait until it was too late. A shriek erupted and Vincent broke into a sprint as the group erupted into a frenzy of movement.

"They're turning!" shouted the large man fighting with Preston. "Get them, now!"

Vincent froze as a collection of shouts burst out behind him. Running down into the pit were a group of healthier people, each stooping to pick up rocks or pieces of broken junk metal that lay around the pit.

"Stop!" cried Vincent, holding up his arms. He was caught between both groups. The healthy people paused for a second, but then a large weight landed on Vincent's shoulders and he fell face forward into the dust. He struggled to twist free. People ran past him meeting around him snarling and biting and slamming stones into faces. The weight on his back released and he crawled free. Blood spattered in the dust around him and then sparks as someone lit an old plank and began swinging it.

"Stop," cried Vincent, "For the love of God, stop it!"

Nobody but Preston stopped. Father Preston let go of the large man and crept down the slope to drag Vincent away.

"It's over Brother Vincent," he said. "Nothing will stop them now."

"We can't let them kill each other," cried Vincent.

"There's nothing we can do," said Father Preston. "The only thing we can do is spread the pesticide and kill them all. That's the only way this stops. Either when the sicker half are dead or when they all are."

Vincent reached to pry a pair of fighters apart but Preston held him back. "You ready to die? It'll be for nothing. Don't throw away your life. It won't stop them."

He let Father Preston lead him out of the tire pit. They stood at the side of the pit and watched it darken with blood. After a moment, Vincent noticed Father Preston's lips moving without sound. "What are you doing?" he asked.

"The only thing I know how to do," said Father Preston, "praying for help."

Vincent nodded. "Will you say it out loud?" he asked. "Will you let me pray with you?"

They stood at the side of the pit, until the screams died out and the violence flagged and all anyone could hear were the murmured words of the two priests praying for the soul of the dead world.

THIRTY-SEVEN

Frank began pulling back the pile of branches they'd left over the rowboat. "That's a good sign," he said. "Maybe our luck is changing. Gray must not have made it here yet. Or ever. The boat's still here."

Nella frowned looking doubtful. "Maybe he found a different one. We didn't check any of the nearby houses."

"The sailboat is still there," he said, pointing through the trees. "You'd think he would have moved it."

"That's true," said Nella, allowing herself to relax a little. They worked together to clear the branches. There was a sense of going home for both, though they knew it was for the last time. The night before had been restless, and they had clung together, trying to find some sense of peace in the growing panic that threatened to swallow them both. But now they faced it, as they had a few months before, standing outside the gray, squat prison saying goodbye in the windy parking lot. It felt the same, there in the warm sun at the edge of the ocean. An almost-relief of having it arrive at last, regardless of what happened next. They carried the boat down onto the gravelly beach, laying their packs into the bottom. The water was chilled and Nella's feet ached on the cold, smooth stones beneath them as they shoved it off and climbed in. She tried to imprint everything, though she knew it would be several more days until the sickness took her. Tried to hold on to the way the light shattered over the waves and the shadow of the water swallowed up the sparkles. Took in the sting of the salt in her nose and the dry tightness it left where it touched her skin. But mostly she tried to memorize Frank. The way he tried to smile at her, though he was as deep in grief as she. The way the scar on his cheek crinkled with every change of expression. The heat of his bare foot next to hers as he rowed. She wished he'd talk so she could save the roll and rhythm of his voice too, but she could think of nothing to ask him and he could think of nothing to say without disrupting the fragile peace between them. She wished, even in the misery of the moment, that they'd just keep rowing. That the day would keep shining and he'd still be across from her, rowing forever. But the moments passed, as they always did, and they were pulling up to the large sailboat before she even realized they'd gone more than halfway.

"Let me go first," said Frank, "just in case." He pulled the gun from her pack and climbed the ladder as she held the rowboat steady. He took a quick circuit of the deck and returned to her. "All clear up here," he said. They pulled the rowboat from the water and secured it. They pulled up the small anchor and Frank unlocked the steering.

"We should check below," said Nella.

"He didn't make it, Nella."

"I still think we should check. Just to be certain."

"All right," said Frank, "Get us going, I'll go look."

"Maybe we should go together. Please, Frank. The boat won't drift, we don't have the sails up yet."

He laughed gently. "Okay, then, we can go together." He took the gun from his pocket and climbed down the stairs. He stood for a moment letting his eyes adjust to the dark interior. They passed through the tiny kitchen, Nella checking under the table and in the cabinets, though she knew a big guy like Gray would never fit inside. Frank smiled but it sank away from his face as he realized how worried she was. He helped her take the cushions from the couch without comment, checking the storage underneath. Still just the fresh water supply. They put the cushions back. She slid past him to the tiny bathroom, flinging the door open as if it would bite her. It was empty. Frank *did* smile as he opened the bedroom door, turning to look at her as he did. "See Nella, he's not here. He probably died of an infection, we're—"

He stopped with a gasp. Nella saw the sharp tines of Frank's antique fishing spear plunge into his gut and he was pushed backward. Gray had ripped it from its mount over their bed and plowed out of the room, Frank stumbling backward until he tripped over the couch and fell backward, shocked and wordless. The gun fell from his fingers as he reached to touch the shaft of the spear.

There was a second of silence as both men panted heavily, one with adrenaline, the other in agony. And then Nella screamed. Gray turned to face her, but the scream didn't stop. She couldn't stop it, it vibrated between the narrow walls and in her chest, deep and ripping as if she'd been the one stabbed. She launched at Gray as he turned to face her, her mind a blank except for the pain on Frank's face as he was struck. *Supposed to be me,* she realized, *Frank was supposed to live. He's supposed to live.* And then it was gone as she sank under a tide of sorrow and anger. Gray stumbled backward in surprise, smashing into the bedroom door frame and sliding down to the floor. It was all Nella needed. She was on top of him. She scraped at his face with her fingers, digging into his skin, leaving ribbons of blood behind. The feel of his skin bursting open on her fingertips was like scratching an itch she'd never been able to reach before. But it wasn't enough. Not for what he'd done.He grabbed for her hands and she reared back and punched. The back of his head smacked against the door frame with a sharp cracking sound and he abandoned her hands to protect his head.

"Nella," Frank was yelling, but she couldn't hear him over her own ragged shriek.

Frank struggled to hold the spear steady in his abdomen so it wouldn't do more damage. The other hand searched for the gun below him. Nella wasn't waiting for him to find it. She closed her hands around Gray's throat, squeezing until her fingers shook and ached. Gray flailed, finally finding the pocketknife from the hunting lodge in his pocket. He snapped it open and swung it at her, slicing her cheek. She didn't let go, instead, whipping her head toward his hand closing her teeth on his wrist with a sickening crunch. She could taste copper and wasn't certain whether it was his blood or hers, whether she'd shattered her teeth or his bone. The only pain that registered was the one in her chest. The knife slid from his hand onto the floor as he wheezed in agony. She released his throat and grabbed the knife.

"Nella," called Frank, his fingers closing around the smooth metal of the gun at last. "Move, Nella."

But she didn't hear him. He saw her arms reach far above her head and then plunge forward. Gray's feet kicked and he tried to push her off. Nella grunted and pulled the knife free, raising it again and smashing it into his chest. His blood was warm and sticky as if sprayed over her. She grunted again, twisting and grinding it further. He half shoved her from his waist, but she didn't stop, yanking the blade free and stabbing again. This time, the blade snapped off in Gray's sternum as he howled. Nella dropped the knife. She punched his face, smearing blood and spit and snot with her fists, over and over. Frustrated that he continued to move, she picked up the broken knife again, the spiral corkscrew loose and falling into her palm. She struck his left ear with it and shoved as far as she could. There was a sucking noise as she pulled the corkscrew free. It fascinated her, drowning out even the sound of Frank's voice. Gray spasmed and lay still, the blood still gushing in pulses around her. Her chest heaved and it wasn't enough to satisfy the rage that made every particle ache with adrenaline. She stabbed again and again, until the corkscrew broke off the handle and her arms sagged, exhausted.

Then she heard Frank crying her name. "Please Nella," he sobbed, "Fight it. You have to fight it. Come back. Come back to me, Nella."

She turned slowly around. There was a click as he cocked the gun with a shaking hand, the other hand struggling to keep the spear straight.

"Say something," he begged, tears streaming from his face. "Tell me you love me. Tell me anything. Please Nella, please come back."

THIRTY-EIGHT

The pit's dusty bottom had turned to mud and people sat on the edge nursing injuries, exhausted. Vincent and Father Preston carefully checked the scattered bodies and carried them to the center. There was nobody left alive on the floor of the pit. A dozen people sat on the sides like vultures watching the priests. None of them stumbled or slurred. None of them rocked or bit their nails. Some of the wounded called out to him for help, but Vincent ignored them. He knew he'd have to help eventually, but even his compassion stretched only so far. They covered the small mound with tires. He tried to light it, but they were short on gas. If he took more, the sprayer would never make it. He couldn't leave them like this. Not just for themselves, they were a health risk too. He thought about using the sprayer on the pile. He'd thought about it earlier too, using the sprayer on the entire lot of them. Right in the tire pit. Just to make them stop killing each other. Father Preston had held him back, kept him sane.

He stared at the people who were left. "You've had your way, hurt people whose only crime was to be sicker than you. Now clean up your mess. We need to cremate them, so no one else will get infected. Go get as many dry branches from the woods as you can and bring them back."

There were some groans. Vincent's temper snapped. "You've brought this on yourself, and worse. Look at what you have done. You attacked them because you were frightened they'd turn. They would have attacked you without second thought. But *you* planned this. You got together and made a plan to hurt them. To kill them. Who is the true monster? You will never be able to atone for what you've done here. Not ever. But you can clean it up. You can prevent it from happening ever again."

People got up slowly, stiffly. Limped along the incline until they disappeared over the lip of the pit.

Several minutes later they began tossing dead branches down to him. He and Father Preston wove them into the tires, piled them over the bodies, until all that could be seen was a dull pile of bracken. Vincent lit it and stood in the choking smoke until he was certain it wouldn't go out. Then he wearily climbed up to the road where the others waited in a sullen clot. Father Preston started the sprayer and headed off. Vincent walked behind it, saying nothing, not even bothering to look around to make sure the others followed. He couldn't remember a more disturbing day, even when he'd been in the midst of Infection himself. They reached the Barrier at dusk, finding half a dozen more people waiting for them, drawn by the promise of a cure. They were helping Father Preston clear the main gate, boulder by boulder. Vincent made the others help too, unburying the City with their bare hands. He finally let them rest once it was too dark to see. It was unsettling, how silent the City was. Nothing came through the Barrier. No music, no conversation, not even the shouts and thumps of fighting. He didn't sleep, just lay rigid, worrying on the cold tar of the road. He'd expected to be able to trust a few of them. He'd expected to be able to get help spreading the poison as people came to accept that they were at the end. But now— all of them had joined in. All of them had slaughtered someone in order to preserve themselves. Father Preston and Lisa were the only ones he could rely on. These people weren't going to wait around to be poisoned either. They'd scatter, run, leak out the hole in the barrier he'd just made and the whole trip would be pointless. He realized his instinct about doing it at the tire pit had been the right one. He told himself it was mercy that made him wait, but some part of him insisted it was weakness. He couldn't kill them all. How could he? He had willingly walked into this role, but he couldn't really remember why. He'd known how it would end, even a month ago. And now it was here. He sat up and crept to the truck. He slid into the cab waking Father Preston.

"I don't think I can do this," he confessed.

Father Preston nodded. "This is not what I wanted either. We're out of options. We can't let them go. They'll expose other groups if they haven't already. We could lock them up and try to care for them, but we both know we only have a week— maybe ten days left until we start showing symptoms ourselves. They'll starve. It will be very painful. Or we can follow through with the plan and it will be over by tomorrow night or the day after."

"How are we supposed to do this without panicking them? Just herd them into a building and hope they stay?"

Father Preston glanced out the window. "We could do it now, Vincent. They are all here in a group. It's too dark for them to wander far even if they woke up. Maybe they won't wake up. Maybe they'll just sleep and never get up."

"And tomorrow? What do we do with the bodies? And how do we get the truck into the City?"

Father Preston peered out the dark windshield. "I'm pretty sure the hole is big enough now, but even if not, it would take you and I no more than an hour to shift enough of what's left. As for the bodies— Didn't the man who gave you the poison say it would wipe out everything, sterilize everything?"

"Yes," said Vincent, "but we can't *leave* them here —"

"It's too much," said Father Preston, "We can't bury them all. We'll never finish before we turn. And there's the rest of the City to cover. We have to let it go. We have to hope that they will rest here, at the gate. Maybe they will be a warning to anyone who comes looting or for curiosity's sake."

"You can't be serious, Father. You know how

important burial is—"

Father Preston laid a heavy hand on Vincent's shoulder. "Yes, I know. I also know that millions of people died during the Plague and were never buried. That people die every day in the empty wilderness beyond our Colony with nobody to bury them or mourn them. I told you I wanted to help. I wanted to be worthy. You told me to put aside ceremony and find out what practical use I could be. We have a task to do. A dreadful, sad, important task. We are the only ones left who can do it. We must save ceremony for another time. God will understand."

Vincent took a deep breath and then nodded. Father Preston handed him a suit of plastic. "I'll wake Lisa," he said, "she can turn on the sprayer for us. You and I can climb to the top of the rubble with the hose."

Father Preston began pulling his own suit on and grabbed a third for Lisa. Vincent slid into the slick plastic, careful to seal each seam. He got out of the truck and slowly uncoiled the heavy hose loop by loop. It hissed against the gravel as he pulled it up the jagged chunks of concrete toward the top of the Barrier, but it was too quiet for any but himself to hear. Father Preston quickly joined him, a rustling, faceless ghost. They hovered over the sleeping Infected from the top of the wall. Vincent winced as the sprayer rumbled to life when Lisa turned it on, but most of the sleeping people simply shifted. The rest didn't even move. He supposed it was too late to worry about it now, if they woke up, he'd still have to finish what he'd started. He turned the hose on, aiming it high so that it fell on them in a thin mist instead of a rain. He could smell it, even through the mask. At first, it was pleasant. The scent of fresh cut grass. It made him think of his father on a Saturday or football practice when he was a child. But the smell intensified, became acrid. They let the mist fall for some time, more willing to risk overdoing it than underdoing it. The first coughs started as Lisa turned off the truck and Vincent recoiled the hose.

He stood guard, waiting for the panic, waiting for the people to start running. Most of them only coughed in great croupy gasps, then turned to reposition and fell asleep again. Some didn't even do that much, their lips slowly bluing and their bodies cooling under their blankets. Vincent was relieved that it was so peaceful. He knew he looked frightening in his suit and he prayed it wouldn't be the last thing that they saw. He stood still until the sky dulled to pale gray. Then he bent over each face and checked. Vincent tucked each one into their sleeping bag, as far as they could fit and zipped them in an apologetic version of a shroud. He didn't want to leave anyone to wake up alone. Lisa and Father Preston carefully moved a few more chunks of rubble until the sprayer could fit through the gate. Satisfied that they were each gone, Vincent trudged behind the sprayer. They stopped inside the gate to pull the spray arm down. Vincent grabbed one of the portable tanks and poured in a canister of chloropicrin. He helped strap it to Father Preston's back, and then prepared his own.

"We have to coat everything," he said, shouting to be certain he was heard through the thick plastic of his mask and over the rumbling truck. "It's been quiet, but that doesn't mean we're alone. Do you have anything to defend yourself?"

Father Preston shook his head. Vincent opened the truck's passenger side door and fumbled around until he found the tire iron behind the seat. Lisa looked pale through the clear plastic face guard. "The sound will probably draw them to you first, Lisa. Just keep moving, the gas will incapacitate them within a few moments. Keep your mask on and your windows rolled up."

She nodded. "What if— what about Immunes?" she

asked.

Vincent shook his head sadly. "If they get to you, it's probably too late, they'll have breathed in too many fumes. But if they can make it. We're meeting a boat at the docks, anyone still healthy that can get there, we'll take. The City is a grid skirted by the barrier. It's large but it's hard to get lost. If you went straight from this point, you'd hit the docks. There's too much ground to cover in one day. Take a left here and keep the docks behind you and to the right as you work your way down. Tomorrow we'll do the other side. You could probably get through the streets today, but you'll have to stay a little close, we'll have to change canisters often."

She nodded and he shut the door, turning to hand the tire iron to Father Preston. "There's only three of us," shouted Preston, "We'll never cover the whole City."

"Five," said Vincent, "Dr. Ryder and Mr. Courtlen will be here tonight. They'll help. And somebody has destroyed the entrances. They knew what was happening. They would have gathered people up for defense or for quarantine. We have to find those places."

"We still won't be able to coat it all. Even if we had the strength to do it, we'd run out of chemical."

Vincent nodded. "You're right. We just have to do what we can. Anywhere that looks promising to a looter, and anywhere that looks like it might have people still living in it, we have to douse. We saw the fires several weeks ago, I think a good portion of the buildings are gone. It's up to us to take care of what we can."

Vincent headed into the sagging entrance of the barracks where the tank had collided. He walked up to the top floor and glanced out the window. Lisa was creeping ahead with the spray truck and Father Preston disappeared into a building across the street and further up. Vincent called a few hellos as he sprayed, not expecting any answer except the hollow echo of his own footsteps. The first building took a while as he became used to the sprayer and tried to hit every surface. As he went on, he picked up the pace and concentrated on surfaces people would have touched, objects that looters would want. The emptiness started to unnerve him a few hours in and he kept glancing over his shoulder and calling out into the dim twilight of the buildings as he went. The chloropicrin became a cloudy fog that spilled from shattered windows and opened doors and rolled along the road in a thick smoke as they worked their way up the hill toward the airport. The buildings gradually petered out and left a rural road to the flat expanse of the airport and beyond. They joined Lisa in the cab until they returned to the City's grid. Vincent gasped as they passed the power plant. It was a twisted bloom of metal and ash. The hospital as well, had been gutted, its walls blackened with soot. A huge pile of ash stood in its parking lot surrounded by military trucks.

"What was *that*?" asked Father Preston quietly.

Vincent shook his head. "If I had to guess— I'd say it was a cremation pile. Marnie said the people they'd let into the bunker had told her that the military was taking sick people away. They had to do something with them… looks like maybe some of them fought back. Or some of the soldiers turned."

Father Preston crossed himself and said a prayer behind his plastic shell.

"This is where the bunker was supposed to be. We have to check," Vincent waited until Lisa pulled into the large covered lot and slid out. The metal door to the basement was twisted open and down, its back dusty with ash. Vincent turned on a flashlight and headed carefully down the stairs. The bunker door hung from one hinge and pieces of the generator's red painted sides were curled and spearing the walls all around the basement. Vincent pushed the bunker door farther open, just in case. All that was left was an empty cement tube and the melted metal of the bunks like ragged spider webs. He sighed and returned to the truck. It had been his best hope at finding survivors.

They went back to spraying after that, finally reaching the town square as the sun set. Vincent was convinced there would be people in the large town hall and he didn't want to quit without checking. He pushed through the large glass doors, remembering the last time he'd been there with Henry, begging for the City's help with Phil. Begging for justice. It was very dark, the large rooms echoing with his footsteps. He picked his way up the stairs in the gloom. The Military Governor's office was at the very top. He knocked on the large doors, calling out a hello. There was a scrabbling and a thump behind them. Vincent reached for the knife at his side. "I don't mean you any harm. We're here to help. Who is in there?"

There was no answer. Vincent curled his hand tightly around the knife, letting the sprayer hose drift behind him. "I'm coming in now, there's nothing to be afraid of—"

He pushed gently on the heavy doors and they opened a crack. It was too dark in the office to see anything through the crack. There was a low moan from the other side. He pushed the doors open further. The right-hand side door caught up on something and wouldn't open farther, so he pushed past the left door and into the large room. The military governor was lying against the other door. His uniform gave him away. Vincent wouldn't have recognized him otherwise. Crouching on the desk, in the ragged, torn remains of what was once a pristine white silk blouse and smooth pencil skirt was the secretary Rickey had thought was so pretty. She snarled and Vincent could see the broken tips of her long fingernails glint in the half light, jagged and bloody. Her face was scraped in stuttering strips where she's scratched herself. Her mouth dripped with drool.

"I'm sorry," said Vincent, sadly and held up the knife as she leapt at him. She flopped onto him and he threw her sideways, withdrawing the knife. Another stroke to the neck, and it was done. He looked around the dark room. Dozens of folders, maps, plans all scattered and crumpled. The heart of the City, and it was dead. He and his friends hadn't been comfortable here. They hadn't agreed with some of what the City did, but its loss was devastating anyway. The Colony was truly alone. The loss exhausted him. He sprayed the room and gradually worked back down to the lobby, sagging with the weight. "Let's find the boat," he said, climbing into the truck.

THIRTY-NINE

The harbor was empty. The plastic suits had become uncomfortably hot and Vincent could hear the others gasping to draw breath. Where was the boat?

Father Preston groaned. "It was Gray. I know it. He killed them."

Vincent shook his head. "They'll be here. They promised."

Lisa killed the engine and they sat in the large arch next to the beach. "There're no docks here," she said. "Looks like they were destroyed. Maybe they couldn't land here."

Vincent got out of the truck and walked down toward the beach looking out over the water. He itched to strip the plastic mask from his face but he turned to see the silvery trickles of the poison gas spilling down onto the sand. He sat on a stone bench until the moon rose. A sleek shadow pierced the horizon and a white speck flashed in the waves. They had waited to be able to see, they were rowing toward the City now. Vincent stood up and walked back to the truck. "They are coming."

Lisa pulled the keys from the ignition. Father Preston gathered the remaining canisters in his arms and they headed down to meet the small, gleaming rowboat. Vincent could tell something was wrong before the boat was even close enough to shout to. There was only one person in it, and the figure slouched and pulled the oars half heartedly, as if it took tremendous effort.

"It's Gray," hissed Father Preston, placing the canisters down and pulling the tire iron from his belt. Vincent held him back.

"Just hold on. Just wait and see. We don't want to hurt anyone we don't have to."

The small boat knocked floating pieces of wood out of the way and hissed to a stop in front of them. The figure inside slumped backward. Vincent ran forward and pulled the rowboat up onto the beach.

"It's Frank, give me the extra mask, quickly, he's wounded."

Lisa fumbled with the package and hurried to slide the face mask over the unconscious lawyer's head.

"Get in," said Vincent, "we can find out what happened once we're out of the range of the poison."

They piled into the small rowboat and shoved off. They were halfway back to the sailboat before Vincent felt safe enough to shake Frank awake.

"What happened? Is Gray on the boat? Do we need to fight?"

Frank stared blankly at him through the mask. He touched the dark bandage on his stomach gently. "Already done," he rumbled, "Nella— he's dead."

Vincent slid out of his mask to get a better look at Frank's stomach. "He did this to you? Why didn't Nella stitch it?"

Frank sobbed.

"Never mind," said Vincent, alarmed, "I can do it when we get to the boat. Is she hurt too?"

Frank pulled the mask off his own face and shook his head. "She's dead. I had to shoot her. It wasn't time yet. It wasn't supposed to happen yet. She was supposed to wait for me."

"Did she do this?"

"No, no this was Gray. She— she lost it when he stabbed me. She was mad. I've never seen anything like it. I begged her to calm down. To just— to *come back*. You know how hard it was once you'd given in, though, don't you remember?"

"I remember," said Vincent softly.

"I kept calling her and calling her, asking her to talk to me. She turned around so slowly. Like she was trying.

Like she was fighting not to hurt me too. She was drenched in his blood but her face was so sad. Like I was already dead and that's all she could see. She was so out of breath, she was taking these heaving gusts of air and shaking. I lifted the gun to show her that I had it. I asked her again, please, just say something. This low growl rose up from her gut, the strength of it vibrating her, making her shake even more. I told her I was sorry— so *sorry*. And I shot her. Because I promised I would. I promised I wouldn't let her go through what I did. I promised." Frank was sobbing into his hands.

"And you bandaged yourself and sailed here?" asked Father Preston, his voice colored with awe.

"I gave my word that we'd be here. I pulled out the spear, hoping maybe I'd bleed out before we got here. I know how to stitch, but I wasn't certain if I was supposed to for something this deep."

"I'll take care of it," said Vincent.

Frank shook his head.

"She'd have wanted you to try. She let herself go to save you. She gave up what time she had left so you'd finish it. If it were her instead, you'd beg her to try, wouldn't you?" asked Vincent gently.

Frank was silent. They'd reached the boat. They pulled up the small row boat and Vincent lit the cabin lanterns. Nella lay on the deck, the ends of her hair fluttering in the wind, giving the illusion of movement. The interior was soggy with blood. Another mangled body and a large spear lay across the large, dark stains on the carpet. He told the others to try and sleep while he helped Frank onto the bed and unwrapped the wet bandages.

Vincent shook his head. "It's bad."

"I know. That's okay."

"I can stitch it, but you have to try."

"What's the point? If she was sick, then I'm sick

too."

"What if you're immune?"

Frank laughed and it was bitter and angry. "Now? I've lost— everything. I failed in every possible way. Why should I be immune?"

"It isn't your fault that she got sick— it wasn't your failure."

"It *was*. All the way in the beginning. She cried because she was frightened that we wouldn't find the Plague, that it would be released and we wouldn't be able to stop it. I promised her we'd find it. But it got released anyway. It got past me. I didn't save her. We were hundreds of miles away when we found out it was loose. I could have kept us away. I could have kept her safe. But I agreed to come back. Even though I knew there was nothing we could do to stop it. I agreed to come anyway. She would have stayed away if I'd insisted. She loved me enough. I came back to die with her. And I didn't even do that right."

"We *are* stopping it. Without you— we wouldn't have even tried. The Colony would be gone or under perpetual siege by the Infected. She let herself go, she stopped fighting the disease so that she had the strength to defend *you*. To save your life. If you want her death to mean something, then you have to try to live. See this through. Help me stop the thing that defeated her. Help me carry any survivors away to start over."

"It's too much to ask," cried Frank.

"I know," said Vincent, "but I have to ask anyway."

He pulled the first aid kit from the wall and began cleaning Frank's wounds.

The morning was gray and the smell of the acrid poison reached even the boat. They pulled on their suits and slowly rowed back to the docks. Frank was limping and Vincent tried to make him stay on the boat, but Frank insisted, saying he couldn't leave it unfinished, not now. Nella would want to see it done. He picked up her body and put it gently between them in the rowboat and then held her as he and Vincent rode on the back of the sprayer. They headed first to Frank's old street, the row houses huddled together against the rest of the City. Vincent and Preston started at the end of his block, but Frank limped down the street with Nella sagging against his chest. The yards of the neighboring houses were blooming with herbs. The air became a battle between summer and the acrid poison that slunk behind him. Someone had planted a sapling in his own yard and he stopped to stare at it.

"I told you, we *aren't* leaving. You agreed not to come back."

He jumped and spun around, trying to see through his fogged up mask. A short, reedy man stood behind him, his face curled into a sharp snarl. He was holding a baseball bat and a teen girl with one leg leaned on crutches behind him. The man's face softened as he saw Nella's body and realized who it was.

"Frank? You came back?" The baseball bat sagged and then dragged on the cement. "Things have gone really wrong here. Is that—"

Frank nodded behind the mask. "I just wanted to bring her home," he said, "I didn't come to hurt you."

"Course not," said the man.

"You need to get out of here. Get a mask or something to breathe through and go to the harbor. I'll meet you there tonight. Stay out of the City. Stay away from the smoke. You'll be safe on the boat."

"What is it?"

"Poison," said Frank, "Poison to kill the plague. So we could keep the rest safe."

The reedy man nodded. "You came back to help,

didn't you? And her?"

"We tried."

"I'm sorry."

Frank nodded. "I'll meet you at the boat," he said and turned back to his door. The house was dark and even the leaky sink didn't drip in the silence. He slowly climbed the narrow steps, adjusting Nella's weight to hold her higher off the ground. He put her on the bed, the blue sailing charts hung over her, the little islands and rock outcrops like stars against the watercolor sea. He thought about lying down next to her. His stitches stretched and ached and he was exhausted. But no one else knew how to sail the boat. He couldn't deny them a chance to escape. He stood a long time, looking at Nella. The rumble of the sprayer moved on and he knew it was time. Frank opened his small canister and sprinkled it, like yellow snow over her. He put the old camp lantern on the bedside table and switched it on. She looked waxen. Not real. It made leaving easier. She wasn't there. Not anymore. Neither was he. He walked down the stairs and back into the street. The bedroom window glowed, keeping the dark away from her. He got into the truck with the others. Lisa drove the other direction this time, hitting the Immune side of town. They overlapped a few streets and a small scattering of bodies told them the poison had been effective overnight.

"Where is everyone?" Vincent asked.

Frank shrugged. "Locked away in their apartments maybe. Nella said—" he broke off and then forced himself to continue. "She said she didn't even know her neighbors. It was like that on this side of town."

But except for a few Infected, they found no one until they closed in on the prison. "Maybe they were all captured and cremated," said Father Preston. "That ash pile was pretty big."

Lisa pulled up to the short gray building that had

been such a large part of Frank's life. There were several buses in the lot. "Of course it would be here," he groaned. "Misery floods from this place. They would have locked everyone up for safety."

"We should check for Immunes before we start spraying," said Vincent.

They walked into the prison together, Frank holding the heavy glass door open for a moment, wishing that first slushy day in March had never happened. That she'd never met him. That she was somewhere safe in her apartment or consulting at a far-flung Cure camp. He wished he could burn the place down like so much of the rest of the City. Instead, he followed Vincent through to the block where the Infected started shrieking at the sound of the opening door.

FORTY

The tire fire burned for a long time. Henry tried not to read into it too much, but it was hard to ignore day after day. Nancy, the other quarantine camp occupant was released on a sunny day at the end of August when the milkweed was bursting and the seeds floating like warm snow over the field. It was Marnie's time too, but she refused to leave Henry. Nancy shook their hands and quietly walked up to the Colony. Henry could hear the shouts of welcome even below the wall. The days grew cooler and Amos sent down some scraps of plywood left over from building. Henry built a small two room shack, trying not to equate it to the wood shed he'd spent too long in. It kept the wind out, but not the loneliness. He missed Molly, but it was easy to pretend she was up in the Colony sorting and drying vegetables as long as he was down in the quarantine camp. He couldn't pretend with Vincent. He heard echoes of him everywhere. If only they knew for sure, he could rest easy either way.

He taught Marnie to read, something she hadn't had since kindergarten. He read anything the Colony would send them, and his head was already filled with plans for next spring. This would be the last hard winter if he and Amos had anything to say about it. There was so much missing. Everyday tasks were harder and took longer than he'd ever expected. But it was the people he missed more than anything else. Their voices, their faces, the comfort of being part of them.

On a blustery, rainy September day, something knocked on their shack. Henry thought it was the food delivery and didn't open the door, waiting for the person to go away. The knock came again. "You know how this works," called Henry, "leave it and I'll come get it after you are gone. Can't risk exposing anyone else."

"But it's the fortieth day," called a voice.

Marnie looked over at him. "Fortieth day?" she asked.

Henry stood up. "What's the date?"

"September 27th," answered the voice.

"The fortieth day," repeated Henry. He flung the door open.

"Wait, what's the fortieth day?" asked Marnie.

Henry was swallowed in a hug.

"It's the last day of quarantine," said a woman smiling at her. She held out her hand. "I'm Melissa. I'm glad to finally meet you. We've heard so very much about you."

Marnie shook her hand and looked over at Henry who was laughing and slapping a thin, angular man on the back. She decided the fortieth day was a good day.

FORTY-ONE

Henry grunted as he dug his feet into the soil, dragging the heavy blades behind him. "Thought you said you picked this area," he grumbled. Amos laughed.

"Sure, but the frost always throws up more. Stephanie and Marnie said the settlement we got the apples from has a pair of horses. One of em's ready to foal. If we can scrape enough together, maybe we can trade for it. It'll be no good for the plow this year but next—"

Melissa ran up to the edge of the field. "Someone's coming," she said, "not a regular visitor either."

Amos shrugged. "Maybe he wants to start trade."

"Rickey spotted him a few days ago on that lumber run. He was coming from the City."

"He's sure?" asked Henry, letting the tiller go slack.

Melissa nodded. "He said he tried to catch up with him that day, but lost him in the woods beyond the barrier. But he recognized him today. Said it couldn't hurt to let you know."

Amos helped Henry slide out of the straps and they walked to the wall where Rickey stood chewing a long piece of grass. "You think he's exposed?" asked Henry.

Rickey shook his head. "Guy was wearing a gas mask as he climbed through the barrier. Wouldn't have recognized him today except for this wood crate he's carrying."

They watched the figure walk slowly up the long field toward them. He closed the distance between them while gazing steadily at his own feet. He stopped where the quarantine camp had been, the wire fence long gone, only a small circle of unmarked mounds beneath an old apple tree where it had been. He looked up at them and Henry took a step back as he drew closer, unconsciously mirroring Vincent's reaction to the same man on a spring day two years before.

"I know it wasn't me you were hoping to see," said Father Preston, pushing a knit cap back on his head, "But I brought a gift from a friend. I hope you will forgive me for not being Vincent."

He lay the wooden crate in front of them. Henry crouched and opened the lid. Half a dozen bottles of yellow liquid were cushioned against a burlap sack and a small envelope. Father Preston scratched the back of his neck. "Frank said to warn you that the pineapple wine has a bit of a wallop. He promises to get better at it, but he thought you'd want some of the first batch. The sugar's from a nearby farm. Frank trades with them an awful lot. I think they'd adopt him if he'd let them. He sent you a letter too, about— about what happened. For my part, I was a fool. I know I can't ever replace what— *who* I've taken from you, or from Frank through my actions, but I hope I can find some way to atone—"

Amos stuck out his hand. Father Preston grasped it and shook. "You made it right," said Amos, "You went with Vincent and the others until the end. You protected this place and your people."

"Have you come to stay for a while?" asked Melissa.

Father Preston shook his head. "Maybe a few days, but I have other people to make amends with. I'm on my way home. I need to find Ruth and Bernard, see if there's anything I can do to help."

"You seem like you've been on the road a while," said Rickey clapping him on the back, "Let us give you a few nights' proper rest and a couple of good meals..." they kept talking as they turned the priest up toward the little cluster of houses, leaving Henry crouched near the crate. He pulled the slim envelope from where it was tucked in the corner and frowned as something oddly shaped made gentle creases in the paper. He tore it open with one finger and stretched out on the gravel road to read.

It was one sheet of paper and a slim badge of leather, ragged at the edges and glued to fraying black ribbon. Henry would have recognized it anywhere.

I know you didn't expect to hear from any of us again, and I've long hoped the lack of radio broadcasts from your area means that we were successful in containing the Plague. We were able to pull three Immunes from the City before we left, but our own party was less lucky. How I wish this letter was written by any hand except mine. Both Nella and Vincent were pushed too hard in the end. She turned early because of a great shock that I wish I'd prevented. You will never need worry about Gray again. Vincent turned out of exhaustion. He was caring for all of us until the end. Father Preston and I buried him in the grounds of an old monastery, south of the City. I was surprised to find that Vincent didn't wear a cross, but I wanted you to have something of him to hold onto. He'd said the patch was part of his life after he woke up with you. Father Preston told me something, a little while after we lost Vincent. He told me that when he was a young man, Father Preston thought to be a truly good man was to make it through life as free of sin as one could. That we were living in a world of it and whoever arrived "cleanest" would have proved their goodness. But he said Vincent convinced him that it wasn't enough to sail above the world's troubles and arrive unscathed at the end. That the true worth of a person was if they could walk right through the muck and lift other people out of it on his own shoulders if he had to. Both Father Preston and Vincent were sure you were among the worthiest.

I know now, how hard it must have been for Nella to write you that first letter— how much she wanted to be there when you woke up so that she could help you, so she could explain that there were things still out there worth living for, no matter how bad your memories were. I know now, because I wish I was there to tell you about Vincent myself. About the empty City, about the empty world beyond. There are others out here, I want you to know that, in case you need to make a new home someday, like me. Kind people and lonely people and some that were barely touched at all by the Plague. As much as I miss her, as much as you must miss him, the world keeps on spinning and people keep going. The time passes and there are still smiles and joys to be found. I told Nella once that surviving the Plague was the easy part. That once the danger had passed, the really brave work had to be done, the picking up and moving on that would rebuild us. I wish I'd been wrong about how difficult it is. I wish I hadn't been the one left behind to do it. But it would make them happy to know we were trying. Even if we fail at first. As long as we keep trying.

  F.C.

NOTE TO THE READER

Dear Reader,

I just wanted to thank you for sticking with me in this dark post-"zombie" world. Whether you jumped in at After the Cure or one of the later novels or stories, I hope that the book and series have entertained you, made you think, or just moved you in some way. I hope that you loved it, but maybe you'd rather throw the kindle at me instead. I can't say I'd blame you, but I want you to know I probably miss the characters as much as you (for you skippers-ahead, I'm not going to say who and spoil it all if you are reading this bit first. I know you are out there!), and I will continue to miss them and this world. Will I be returning to them? Maybe, probably. Ruth is still out there, somewhere. In the meantime, I hope you'll drop me a line and tell me how you feel, I'd love to hear from you, whether you are railing against me or just want to know what the weather in Maine is at the moment. You can always find me at dk.gould@live.com and I promise I will do my best to answer any questions you might have or just say hello and make a new friend in zombie- er, *Infected* and post apocalyptic appreciation. Or you can pop in to the After the Cure facebook page to see what's new, like audiobooks, new stories or what I'm up to next(or to find out about other awesome science fiction and horror books that I've run across and want to share): https://www.facebook.com/Afterthecurenovel

Of course, I always appreciate sharing how you feel with the rest of the reading world too, and if you felt sad, angry, happy, satisfied, frustrated or excited for more, I hope you'll leave a review for this, and *any* book you read. Finding out someone loved or loathed a book is usually how I find my next read!

So many of you have written to me in the past few

years to tell me what you thought, to yell at me about those nasty villains or a favorite character's choices, and I want you to know I've loved and appreciated every single note. Your support, your suggestions and your enthusiasm has meant the world to me, and my sincerest hope is that I haven't disappointed. I hope we'll talk soon, about this book or any other!

January 22, 2016
Deirdre Gould

OTHER BOOKS

Other Books

In the After the Cure world:
After the Cure (book 1)
http://www.amazon.com/After-Cure-Deirdre-Gould-ebook/dp/B00ERVTFCM
The Cured (book 2)
http://www.amazon.com/gp/product/B00J2EJAOM
Krisis (book 3)
http://www.amazon.com/gp/product/B00TA9YHR4
Poveglia (book 4)
http://www.amazon.com/gp/product/B0127Z5CZI

Curing Khang Yeo (companion story)
http://www.amazon.com/Curing-Khang-Yeo-Deirdre-Gould-ebook/dp/B013V3NIII
Andy and Igor (companion story)
http://www.scullerytales.com/?p=1279
Pet Shop (companion story in Tails of the Apocalypse)
http://www.amazon.com/Tails-Apocalypse-David-Bruns-ebook/dp/B016E5JIRU

Non-Zombie Stuff:
System Failure in The Robot Chronicles
http://www.amazon.com/Robot-Chronicles-Samuel-Peralta/dp/1500600628
Iteration in The Future Chronicles
http://www.amazon.com/Future-Chronicles-Special-Samuel-Peralta/dp/0993983251
The Moon Polisher's Apprentice: The Moth Queen
http://www.amazon.com/Moon-Polishers-

Apprentice-Part-Queen-ebook/dp/B00J8U6WB4/

44568049R00155

Made in the USA
Middletown, DE
10 June 2017